THE GHOST
OF A MEMORY

HAUNTING DANIELLE

HAUNTING DANIELLE - BOOK 25

THE GHOST

OF A MEMORY

USA TODAY BESTSELLING AUTHOR

BOBBI HOLMES

The Ghost of a Memory
(Haunting Danielle, Book 25)
A Novel
By Bobbi Holmes
Cover Design: Elizabeth Mackey

ISBN: 978-1-949977-60-8

Dedicated to Karen Dickey,
for all her help with the
Haunting Danielle series.
It is much appreciated.

ONE

M ax stood in the open doorway of the attic bedroom and watched as the intruders ransacked Walt's desk. Had he been a dog like Sadie or Hunny, he understood they would have been more concerned with his presence. One had stopped by him when entering the room, taking a moment to lean down and stroke his fur. Then the other one had hurried through the doorway, shoving his companion farther into the room, almost stepping on him.

But Max had avoided getting trampled and remained by the doorway, observing and wondering. He had been sleeping when they had first entered the house. Considering the thunder and lightning that had been rattling the roof overhead, he didn't imagine he would have heard them coming in even if he had been awake. Max had been on the stairs leading to the attic when they first woke him; the sound of their shoes stomping up the wooden steps shook him from his afternoon nap.

Minutes later the rain had stopped falling, as did the thunder. Light now streamed in the bedroom window, suggesting the rain clouds had spent themselves and moved aside, allowing sunlight to brighten the afternoon sky.

Curious, Max strolled panther-like to the king-size bed, his eyes never leaving the two masked people dressed in dark clothing. They hurriedly opened and closed drawers, searching through file folders.

Jumping up on the mattress a moment later, his black tail swishing back and forth, Max walked closer to the two strangers to get a better look. He sat on the edge of the mattress and observed, wondering why they were here.

Intently focused on their task, the two intruders did not seem to notice their audience, at least not until Max let out a loud, demanding meow. They paused a moment, glanced over at the curious golden eyes, and then returned to their search.

Max meowed again.

The taller of the two, the one who had barreled into the room and had almost stepped on Max, looked over to the persistent cat. Their eyes met. "Creeps me out, the way he keeps staring at me."

Max, who did not understand the meaning of the spoken words, thought the voice sounded male, like Walt's voice.

The shorter intruder, the one who had taken a moment to stroke Max's fur when they had first arrived, glanced over to him and said, "He's just curious."

Again, Max did not understand the words, but he thought the voice was softer, like Danielle's.

"And you know what they say; curiosity killed the cat." The taller one snickered.

"Oh, stop. You wouldn't hurt the cat."

With a shrug he said, "It's just lucky for him he can't talk. Or I'd be shoving him in a pillowcase for a little swim in the ocean. We don't need anyone to tell the Marlows we were here."

"I doubt the cat will tell anyone about us. And you might as well get used to him. If you don't want Walt Marlow to figure out we were here, you can't be doing anything to his cat. And we could be here for hours before we find it."

"At least the Marlows are out of town, and we have the house to ourselves. I'm just glad they don't have a yappy dog. But I'm tempted to toss that nosey cat in another bedroom and shut the door. That staring is getting on my nerves."

As if Max understood what the man said—which he hadn't—he plopped down on the bedspread and began grooming himself, seemingly no longer interested in the pair.

The shorter intruder laughed and said, "Feel better now?"

With a shrug, the taller one slammed close the drawer he had been searching. Resting balled fists on his waist, he glanced around the room. "I don't think it's in here."

"We still have the downstairs to go through. And I told you, I bet it's in the library."

"We were told Marlow does his writing up here. I just figured this is where he'd keep it."

The shorter intruder glanced around the room and then fixed a stare on one wall. "Before we leave, I want to check out that hidden staircase."

"Where do you figure the door is?"

"Not sure. But according to an article I read, there's a hidden panel in one of the inside walls. Maybe we'll find what we're looking for stashed in the hidden staircase."

As the shorter intruder looked for the hidden panel, her companion walked over to the window. They had been careful to avoid going near it, not wanting a neighbor to notice someone in the house. The blinds were only half drawn. Standing to one side of the window, he peeked out the opening, curious to see what the weather looked like outside. It had been storming when they had first arrived at Marlow House, yet the rain had stopped before entering through the kitchen.

"I found it!" she said.

"Crap," he cursed under his breath, still peering out the window.

With a frown, she turned to him and asked, "What's wrong?"

"Someone just pulled up in front of the house," he said.

"Get away from the window. You don't want them to see you!"

"Don't worry, they can't from there. But they're getting out of the car."

"Is it the Marlows? They aren't supposed to be back for a couple of days."

He shook his head. "No, it's a woman. She's walking up to the front door."

"She'll go away once she realizes no one is home." The shorter intruder remained standing by the panel door she had opened. Yet instead of looking into the dark passageway, she looked at her companion, who continued peering out the window.

"She just walked up to the house. I can't see her. She must be on the front porch. But she hasn't rung the doorbell yet."

"Maybe it doesn't work?" she suggested, turning back to the opening. Pulling out her cellphone, she turned on the flashlight app and used it to illuminate the hidden stairwell as she looked inside.

"I still don't see her. She hasn't gone back to her car," he said, focusing his attention on the sidewalk below.

"Oh, this is so cool! You should check this out!" she said, walking into the stairwell, using her cellphone flashlight to light the way. "But I don't see anything stored in here."

"Something's not right," he mumbled. Turning from the window, he walked to the open doorway and stepped out onto the landing. Then he heard it, the front door slamming close. A moment later, he could hear someone coming up the stairs leading to the second floor. After the person reached the second floor, the footsteps sounded as if she was heading toward the stairs leading to the attic bedroom. Turning abruptly, he rushed back into the room and to the hidden staircase his accomplice had just entered.

"You should—"

"Quiet," he hissed, entering the hidden staircase and closing the panel behind him, yet leaving it open an inch. "Someone is here."

Standing on the top landing in the hidden staircase, flashlight in hand, she turned to him. "Are you sure?"

"Turn the flashlight off," he told her.

"But it's dark in here."

"Do as I say," he ordered.

She turned off the flashlight. They stood in darkness. A sliver of light made its way around the open edge of the panel door. Finally, a woman's voice said, "Max, is this where you're hiding?"

Leaning close to the panel door, now open just a sliver, they listened.

"Walt and Danielle are coming home today," they heard her say. "They should be here in a couple hours. And I need to get the clean sheets put on their bed, so get off."

Gingerly he closed the panel door completely, careful not to make any noise. It sent them into total darkness. He reached for his companion's hand, urging her to turn the flashlight back on. It took her a moment to do it, but once they had light again, he motioned down the stairs. Together they walked to the second floor, careful not to make any unnecessary noise, for fear the woman might discover them.

When they reached the bottom of the stairs, she asked, "What are we doing?"

"We're getting the hell out of here. Before she comes back downstairs or the Marlows show up."

"How do we do that?" she asked.

"There has to be another panel. According to one article, this leads to a bedroom," he said.

A moment later she held the flashlight while he felt around for another panel doorway. When he found it, he slid it open, not realizing how fortunate they were. Walt and Danielle sometimes kept it locked from the other side so their guests would not feel uncomfortable using a bedroom with a closet leading to a hidden staircase to their room.

But it was unlocked, and once open, they stepped into the closet of the master bedroom on the second floor. He closed the panel behind him, not wanting anyone to discover they had been there. They needed to return later, to continue their search, and they didn't want the Marlows to take extra precautions to avoid a future break-in.

When they slid open the closet door a moment later, preparing to walk into the bedroom, the black cat with the white-tipped ears unexpectedly greeted them. Sitting before the now open closet door, the cat looked up and meowed.

"Oh, gosh, he scared me!" she gasped.

"Stay here," he told her, rushing out of the closet and past the cat, to the open bedroom door leading to the hallway. He peeked out into the hall but saw nothing, yet he heard singing. It came from the hallway leading to the attic stairs. If he wasn't mistaken, it was more accurately coming from the attic.

He looked back to his companion and motioned for her to follow him. Turning off the flashlight app, she rushed to his side. He took her hand, and together they ran down the hallway, to the stairs leading to the first floor, while the cat watched.

TEN MINUTES LATER, after running out the kitchen doorway and through the side yard to the alley, they reached their car. The shorter one held a soaked towel, which she had picked up from where they had dropped it on the kitchen porch earlier that day. It had been used to wipe off their wet shoes before entering the house. She was grateful the woman had used the front door instead of the kitchen door, or she might have noticed the towel sitting on the back porch. She tossed the wet towel on the floor by her feet. Pulling their masks off after getting into the car, her companion hastily started the engine, and a moment later they drove away.

"That was close," she said breathlessly. "Was that their housekeeper?"

"Apparently so. And it sounds like they're coming back today, so we'll have to figure out something else."

"We were told they weren't coming home for a couple more days."

"Apparently they changed their plans."

"There's one good thing," she said.

"That you found that opening into the staircase before she walked in on us?"

"Well, that too. No, I was thinking it's a good thing cats don't talk. Or he'd tell Walt Marlow about our little visit."

TWO

Before leaving the Portland airport, Danielle adjusted the passenger seat in her car to make it more comfortable to nap. But there had been no sleeping. She and Walt had been chatting away since leaving the airport and heading home to Frederickport.

"I'm glad you like to drive." Danielle snuggled under the small throw blanket she kept in her car.

"I don't mind driving. And I seem to recall men did most of the driving when I first got my driver's license." Hands firmly on the steering wheel, Walt flashed Danielle a quick smile before looking back down the road.

"Yeah, well, it's probably considered very un-feminist of me to expect you to do the driving."

"I promise not to tell your fellow feminists."

She giggled. "That's kind of you."

"Eager to get home?" Walt asked.

"I am. It was a wonderful trip, and Hawaii was as amazing as our honeymoon, but I'm looking forward to getting home to my bed. Seeing Max and the others."

"Where do you want to stop to pick up something to eat?"

"I've been having this insane craving for Pearl Cove's clam chowder. But that isn't exactly fast food."

"Did you say craving?" he teased.

Danielle laughed. "No, I'm not pregnant."

"You might be if you stopped taking birth control."

"We need to enjoy this time together before we start a family."

"But you want to start one?" Walt asked.

"Of course." She loosened her seatbelt, leaned over, and kissed his cheek.

"We've been married over two years," Walt reminded her.

Settling back in her seat and adjusting her seatbelt, Danielle said, "So much has happened in that time; it's like we really haven't been able to enjoy being just us."

The next moment Danielle's cellphone rang. She picked it up from where she had placed it in the center console. Before answering, she looked to see who was calling and told Walt, "It's Chris."

"Hey, Chris," Danielle said into the phone a moment later.

"Lily said you were back," came Chris's reply.

"Almost. We should be home in about twenty-five minutes."

"Have you guys had anything to eat yet?" Chris asked.

"Not since we landed. We ate nothing on the plane. Figure we'll stop at a drive-through when we get to Frederickport and pick something up to take home."

"That's why I'm calling. Some of us are getting together at Pearl Cove for dinner. About a half hour. Why don't you meet us there?"

Danielle glanced down at her clothes before looking over at Walt. "Chris wants us to meet them at Pearl Cove for dinner."

"You said you were craving their clam chowder," Walt reminded her.

Danielle grinned and turned her attention back to the phone. "Okay, but we're not stopping home first. We're not exactly dressed for Pearl Cove, but I doubt they'll turn us away."

Chris laughed and said, "You'll be fine. How was your trip?"

"It was great, but good to get home. Who'll be there tonight?"

"Ian and Lily, Adam and Mel, and Heather."

"Are they bringing Connor?" Danielle asked.

"No. Joe and Kelly are babysitting tonight."

AFTER WALT and Danielle walked into Pearl Cove thirty minutes later, the hostess led them to a large booth in the far corner, overlooking the ocean. The sunshade helped block the glare from the setting sun. Already seated at the booth were Chris and Heather.

The minute Walt and Danielle arrived table side, Chris stood up and gave Danielle a quick hug before shaking Walt's hand. Heather remained sitting, her black hair tied in a knot atop her head.

"Nice suntan," Heather noted as Walt and Danielle slid into the booth with them.

"Did you do any surfing?" Chris teased.

"No, but Walt took me sailing." Danielle picked up one menu.

"That's romantic," Heather said.

Danielle flashed Heather a grin. "Yes, it was."

A moment later Lily and Ian joined the table, resulting in more hugs as the friends exchanged greetings. Before the pair sat down, Adam and Melony arrived.

"Hey, what are you doing here?" Adam asked Danielle the moment he saw her.

"Some greeting." She laughed.

"I thought you were staying two weeks?" he said. "It hasn't been two weeks yet."

"Ten days, not two weeks," Danielle said.

A FIFTY-SOMETHING COUPLE sat alone at their table, each looking over their menus. Commotion from one of the nearby booths caught the woman's attention.

"Beau, isn't that your Realtor?" she asked her husband.

The man looked up from his menu and turned his attention to the group of thirty-something people at a large booth. He was close enough to see them, yet not close enough to hear what they were saying.

"Yes, it is. Adam Nichols," Beau said.

"His date is stunning. Is she a model?" she asked, referring to the tall leggy blonde standing at Adam's side.

Beau chuckled. "Hardly. That's Melony Carmichael. She's a criminal attorney and a damn good one."

"That's not Jolene and Doug's girl, is it?"

"It is."

Setting her menu on the table, she glanced briefly to where Melony stood before looking back to Beau. "I remember their daughter became a lawyer. That always surprised me. She was a wild thing, as I recall."

Beau shrugged and turned his attention back to his menu.

Curious, she glanced back to Adam's booth. She noticed the blond man at the end of the table, sitting next to a goth-looking girl. *An odd pair*, she thought. He reminded her of someone from a beach band. "Who are the others?"

He looked up. "Why do you care?"

She shrugged. "Only curious. And we're now property owners in Frederickport; it doesn't hurt to meet the locals. Isn't that what you're always telling me?"

He set his menu on the table and glanced over to Adam's booth.

"The guy at the end, I met him at Adam's office. That's Chris Johnson, and next to him is his assistant, Halley or Hillary, something that starts with an H. I don't remember. They work for the Glandon Foundation."

"So they aren't a couple?" she asked.

"I doubt it."

"That makes more sense. They seemed rather mismatched. What does he do at the Glandon Foundation? Isn't that a nonprofit organization?"

"Yes. And after meeting Johnson and his assistant, I'm convinced their charity extends to giving cushy jobs to people with no qualifications. They both seem more suited for work in a head shop."

"Perhaps they hired him for his looks," she said with a chuckle before picking up her water glass and taking a sip.

"I seriously doubt *she* was," he said with a snort, nodding to the assistant. "I haven't met them, but someone pointed them out to me, the little redhead with the tall guy. The tall guy is Jon Altar."

"You're kidding me? I heard he lives here."

"I meant to tell you. I learned Altar is a pen name; his actual name is Ian Bartley. From what I understand, his wife is a teacher."

"And the other couple?" She nodded to the brunette and her companion.

"I've no idea who they are," he said with a shrug.

FIFTEEN MINUTES LATER, after their server took their orders and delivered their cocktails, Beau excused himself to visit the restroom. En route, he passed Adam's table, stopping a moment to say hello.

"Beau, I thought that was you over there," Adam said, standing up briefly to shake Beau's hand.

"Evening, Adam," Beau greeted him.

Sitting back down at the table, Adam said, "Everyone, this is one of my clients," he hastily added, "and friend," before saying, "Beau Stewart." Adam motioned to Chris and Heather and said, "You've already met Chris and Heather."

"Nice to see you again," Beau said with a nod, while Chris and Heather returned a brief greeting.

"And next to Heather is Danielle Marlow and her husband, Walt."

Beau cocked his brow at Walt. "The author?"

Walt smiled. "Guilty."

"Walt's not the only author in the group. This is Lily Bartley and her husband, Ian Bartley, but you might recognize him as Jon Altar."

"Ahh, it's a pleasure," Beau said, shaking Ian's hand. "My wife is a great fan of yours."

"And you wouldn't be the same Beau Stewart who some say will be our next senator?" Ian asked.

Beau laughed and said, "Now I'm the guilty one."

"IS HE MOVING TO FREDERICKPORT?" Danielle asked after Beau left their table and was out of earshot.

"No. He purchased land for a vacation home. He bought it from his cousin."

"Why did he have to use a Realtor if he was buying it from a relative?" Heather asked.

"Because the cousin listed the property and didn't sell it directly to him. Although, I have a feeling he might have if it hadn't been for his family," Adam said.

"What do you mean?" Danielle asked.

"The guy who owned the property is ill. Beau knew his cousin wanted to sell. His kids aren't interested in living there, and his wife died a while back. Beau tried to buy the property directly from him, but I suspect the guy's kids felt Beau was trying to take advantage of their father, so they convinced him to list the property. Which I'm rather glad they did." Adam snickered.

"Because then you get a commission?" Danielle teased.

"Exactly. Although I imagine the kids—although I use that term loosely, I'm certain they're older than me—anyway, they were a little annoyed, because after it closed escrow, they realized their dad would've probably ended up with more money had they not used an agent and had to pay six percent in real estate fees. Beau ended up paying his cousin what he offered the first time. There wasn't a lot of action on that property, and to be honest with you, I wouldn't be surprised if Beau only bought it to help his cousin out. He's too sick to take care of the place, and frankly it's a mess. Needs demolishing."

"If the place is in that bad a shape, and their father is ill and they don't want it, I'm surprised they would have had an issue with a cousin getting it," Lily said.

Adam shrugged. "Just between us, there's no love lost between them. The Stewarts are loaded, and the cousin who sold him the property—I guess you could call him the poor relation. I think his kids didn't want Beau to get his hands on the property."

"You're right about Stewart being loaded," Ian said. "I did a little research on him a while back when they started talking about him running for Congress. Back then it seemed he came up out of nowhere. I wondered who the guy was."

"Where did he get all his money?" Danielle asked.

"Family money. His father was a developer, and they own a ton of property in Oregon. He took over the family business after his father died," Ian explained.

Danielle looked at Adam and arched her brows. "Ahh, good client, Adam. More real estate transactions with him in your future?"

"I wish, but he has his own team. He used me because he wanted someone local," Adam said.

"If he has so much money, why in the world would he want to go into politics?" Heather asked.

"Maybe he wants to give back and help his community," Danielle suggested.

Ian let out a snort. "Sometimes you can be so naïve, Danielle."

Danielle frowned at Ian. "What is that supposed to mean?"

"Power. Men like Stewart do it for the power," Ian said.

THREE

Beau Stewart studied his wife as she walked to the women's restroom, leaving him alone at their table. He liked that she normally wore stylish dresses, stayed trim and fit, and visited the beauty parlor once a week. Many considered her tall at five nine, yet he still stood a good six inches over her. She had been his high school sweetheart, which proved to be a valuable asset now that his interests had turned to politics.

They had just finished dinner. He tossed his napkin on the table and picked up his cellphone while his gaze drifted over to Adam Nichols's table. The group seemed to enjoy themselves, chatting away, laughing, while sharing plates of dessert the server had brought minutes earlier. None seemed especially concerned over germs, as forks and spoons darted across the table, snatching bites of cake and ice cream in various flavors. Beau had never been a fan of someone else taking food from his plate.

He placed his call, his gaze darting from Adam's table to where his wife had headed and back to Adam.

His party answered a moment later. Beau said, "You will never guess who I just met...Walt and Danielle Marlow...Pearl Cove... Yes, they're obviously back in town...I learned something interesting, they're having a fundraiser at Marlow House on the fourth...It's some anniversary...Does it matter? Yes, that's what I was thinking…" He glanced up and spied his wife returning to the table. "I have to go. Talk to you in the morning."

"Who were you talking to?" his wife asked when she returned to the table and sat down.

"It was our son; he couldn't find the television remote, again. By the way, I forgot to tell you, when I stopped and said hello to Adam, they told me about a fundraiser they're having over at Marlow House on the fourth. You said you wanted to see inside, and the event includes a tour."

"I read about that," she said. "I intended to mention it to you. They're raising money for the local Humane Society."

"We should go," he told her. "It would be an excellent opportunity to meet some locals."

A moment later the server came to the table and removed their dinner plates and took their dessert order. After the server left them alone, his wife started telling him something when two women walking from the direction of the restrooms caught his attention. His wife continued to chatter on, oblivious to her husband's momentary lapse. One looked Beau's way, and their eyes locked briefly. He didn't know her, but there was something eerily familiar about the woman.

She quickly looked away, breaking their brief silent exchange, and began whispering to the woman at her side while they continued on their way. After they passed their table, Beau turned around and studied the two women as they headed for the entrance of the Pearl Cove lounge. Right before entering, the one who had met his gaze looked back. Once again, their eyes met.

KIARA GRABBED her cousin's hand and picked up her pace, walking hastily toward the table in the lounge where her brother, Laken, waited.

"What are you doing?" Raven asked with a laugh, allowing Kiara to hurry her to their destination.

"Didn't you see who that was?" Kiara asked as she reached the table. Dropping hold of Raven's hand, she took a seat across from Laken.

"Yes, Walt and Danielle Marlow…" Raven began.

"No!" Kiara shook her head. "No, I mean, yes, they were there too. I saw them. You practically put a hole in my side with your elbow."

"I barely nudged you," Raven argued.

Laken sat up straighter at the table. "The Marlows are here?"

Cocking a brow, Kiara looked from her brother to her cousin. "Yes, they are. And so is Beau Stewart. And he was staring at us!"

"No secret he's in Frederickport. I'm not surprised to run into him," Laken said. "I'm more interested in hearing about the Marlows."

"But the way he was looking at me…" Kiara shivered.

"You said he was staring at us," Raven said.

"Well, I guess he was, but then he wasn't. He looked me directly in the eyes. It was creepy. And then right before we walked into the lounge, I looked back, and he was still staring at us."

"You mean at you," Raven reminded her.

Kiara glared at her cousin. "And that was not a nudge. You slammed your elbow in my side."

Raven shrugged. "You were always delicate."

"Would you two stop," Laken snapped. "If the Marlows are here, that means they're back in Frederickport."

"Obviously," Kiara said, slumping back in her chair. "Now what?"

"We should do what I suggested in the beginning," Raven said.

"What, knock on their door and tell them we think they have something we need?" Kiara asked.

"I don't understand why not," Raven said. "You guys always want to do things the hard way. I don't think this needs to be that difficult."

"And if Marlow is such a decent guy, why hasn't he done something by now? Instead of using it to make money. And from what I understand, it isn't like he needs money. He's no different from Stewart," Laken said.

THE SERVER HAD REMOVED ALL the dirty dishes from their table and delivered the check, which Chris promptly snatched. There was a brief argument from several in his party, who wanted to pay, but he reminded them dinner out was his idea.

"Thanks, Chris. I have to say this was much better than takeout," Danielle said. "But we need to get home and unpack, and I'm looking forward to seeing Max."

"Don't forget, tomorrow night we're having a barbecue at our house," Lily reminded them.

"Wow, going out two nights in a row," Heather said.

"I figure people will start arriving for the Fourth this weekend, and we won't be able to use the beach for a while. Not unless we want to fight the crowds," Lily said.

"All my rentals are full this next week, so you have a point," Adam said.

Danielle stood up with Walt. "If you'll excuse us, we're exhausted. We've been up for hours. And we really need to get home and unpack."

"IT WAS NICE SEEING EVERYONE," Walt said as he drove the car with Danielle to Marlow House.

Danielle yawned and said, "I have to say, Adam seems to have gotten over whatever issue he once had with you."

"I like Adam. I also like how he once informed me I wasn't to take advantage of you—the protective brother." Walt chuckled.

"I used to think he was such a jerk. Melony is good for him."

"His friendship with you is good for him."

Danielle smiled at Walt.

"It surprised me we didn't see Marie or Eva tonight. I was sure they would stop by the restaurant," Walt said.

"When I went to the bathroom with Heather, she told me Eva and Marie have been spending the last few days in Astoria, something going on with the theater there. According to Heather, we won't see Marie or Eva until after the fourth."

"I thought Marie was taking care of Max?" Walt asked.

"Marie asked Heather to check on Max for the last few days," Danielle explained.

A few minutes later Walt turned down the alleyway leading to their garage. When they reached it, Danielle used the remote to open the garage door. Walt pulled the car in and parked next to the Packard. After he turned off the engine, the garage door came down.

A few minutes later they had the luggage out of the vehicle and piled just outside the garage door, in the backyard. Danielle reached for her suitcases when Walt shooed her away. She stepped back for a moment and smiled at the luggage. It floated up from the ground, carried by invisible hands, and floated effortlessly across the yard from the garage to the kitchen door.

Danielle laughed and said, "Someone might see!"

Walt nodded over to Pearl Huckabee's house next door. "The only one who could see is Pearl. Her upstairs is pitch dark. During this time of night, I imagine she's downstairs with her television on, and she can't see in our yard from there."

SEVERAL MINUTES EARLIER, Pearl Huckabee stood in the darkness at her bedroom window, about to close the blinds, when she noticed lights from the Marlows' garage next door. She understood they had been out of town for over a week and wondered if they had just returned. Looking across her neighbor's yard, the sky lit by a full moon, she spied the Marlows walking from the garage into the backyard.

She was about to turn from the window when motion in front of Walt and Danielle caught her attention. It looked like their luggage —and it was flying. Flying across the yard as Walt and Danielle followed it, hand in hand.

Pearl closed her eyes, took a deep breath, and turned from the window, not looking back. "Why did I let my doctor talk me into trying medical marijuana? Never again."

LEANING against the pile of pillows stacked along the headboard, Walt stretched out under the crisp clean bed linens, his chest bare, and the top sheet and blanket pulled up to his waist, covering the lower portion of his body. Danielle had insisted he take his shower first while she unpacked the luggage. She was now in the shower; he could hear the water running. Max sat at his side, looking up at him with golden eyes and conversing in the way they did. Not with words, but with silent telepathy.

"Did anything interesting happen while we were gone?" As was his habit, Walt asked aloud even though it wasn't the verbal words

Max understood. "What do you mean…Why didn't you say some-thing before?"

Danielle walked into the bedroom a few minutes later to the sound of Walt grilling Max, a one-sided conversation that immedi-ately piqued her curiosity.

"What's going on?" she asked while running a brush through her damp hair.

Walt looked up from Max to Danielle. "Someone broke in the house."

"When?" Danielle frowned, looking from Walt to Max.

"This afternoon. They came up here and searched through our things."

Danielle stopped brushing her hair and glanced around the room, looking for anything out of place. "Someone was in our bedroom?"

"From what Max said, it sounded like they only had time to go through my desk. But Joanne showed up, and they slipped out through the hidden staircase."

"Oh no! Joanne walked in on them? How many were there?"

"If Max can count correctly—after all, he is a cat—it sounds like there were two of them. A man and woman, by the sound of their voices."

"What did they look like?" Danielle asked. "Does he have any idea who they were?"

"No. Max isn't good at describing people. And it sounds like they wore something like a ski mask over their heads, concealing their faces. At least, that's how he describes it."

"Oh my gosh, Joanne could have gotten hurt. Did they take anything?"

"According to Max they didn't. But they were obviously looking for something."

FOUR

The next morning Walt and Danielle walked across the street to the Bartleys' house. Ian answered the door while his golden retriever, Sadie, exuberantly welcomed the pair. They followed Ian into the house after he greeted them and said, "Lily's in the nursery."

"Hey, guys," Lily called out when the three walked into the nursery a few minutes later. She was busy arranging something on the dresser while Connor stood in his crib, hands on the rail, bouncing in excitement when he spied the newcomers. Danielle went immediately to the crib and picked up the baby, giving him kisses and hugs.

"They were telling me someone broke into Marlow House yesterday," Ian told Lily, while Walt walked to Danielle and Connor, giving the baby's ruddy cheek a quick kiss.

Lily pivoted from the dresser and faced her husband. She glanced over to Danielle and Walt, her son content in Danielle's arms. "You're kidding me?"

Walt recounted what Max had told him the night before.

"And nothing is missing?" Lily asked.

"According to Max, they took nothing, and nothing seems to be missing," Danielle said.

"How did they get in?" Lily asked.

"I'm thinking the pet door," Danielle said.

"You can get one of those remote-control thingies for Max's collar that opens the door, making it harder for a burglar to get in. It was probably someone who knew you were out of town," Lily said.

"I don't keep a collar on Max. They're dangerous for cats. He could hang himself. And I don't think they were there to steal anything. They were looking for something," Danielle insisted.

"What are you going to do about it?" Ian asked.

"I called the chief this morning and told him. There's nothing he can really do about it. And we can't mention anything to Joanne about what she walked in on. That would be a hard one to explain," Danielle said. Connor squirmed in her arms. She wrestled with him a moment before Ian took his son from her, placing him on the floor with some toys.

"Sounds like Joanne walked in on them before they found something to steal," Lily suggested.

"Since when do thieves look through file folders? Why not my jewelry box that was sitting in plain view?" Danielle asked.

"They could be looking for something more valuable, like credit card numbers, social security numbers, stock certificates?" Ian suggested.

"I suppose," Danielle said glumly, taking a seat on the rocking chair.

"We were wondering if you noticed any strangers—assuming they aren't someone who has been at the house before, since Max didn't recognize their voices—in the neighborhood yesterday. A man and a woman?" Walt asked.

Lily shook her head. "Sorry, I didn't see anyone." She looked at Ian, who repeated the same thing.

"On the positive side, they didn't hurt Joanne, and they left empty-handed," Walt said.

Danielle glanced to the dresser and noticed something that hadn't been there the last time she had been in the nursery. "Is that one of those Echos?"

Lily glanced at the electronic device and grinned. "Yes. I just hooked it up. Check this out. Alexa, turn on Connor's lights." Overhead, the lights turned on. Then a voice coming from the dresser said, "Okay."

Confused, Walt looked up to the ceiling light. "Who was that? What did you just do?"

"See, I'm almost as good as you and Marie," Lily boasted while Ian rolled his eyes and sat down on the floor with his son.

Danielle glanced over to Lily and cocked her brows. "I can't believe you got one of those."

Walt frowned.

"Yep. Now watch this. Alexa, play nursery rhymes," Lily said.

The voice from the dresser said something before nursery rhymes began playing.

Lily laughed and said, "Alexa, stop."

"You told me you would never get one of those things. Said something about them being able to listen to you," Danielle said.

"Ah, now I remember what that is," Walt said, pleased with himself he had figured it out.

Lily shrugged. "I just got one for this room. I figure they won't be getting any state secrets from the nursery." She looked at Walt and asked, "This couldn't pick up Marie's voice, could it?"

"No. It's not sound waves like a voice from a living person," Walt explained.

Lily nodded. "That's what I figured."

"Why did you get it?" Danielle asked.

"I decided it would be convenient when my hands are full with Connor. Turning lights on, listening to music or having it read to me. I haven't checked all its features yet," Lily said.

⸻

WILBUR OPENED his eyes and looked up to the sky. Disoriented, he wasn't sure where he was—or what day of the week it might be. Blinking several times, he awkwardly sat up and looked around at his surroundings. It surprised him to find himself stretched out on the beach. He looked behind him and spied a row of houses. In front of him was the ocean, its waves breaking on shore before retreating in a steady rhythm. It was then he noticed it, the gunnysack, washed up on shore a short distance from where he now sat. It was the reason he was here.

He remembered now. Beau. Beau had tried to kill him. He wasn't sure why. None of it had made any sense. They had a deal, and Wilbur had been more than generous. Now, he needed to get somewhere safe, find another hiding place, until he could work it all out. He stood up and glanced around. The beach was virtually empty save for a guy running down the shore in his direction.

Wilbur considered retrieving the gunnysack but decided it best to leave it until he figured out where he was going. The last thing he needed was to have someone question the bag and ask to see inside. How could he explain any of it? Especially since he didn't understand himself.

He silently observed the runner. It wasn't one of Beau's men, of that he was fairly certain, and he didn't see where he could carry a gun. Finally, he turned his back to the man and started walking toward the houses. Perhaps he might find someone who would help him.

He had walked a short distance when pounding feet on the sand and heavy breathing caught his attention. Turning to the sound, it surprised him to find the runner barreling toward him, and he didn't appear to be slowing down or about to change course.

"Hey, look out!" Wilbur shouted. In the next moment the man ran straight through Wilbur's body, continuing south down the beach without breaking stride.

Wilbur stood speechless for a few minutes, watching the runner's back as he continued down the beach.

"It was another ghost!" Wilbur blurted. "Another damn ghost!"

Wilbur didn't understand any of it. He had never seen ghosts before, not until Beau had tried killing him. But Wilbur had survived the attack, nursed himself back to health, and since that time had seen ghosts. He had read about the phenomenon of acquiring a gift after experiencing a traumatic event. But this was one gift he would rather not have.

"People will think I'm crazy," he muttered under his breath. "If I'm to convince anyone what Beau has done, I can't tell them I see ghosts."

While pondering his current situation, he failed to notice a second runner coming in his direction. It was not until he heard more pounding feet on the sand did he turn toward the runner. This one was a woman, with long black braids, each bouncing up and down as she made her way toward him.

Preparing to jump out of the runner's way should it be another ghost; relief washed over him when she took a detour around him and flashed him a smile and said, "Good morning."

He returned the smile and said hello as she continued on her way, in the same direction as the ghost runner. Relieved it wasn't another spirit, he continued on to the houses, hoping to find someone who could help him. Wilbur was about six feet from one house when its back door opened, and out walked a man wearing a blue baseball cap with a large red C on its crown. The man stood in the doorway, holding the door open, looking in Wilbur's direction with a smile.

Believing the man looked trustworthy, and willing to give it a shot, Wilbur said, "Excuse me, I'm in trouble. Can you help me?"

The man said nothing, but held the door open wider, as if inviting him inside.

Wilbur flashed the man a smile in silent thanks and quickly ducked into the house. He was about five feet down the hallway when the man yelled, "Sadie! Come on!"

The next moment a large golden dog came running down the hallway, stopping a moment to look at him.

Wilbur glanced down at the dog and thought it looked friendly and nonthreatening, yet he had the strangest sensation the dog had just asked, "Who are you?"

The next moment the man holding the door open called out, "Sadie, come!"

The dog quickly lost interest in Wilbur and continued on its way, running out the back door. The next moment the door shut, and Wilbur found himself alone in the hallway. Somewhat confused, Wilbur continued down the hall and then heard voices. He looked into what appeared to be a living room. There was a petite redhead holding a baby, a brunette standing next to her, and a man…Walt Marlow!

Wilbur immediately recognized Walt Marlow. His eyes widened.

I can't let Marlow see me, he thought. Fortunately, none of them noticed him standing in the hallway entrance.

Spinning around, he started back down the hallway when he spied the door he had initially entered opening. Not sure what to do, Wilbur darted through the first open doorway. It was a baby's nursery. In a panic, he looked around and spied a closet, its door partially open. He ran to the closet and dived in. Wilbur huddled in its dark corner, once again terrified.

WILBUR HAD no idea how long he had been in the closet when a woman's voice broke the silence. Peeking out into the nursery from the closet, he spied the redhead carrying the baby.

"Alexa, turn on Connor's light," she said.

The next moment the overhead light went on, and a woman's voice said, "Okay."

Wilbur glanced around the room, looking for this Alexa. He saw no one but the redhead and baby.

He watched as she changed the baby's diaper and put him down in the crib.

The redhead said, "Alexa, play lullabies."

Alexa said something and then music began playing.

"Alexa, turn the volume down," the redhead said.

The music's volume lowered.

The redhead leaned over the crib and kissed the baby. Standing back up, she said, "Alexa, turn off Connor's light."

The overhead light turned off, and again the invisible woman said, "Okay."

Trembling in fear, Wilbur watched as the redhead left the nursery, shutting the door behind her and leaving him alone with the baby and Alexa.

This place is haunted, Wilbur thought as he huddled farther into the dark corner. *But this Alexa ghost is invisible and has powers. That's much worse than the others.*

FIVE

O n Friday evening, the friends on Beach Drive gathered at the Bartleys' for a barbecue. It included Walt, Danielle, Chris, Heather, and a few who did not live on Beach Drive, such as Adam and Melony, and Ian's sister, Kelly, along with her boyfriend, Officer Joe Morelli. Ian and Lily had invited the chief and his sons, but they had somewhere else they needed to go.

Ian and Walt had arranged extra folding chairs on the back patio before their friends arrived. Walt sat in one chair, drinking a cold beer, when Sadie came to sit by his side. She looked up at him. Their eyes met. They were still staring at each other when Danielle took the empty seat next to Walt, a glass of wine in her hand.

"You and Sadie having a pleasant chat?" she asked.

Turning to his wife, Walt whispered, "Have you seen any ghost around here?"

"You mean Eva or Marie?" Danielle asked.

Walt shook his head. "No. A man. A stranger. Sadie saw someone in the house earlier."

Danielle glanced to Ian and Lily's house, then back to Walt. "What man?"

Walt shrugged. "It was when Ian took Sadie outside when we were here this morning. He was in the hallway, and from what Sadie picked up, he was looking for someone to help him."

Danielle looked to the house again and back to Walt. "You think he's still in there?"

"If he is, I would think one of us would have seen him."

Danielle motioned to Chris, who stood next to the barbecue grill, talking to Ian. A moment later, Chris walked over to them. Walt asked him about the mystery ghost.

"I walked through their house, didn't see anyone other than the regulars," Chris said, keeping his voice low so the non-mediums wouldn't hear. "I would have said something if I had seen someone out of place. But if that was this morning, I wouldn't be surprised if whoever it was moved on already. Sometimes that happens. A spirit pops in, lost and confused, and then disappears, never to be seen again. But I'll ask Heather."

Walt and Danielle watched as Chris walked to Heather, who stood talking to Kelly. Chris pulled her aside for a moment and whispered in her ear. Heather looked over to Walt and Danielle and shook her head, no.

"I don't want to freak Lily. Let's not say anything to her," Danielle told Walt as Chris walked back to the grill, and Heather resumed her conversation with Kelly.

"No reason to. You're right, it would just upset her," Walt agreed.

SINCE CHRIS AND IAN GRILLED, the others cleaned up after dinner, while Ian and Chris took their dogs out on the beach to play Frisbee. With so many hands pitching in, it didn't take long to finish and return to the back patio and enjoy more beer and wine while snacking on the pan of brownies Danielle had contributed. Danielle eventually took a seat next to Walt on the patio while their friends walked out to the beach. They watched their friends playing Frisbee. The only ones not playing were Lily and Kelly, who sat on a beach blanket—a safe distance away from the Frisbee players—with Connor, who played with a plastic bucket and shovel.

"Do you want to join them?" Danielle asked Walt, nodding to the Frisbee players.

Reaching out, he brushed his fingers down the side of her face and said, "I feel like sitting a bit, if you don't mind. I'm a little tired.

I'm afraid I didn't get much sleep last night after Max told me about our intruders. But if you want to go play…"

Danielle shook her head and leaned closer to Walt, resting her head against his shoulder. "No. I didn't get much sleep last night myself." She and Walt stared out to the beach while their friends threw a Frisbee, and Hunny and Sadie did their best to snatch it from one of the humans.

"I threw a Frisbee once, in my first life."

She turned to look at him. "They had Frisbees back then?"

Walt grinned.

"Oh, you mean you threw some disk around that looks like a Frisbee?" Danielle asked.

"No. It was a Frisbee. But they spelled it differently," Walt explained.

Danielle frowned. "What do you mean spelled differently?"

"I visited a friend once when I was in college. He lived in Connecticut, where he attended university, not far from the Frisbie Pie Company. I believe they spelled it f-r-i-s-b-i-e instead of two *e*'s. His friends used to make a game out of tossing around one of the empty pie tins. Not much different from what they're doing out on the beach right now. But before throwing the tin, it was protocol to shout *Frisbie* to give others notice of the incoming missile."

"You're making that up," Danielle accused.

Walt shook his head. "No. When Chris first brought a Frisbee home for Hunny, it reminded me of my friend in Connecticut. Curious to discover if there was any connection, I did a little research online. One article said the pie-tin-tossing game inspired today's Frisbee, yet claimed the story was unproven. But I was there. I know it was true."

Danielle grinned. "I like that story. Even if it isn't true."

"But it is," Walt insisted.

Danielle leaned closer and kissed Walt's cheek. She looked back to where her friends tossed the Frisbee around on the beach.

———

THEY HADN'T NOTICED it before—none of them had—the gunnysack that had washed up on the beach earlier that morning. The surf had pushed it up behind some rocks, concealing it from view. But the surf had since dragged it away from the rocks, sending it down the shore a couple of hundred yards before pushing it back on the sand.

Hunny saw it first and abandoned the Frisbee that had just flown over her head to Joe. A moment later Sadie spied Hunny running toward the surf and wondered what she was chasing. No longer interested in the Frisbee, Sadie ran after her canine pal.

Chris's attention moved from the Frisbee in Joe's hand to the two dogs racing to the ocean, ready to pounce on some debris that had washed up on shore. He let out a sigh and took off jogging toward the dogs, not wanting them to tear up its unknown contents. Toxic and questionable material occasionally washed up on shore.

Moments after Chris took off, Ian saw where he was going. Sharing Chris's concern, Ian ran toward the dogs. The rest of the friends stopped playing the game and watched Chris and Ian.

Hunny reached the bag first and took hold of one end, dragging it up the beach. Sadie joined her a moment later and grabbed the other end. By the time Chris and Ian reached their dogs, the canines were engaged in a lively tug-of-war, doing their best to tear open the bag and spill whatever contents it had on the sand.

Back on the patio where Walt and Danielle had been sitting and watching their friends, Walt stood.

"I should probably help them. I wonder what those two have gotten into," Walt said before taking off in a jog, heading to the dogs. Danielle followed at a slower pace.

HUNNY AND SADIE refused to listen to their humans, who repeatedly shouted for them to let go of the drenched burlap bag. The smells were too enticing, and the prize inside too tempting. Plus, this game of tug-of-war made it impossible for either dog to break concentration and listen to their humans. Each dog understood if she did that, she would lose hold of her end and the other dog would get the prize.

The rest of the Frisbee players gathered nearby, watching and chuckling at Ian and Chris's inability to get control of their dogs— normally exceptionally well-behaved animals. The moment Walt reached the group, the bag tore open and its contents spilled out onto the beach.

The dogs went wild with excitement—*bones!* Just as they each grabbed a large bone, Walt noticed it, as did everyone else, a skull—a human skull. Both Chris and Ian tried to take the bones away and bring the dogs to heel, but Sadie and Hunny, engrossed in their game of keep-away, ignored their humans.

Walt stood nearby, trying to get the dogs' attention with his telepathy, yet their current game was too distracting. Narrowing his eyes and annoyed at being ignored by Sadie and Hunny, he focused his attention on the bones the dogs held. The next moment the bones flew from the dogs' mouths, landing several feet away.

Startled by the abrupt loss, Sadie and Hunny looked toward the humans. Their eyes met Walt's. If the dogs had been balloons, one would suspect someone had just deflated them. Abandoning their newly discovered treasure, they lowered their heads and silently walked to their humans. Hunny sat next to Chris, while Sadie sat next to Ian.

Normally Joe, Kelly, Adam and Melony—the friends unaware of Walt's gifts—would have wondered what the hell had just happened, but the attention of all four fixed on the human skull sitting atop a pile of bones. They'd failed to witness the bones being jerked from the dogs' mouths.

Hesitantly, they approached the gruesome discovery.

"Are those real?" Heather asked as she got closer.

Joe leaned down and examined the bones. "Looks real."

Silently, without saying a word, Joe picked up the skull and looked at it a moment and then set it on the beach. As if they had all come to some silent agreement, they each began picking up the random bones the dogs had scattered and placed them by the skull —puzzle like—recreating what had once been a human skeleton.

When finished, they stood in a circle around the eerie sight. There was no doubt what they were all looking at, the skeletal remains of a human.

"I need to call this in," Joe said.

———

"SADIE AND HUNNY seem to have a knack for uncovering human bones," Officer Brian Henderson said as he stood some distance away from the skeletal remains while the coroner examined them.

"At least I didn't trip over the damn thing," Heather said. "And I jogged up here this morning."

"It's not a thing," Kelly reprimanded her. "That was some poor person." She looked to Joe and asked, "Do you have any idea who it is?"

Joe shrugged. "How would I know? He wasn't carrying an ID."

With a frown, Kelly swatted Joe's forearm. "Brat."

"By the condition of the bag, I don't think they were in the ocean for a long time. Couple of days at best," Brian said.

"This is just creepy," Lily said. She handed a sleeping Connor to Ian, who stood by her side with Sadie. "How long does it take for a body to decompose and leave skeletal remains?"

"In the right conditions, it can take under a month," Brian said.

SIX

Alone, he walked toward the entrance of Pier Café on Saturday morning. They had agreed to meet at the restaurant to go over the plans. Before entering the building, he spied the newspaper stand by the door. He hadn't intended to buy a paper until he saw the headline: *Skeletal Remains Wash Up on Frederickport Beach.* Hastily he pulled money from his pocket, purchased a newspaper, and entered the restaurant.

The others hadn't arrived yet, but the waitress with the rainbow-colored hair told him to sit wherever he wanted. He took a seat at the far end of the café, trying to keep a distance from the other diners, wanting as much privacy as possible when they arrived.

He sat down at the table and opened the newspaper when the rainbow-haired waitress asked if he wanted coffee. After he told her yes, she flipped one of the empty coffee cups sitting on the table right side up and filled it while saying, "That's really something about those bones washing up on shore. It wasn't far from here."

The man looked at her over his newspaper. The name tag on her blouse said Carla. *Chatty Carla*, he told himself.

"They were in a gunnysack," Carla continued. "But Hunny and Sadie tore it up. They're dogs. Heather told me about it. She was here this morning having breakfast. That's Heather Donovan, she lives down the street. To be honest, I'm surprised she wasn't the one who found it, not the dogs. She has a reputation for finding dead

31

bodies when she jogs. I'm surprised that girl hasn't bought a tread-mill and given up running on the beach. If it was me, I would've given it up after tripping over the first body. Don't you agree?"

He stared at Carla a moment before asking, "Did you say they were in a gunnysack?"

"Yes. And according to the police, they hadn't been in the ocean for long, just a couple of days. I wondered how long it would take for a dead body to decompose like that. And according to Heather, she stopped in here earlier after her morning jog—like I said, that girl is still jogging on the beach, which I certainly don't understand. But according to Brian, that's Brian Henderson, he's on the local police force, a body can decompose down to a skeleton in less than a month. So obviously someone murdered that poor guy in the last month and dumped his skeleton in the ocean. Do you think they put him in acid or something?"

The man blinked at Carla, yet he did not answer her question.

A bell from the kitchen rang, breaking Carla's stride. She glanced over her shoulder toward the kitchen and then looked back to him and flashed a smile. "I have an order up. But I'll be right back to take yours." She turned and hurried off.

Shaking his head while mumbling to himself, he looked at the newspaper and began reading the news article about the discovery of skeletal remains. He had just finished the article when a younger man joined him.

"Where's your sister?" the older man asked.

The recent arrival sat down hastily and said, "It's just me. Something came up."

"Something like bones washing up on shore?" he asked, slamming the article he had been reading on the table, headline side up.

The younger man looked down at the paper and cringed.

"What in the hell were you thinking?" the older man demanded.

"You told us to dump them in the ocean. I didn't think it would wash up on shore. At least not in Frederickport."

"And they wouldn't have washed up if you took them out of the gunnysack before you dumped them," the older man snapped.

"That's not true. Stuff washes up on shore all the time. We figured if they were all put in a bag, it would weight it down and sink to the bottom of the ocean," the younger man argued.

"They didn't."

"What's the big deal? No way anyone will figure out where they came from."

Before he responded, Carla returned to the table and took their order. When she left the table, the older man said, "I'm not worried about them tracing the bones, I'm worried about them tracing that damn gunnysack."

"Even if they do, they can't prove anything."

"I want nothing that can link us to this. Have you forgotten what this is all about? That's why we're here. And you throw those damn bones in the ocean without taking them out of the bag."

"We had to do it at the end of the pier, and there were people around. I couldn't let anyone see me taking them out of the bag and dumping them."

The older man grew silent and stared at his companion. After a moment he said, "Are you telling me someone may have seen you throw that bag off the pier?"

"No! Not at all. We were careful. I hid it under my jacket, and when we got to the end of the pier, we looked around, made sure no one was watching, and then dropped it in the water. It took a moment to sink. But no one was around to see it. I promise."

AS THE TWO men sat alone at a table at Pier Café, discussing the skeletal remains, Danielle accompanied Walt to the Frederickport Library. They had invited him to speak to one of the local book clubs that met each Saturday. Driving the Packard, Walt pulled into the parking lot of the library and turned off the ignition. He turned to Danielle, who sat in the passenger seat.

"I'm surprised they want me to speak to their group. Looks like the *Moon Runners* movie is officially dead," Walt said.

"Your book made the *New York Times* bestseller list. Movie or not, you're a local celebrity."

"I don't particularly enjoy giving interviews. People start asking me questions—like do I still have amnesia, or what can I remember."

Danielle silently studied Walt for a moment, cocking her head slightly. Finally, she asked, "If you could make things different, what would you change?"

Walt considered the question and smiled. "I suppose nothing, because then I wouldn't be sitting here with you now. There is no way to rewrite history that might bring us together. Perhaps having you born years earlier, meeting you instead of Angela. But then you wouldn't be you, would you? We're shaped by our circumstances, our environment, family and friends. There was no other way to shift the world around to bring us together than the way it happened."

"Oh my, you are being philosophical today."

Walt chuckled. "Yes, I suppose I am."

Danielle leaned across the seat, gave Walt a kiss, and said, "Come on, let's get going. Your fans await."

KIARA SAT with her cousin Raven in the magazine section of the library. They had arrived early, and the meeting room where the book club was holding the talk had not yet been unlocked. Raven sat next to her on the sofa, flipping through a magazine she had picked up from a table.

"Are you sure they'll let us in there? We aren't members of the book club," Kiara whispered to Raven.

Raven glanced up from the magazine. "Yes. I told you. The flyer said it was open to the public. The book club is sponsoring the talk."

"I wish Laken had come," Kiara said.

"We can handle this," Raven insisted.

Kiara let out a deep breath. "I guess I'm just nervous."

Raven dropped the magazine to her lap and elbowed her cousin.

"Would you stop doing that!" Kiara said.

"Oh...sorry, but look who walked in." Raven nodded to the front of the library. Walt and Danielle Marlow had just entered, and they were talking to a woman.

Kiara looked over to the Marlows. "It's bizarre how much he looks like the other Walt Marlow."

"I'm hoping after today you and Laken see I'm right and we can just go up to Marlow and ask him."

"But like Laken said, why hasn't he already?"

"Why would he? It was so long ago. It's nothing to him," Raven reminded her.

"Unless the first Marlow was more involved, like Laken thinks.

And if that's the case, Walt Marlow wouldn't want his family's reputation tarnished. He's some big-shot author now."

———

LOCATED off the major section of the library, the meeting room slowly filled with people. Members of the book club had arranged rows of folding chairs for those attending today's presentation. Walt stood silently behind the podium at the head of the room. Danielle took a seat in the back row, enabling her to better see those entering the room. Walt flashed her a smile before looking back to the open doorway, watching book club members and their guests trickle in.

Among the early arrivals were two young women; Walt guessed they were a few years younger than Danielle. One looked directly at him. Walt couldn't help but stare. She looked eerily familiar, as if he knew her. But that was not possible. Since moving to this side, there were only a handful of black people he had encountered, and she was not one of them. She whispered something to her companion, who looked his way. The pair took a seat in the front row.

Walt glanced away from the familiar-looking woman and told himself he must have seen someone who looked like her on television. He watched as the chairs filled. The meeting started at the scheduled time, beginning with the president of the book club introducing Walt to the group. Walt discussed the writing of *Moon Runners*, its publishing path, and the movie deal that had fallen apart. When he finished his presentation, he took questions.

After Walt answered about six questions, the familiar-looking woman raised her hand. Walt called on her.

"What was your inspiration for *Moon Runners*?" she asked.

"I'm interested in local history, and I always found that era intriguing, so I started researching that time period, and the story idea came to me."

"Are you saying you based the story on actual events?" she asked.

"Only in the sense the backdrop to the story was prohibition and bootlegging, which occurred during that era, and inspired my storyline."

Her friend raised her hand, and he called on her. "Earlier when someone asked if you ever got your memory back from your accident, you said you hadn't. So, when you say you were always interested in that era, I have to assume you meant since you settled in Frederickport two years ago. Was this interest triggered by something you happened upon when you moved here. Perchance a diary of the original Walt Marlow or his letters?" she asked.

Walt stared at her a moment before saying, "As far as I'm aware, Walt Marlow didn't leave a diary behind. I've never seen any of his letters, and I'm unaware of any the local museum might have."

"So the story was completely from your imagination?"

"I guess you could say that," Walt said.

"HE'S LYING," Kiara told her cousin when they left the library later that morning.

"Maybe Laken is right," Raven said.

SEVEN

"You lied to those women," Danielle teased after she settled in the passenger seat of the Packard and watched Walt take his place on the driver's side. He closed the car door. Removing his fedora hat, Walt tossed it in the back seat and looked her way. "I couldn't very well tell them an actual life event inspired the plot. It would be different if there was some record of what happened back then—but there isn't. I looked."

"Not that. I meant when you said there were no letters. I have the letters Marie gave me that you wrote to her father, remember?"

"I forgot about those. But they included nothing that would have inspired *Moon Runners*."

"Aside from lying to those women, I thought you did an outstanding job," Danielle said cheerfully.

"The one who asked me what inspired *Moon Runners*, I could swear I know her. I understand that's impossible, but there is something so eerily familiar about her."

"It's probably because you saw her the other night," Danielle suggested.

"I did?" Walt asked.

"At Pearl Cove. She walked by our table, looked right at us."

"I don't remember seeing her," Walt said.

"From what I recall, you were arguing with Chris about some-

---

thing at the time. But you must have seen her. You just said she looked familiar."

Walt frowned. "She does. But I don't recall seeing her at Pearl Cove. Have you seen her before Pearl Cove?"

Danielle shook her head. "No. I don't think so. At least, not that I can remember."

"Perhaps she's on television," Walt suggested.

"Or you knew her from another life?"

Walt chuckled. "Entirely possible."

"Aside from getting frustrated trying to place her—personally, I hate when that happens—did you have a good time?"

"Yes. It was a friendly group. And I'll admit I enjoyed that more than sitting down with a professional interviewer. It's interesting to hear what my readers are thinking."

"They were sure eager to hear more about your next book. But you didn't give them much."

"I don't like discussing a work in progress with strangers," he said.

"I know."

"I wonder, if I'm interviewed in ten years, will someone still be asking me if my memory came back?" Walt asked.

"Amnesia has always been one of those…sexy ailments."

"Sexy?" Walt frowned.

"I guess sexy is probably the wrong word. But it was a favorite in the soap opera world. Mom used to watch them. There always seemed to be someone who had amnesia, a handy plot device, and later, when I was older, I realized I had never known anyone who ever had amnesia. I still don't."

Walt glanced at his watch. "We'd better get going. Edward will be waiting for us."

WHEN WALT and Danielle walked into Lucy's Diner fifteen minutes later, they found Police Chief Edward MacDonald already sitting at a booth, with a glass of iced tea sitting on the table before him and a menu in his hands. When he noticed them, he closed the menu, set it on the table, and stood up, extending a handshake to Walt and a quick hug to Danielle.

"Looks like Hawaii agreed with you," the chief said after they all took a seat in the booth.

"It was wonderful, but good to get home," Danielle said.

"Even after learning someone broke into your house and what the dogs found in front of Lily and Ian's last night?" the chief asked.

"Some things never change," Danielle said with a snort as she picked up a menu and opened it.

"Have you learned anything new about what they found?" Walt asked.

Before the chief answered the question, the server showed up at the table and took their drink orders. When she left, Danielle repeated Walt's question.

"The remains belong to a man," the chief explained. "Cause of death, he was shot."

"How do you know?" Danielle asked.

"The bullet lodged in the skull was the first clue."

"There was a bullet in the skull?" Danielle frowned. "No one mentioned that, but most of us didn't look that closely. Once your team showed up, they asked us to keep our distance."

"Any idea how long he's been dead?" Walt asked.

"No. But the bag wasn't in the ocean for more than a few days," the chief began.

Danielle nodded and said, "Brian mentioned something about the condition of the bag, that it didn't look like it had been in the water for long."

"More than the condition of the bag told us how long it had been in the water. The bag had a tag inside. It's a new company, just made its first delivery to Frederickport a little over a week ago. Brian's working on tracking who purchased any," the chief explained.

"Brian said a body can decompose down to skeletal remains in a month under the right conditions. Do you have any missing person report for a man in the last couple of months?"

"I have a hunch his death occurred longer than a few months ago," the chief said.

"Why do you say that?" Walt asked.

"Because of the bullet in the skull. It's from a .35 Smith and Wesson center-fire cartridge," the chief explained.

"What does that mean?" Danielle asked. "I'm not a gun person."

"They stopped making them in the 1920s. In fact, if you can find any, they're considered a collector's item."

"So either someone shot this guy almost a hundred years ago, or they used an antique gun and a valuable bullet to do it?" Danielle asked.

"Unfortunately, it's difficult to determine when our victim died. It might have been a couple of months ago—or a hundred years ago. And the only reason the coroner identified the bullet so quickly, he's a collector and owns a .35 Smith and Wesson."

"Is the coroner our killer?" Danielle teased.

"Since meeting you, Danielle, I've learned anything is possible," the chief said.

BEAU STEWART STOOD on the sidewalk and opened the door to Lucy's Diner. He held it open for his wife as she entered the building, before following her in. Once inside, he glanced around, looking for somewhere to sit. The sign up front said "seat yourself." He spied the Marlows sitting with Police Chief MacDonald, and a few booths down from them was an empty table. There was also an empty table in the opposite direction, but he wanted an opportunity to talk to the Marlows and the police chief. Placing his palm along the spine of his wife's back, he nodded in the direction he wanted to go, gently nudging her that way. She flashed him a smile before taking his lead.

Once he arrived at the Marlows' table, he stopped to say hello and introduce his wife to Walt and Danielle.

"We met the other night," Beau explained.

"Yes, you're one of Adam's clients," Danielle said with a smile.

"I'd like you to meet my wife, Francine," Beau introduced. They exchanged greetings, and it became clear to Danielle the chief had already met the Stewarts.

"I understand you're staying at one of Adam's rentals. Are you renovating your new property here and moving to Frederickport full time?" Danielle knew they weren't planning to move to Frederickport, but she was just trying to make conversation.

"Yes and no," Francine said. "It's a beautiful piece of land, but the buildings…" She gave an exaggerated shiver. "And no, Frederickport will be a vacation home. Our children will love it."

"How old are your kids?" Danielle asked.

Francine laughed. "I imagine about your age."

Before Danielle responded, Beau asked the chief, "What is this I hear about human remains washing up on the beach?"

"A gunnysack filled with human bones washed up north of the pier," the chief said.

"I read the article," Francine said. "Horrible. Have you been able to identify the poor person?"

"It'll be a while before the tests are back," the chief explained.

"I don't even want to think about it!" Francine shivered. She looked at Danielle and said, "I understand you're having a fundraiser on the fourth, for the Humane Society."

"We are. I hope you can make it," Danielle said with a smile.

"Is it true it includes a tour of Marlow House? I was heart-broken when I heard it was no longer a B and B. I would have loved to have stayed there while we're in town."

"Yes, it includes a tour," Danielle told her.

"We'll be there!" Francine said. "I can't wait to see inside."

"I IMAGINE Adam told you they bought that run-down place outside of town, about a half a mile from where that house burned down last year," the chief said when the Stewarts left their table and were out of earshot.

"You mean the one with the broken-down red barn?" Danielle asked.

"Yes."

"He didn't mention where exactly, just that it was owned by Beau's cousin," Danielle said. "If the Stewarts have money, I'm surprised they bought that place. It's not even walking distance to the beach unless you want a good hike. I'd think for a vacation home, you'd want something closer to the beach," Danielle said.

"From what I've heard, that land has been in the same family for years. I think that's the actual reason Stewart bought it, to keep it in the family. But his wife is right, the buildings are in dreadful condition. In fact, the city was getting ready to condemn the property."

"I thought the cousin sold it because he's ill?" Walt asked.

"He is," the chief said before adding, "From what I understand, Stewart initially went to his cousin when he heard the city was getting pressure to do something about that property. He even helped him work out an arrangement with the city, allowing him to sell it, providing the new owners agreed to clean up the land within two years. But then the cousin's adult children got involved, and they convinced their father to list the property. Stewart ended up with it anyway, at the same price he initially offered."

EIGHT

Every time Wilbur tried slipping from the nursery to leave the house, someone walked down the hall. One time he was sure the man with the blue baseball cap had seen him, but he walked by, apparently so engrossed in his thoughts he failed to see the stranger standing in his hallway. But it was the dog Wilbur did his best to avoid.

Wilbur did not understand how long he had been in the nursery closet. He had left it many times trying to escape the house holding him hostage, but each time he retreated to the sanctuary. He looked from his hideout out into the nursery, through a pair of half-closed closet doors. The baby slept peacefully in his crib. The mother, or at least who Wilbur assumed was the mother, had come in several times, and each time summoned up that ghost Alexa to do her bidding. Perhaps the redhead was a witch, Wilbur wondered. He had heard there were some witches living on the north side of Fred-erickport. Was it possible Alexa was not a ghost, but a demon, a demon the redheaded witch used for her own wicked means? The thought gave Wilbur chills.

Retreating into a dark corner, he sat glumly, asking himself how he had gotten into this mess. Inheriting that property had caused him nothing but grief. Had his sister been right all along? If he could contact his sister, would she even help him now?

He heard something in the nursery and peeked out into the

room. The baby was no longer sleeping but now standing up in the crib, holding onto the railing and bouncing up and down while giggling. Easing from the closet, Wilbur stood up and crept to the crib. When the baby noticed him approaching, he broke into a smile instead of crying, which pleased Wilbur.

"Hello, little man," Wilbur whispered.

The baby gurgled, his eyes bright, as he clung to the crib rail and continued to bounce.

"You are such an innocent thing," Wilbur said, glancing quickly to the closed bedroom door, back to the baby. "I need to protect you. I'm sure you love your mama, but I don't think she's considering your best interest, dabbling in the supernatural."

He wondered if someone was listening to him. Was it possible Alexa watched him? Mustering his courage for the sake of the baby, he said, "Alexa, are you there? Can you hear me? If you can hear me, turn on the light."

Nothing happened, and Wilbur felt a flood of relief. Had he been able to summon the demon—or ghost—then what? He wanted to make sure this Alexa wasn't lingering nearby.

"My sister may not want to help me, but she would never turn her back on an innocent baby," he whispered to the drooling child. He heard someone turn the doorknob. Without thought, he pivoted to the closet and raced for cover. Once again hidden, he heard the door open and the woman's voice.

"Connor, you're awake!" she said cheerfully. "Alexa, turn on Connor's light." From his closet sanctuary, Wilbur saw the glow from the room's overhead light.

"Okay," said Alexa.

The next moment the dog, who had followed the redhead into the bedroom, stuck his head into the closet and looked at Wilbur. The dog barked.

"Sadie, what are you barking at?" the redhead's voice asked.

Moving farther into the closet and hiding behind a box of toys, Wilbur prayed the woman would not see him. The dog barked again, and Wilbur had the insane notion the dog had just asked, "Who are you, and what are you doing in my house?"

The closet door slid open the rest of the way, and the woman peeked inside. "What are you barking at, Sadie? I hope it isn't a mouse. Dang, why did Ian have to go to Vancouver today? Come on, I'm taking you to see Walt and find out once and for all what your problem is."

The woman dragged the dog from the closet and shut its door, leaving it open half an inch. Wilbur peeked out into the room. The dog was nowhere in sight. He suspected she had put him out into the hallway. He watched as she changed the baby's diaper and clothes, and then picked him up, leaving the room.

Was she also leaving the house? he wondered. Was this his chance to get away? He started to open the closet door and found himself standing in the nursery. He looked back at the barely open closet door. Scratching his head in confusion, he stared at the door a moment and mumbled, "How did I squeeze through that small opening?" With a shrug, he turned toward the bedroom window. When he reached it, he peeked outside and spied the redhead walking across the street. She carried the baby in her arms, with the big golden dog by her side.

"Good, they're leaving," he said aloud. Considering what she had said about someone named Ian going to Vancouver, he assumed he was now alone in the house.

Hurrying, he reached for the bedroom door, and in the next moment he stood in the hallway. He didn't give much thought to the fact he didn't remember opening the bedroom door to get out of the room, but crazy things like that had been happening lately. Running down the hallway toward the door he had initially entered, he didn't stop to open it and found himself standing outside again, looking out to the ocean.

He remembered the gunnysack. "I have to find that bag," he told himself. "Then I can go to my sister."

WHEN LILY ARRIVED at Walt and Danielle's house a few minutes later, Danielle answered the front door.

"How did Walt's thing with the book club go?" Lily asked as she followed Danielle to the parlor.

"It was nice. I thought it was just for the book club, but I guess they had flyers up at the library, opening it to the public," Danielle said.

"Yeah, right. Walt didn't want us to go," Lily said as she entered the parlor.

"I didn't want you to go where?" Walt asked from where he sat on one of the parlor chairs, a book in hand.

"Your presentation today," Lily said as she walked all the way in the room with Connor.

"I thought Ian had to go to Vancouver today?" Danielle asked.

"He did. I was teasing," Lily said as she struggled with a wiggling Connor in her arms. Now almost ten months old, he was difficult to carry for an extended period.

Walt set his book on the end table and put out his arms. "Why don't you give me the little guy?"

"I need you to talk to Sadie first." Lily sat on the sofa, plopping the baby on her lap. He leaned back on his mother's chest and began examining his hands while making fists.

"What's going on?" Danielle asked, taking a seat on the sofa with Lily. She reached out and tickled the baby, who climbed off his mother's lap and into Danielle's arms.

"Sadie's acting weird. I think there might be a mouse in the nursery. Can you please talk to her, Walt? See why she's barking at the closet. Do I need to borrow Max or something?"

Danielle chuckled. "Max might like that."

Walt looked down at Sadie, who was already sitting at his side.

"Well, girl, what's the problem?" Walt asked. "Lily tells me you have been—" Walt stopped talking and stared at the dog. After a moment he said, "The same one?"

"The same one what?" Lily asked.

Walt let out a sigh and looked over to Lily. "Danielle and I need to go over to your house and check out that closet."

"What do you mean?" Lily asked.

"Oh…I think I know," Danielle muttered.

Lily frowned at her friend. "Know what, Dani?"

"I'm afraid there's a ghost hanging out at your house," Walt said.

"I assume you're not talking about Marie or Eva?" Lily asked.

"It's a man. Sadie first noticed him yesterday morning in your hallway. She mentioned it to me last night."

"And why didn't you tell me?" Lily screeched.

"We didn't want to worry you," Danielle explained. "Sadie saw him once yesterday morning, and no one else did. Chris said it was probably just a spirit who was passing through and got lost. It happens sometimes."

"No one saw him because he has obviously been hiding in the nursery closet. In Connor's room!" Lily said.

"It doesn't sound like he has any powers," Walt said.

"Powers or not, I don't want some creepy man hanging around my son! I don't care if he is dead!" Lily blurted.

Walt stood up. "Okay, we'll go over there, check it out. You stay here. Keep Sadie with you, that way she can let you know if he shows up here."

"Wonderful!" Lily cried. "Now he's stalking us!"

"Walt didn't say that. Calm down, Lily. We'll go check out your house," Danielle said.

THEY SEARCHED the nursery closet first and found no ghost. After the nursery they went through the entire house, looking in closets, behind furniture, anywhere a ghost might hide.

"Perhaps he's here and playing ghost hide-and-seek," Danielle suggested.

"I wondered that myself. Slipping through walls as we enter a room."

"One way to catch a ghost—have extra eyes watching," Danielle said.

Walt nodded in agreement. Danielle pulled out her phone and called Chris and Heather. It was Saturday; they should both be home.

Less than fifteen minutes later, Chris and Heather showed up at the Bartleys' house. Strategically the four mediums moved through every room yet did not find the mystery spirit.

"I bet he's on the roof, laughing his butt off at us," Heather said after they exhausted their search. They stood in the Bartley living room.

"Or we could just do this," Chris said. His friends looked at him. Chris shouted to the room, "Come, show yourself! We know you're here! We just want to help! The dog saw you hiding in the baby's room! The dog saw you! We can help you! Show yourself!"

They all waited quietly. Nothing happened.

"Gee, that worked," Heather said with a snort.

Chris shrugged. "It was worth a try."

"All I can do at this point is have a talk with Sadie. If he shows up again, she'll tell Lily so we can come right over," Walt said.

"And how are you going to do that?" Heather asked. "It's not like Sadie communicates with Lily like she does you."

"I'll work something out," Walt said.

"It would be nice if Marie came back," Danielle said. "I assumed she would have at least popped in to say hello by now, since Walt and I are back from our vacation."

"The production runs through the fourth, and after Eva invited Marie along, Lily talked her into going. She thought it would be fun for Marie," Heather explained.

"And how did Lily do that?" Danielle asked, knowing Lily could not see or hear Marie.

"I played interpreter for Marie's side," Heather explained with a grin.

"Lily might be regretting that about now," Chris said. "I imagine she didn't figure she'd be swapping one ghost for another."

NINE

W ilbur walked to the end of the pier and sat on an empty bench. Tourists and locals leisurely strolled up and down the pier. A few anglers stood along the railing, tossing their lines to the water below. Some people chatted with friends, and others watched the birds. None seemed to pay Wilbur any notice, which he found comforting. He felt more at peace than he had in a long time, because he had finally freed himself of Beau.

Minutes earlier he had walked by an ice cream shop and café. Both seemed to be fairly busy. He wondered why he wasn't hungry. He couldn't remember the last time he had eaten. But that was probably for the best; he didn't have any money on him.

According to the signs, he was still in Frederickport. He was fairly certain Beau assumed he was dead—that he had drowned. If Beau believed for a moment Wilbur had survived, he would have sent someone to find him. Wilbur leaned back on the bench and closed his eyes, thinking of his sister. He needed to get back to Portland and put this nightmare behind him.

He remained sitting on the bench, leaning back, eyes closed, when he heard someone sitting down next to him. Glancing over, he saw a tall man and a woman sharing his bench. The man looked to be in his fifties, slender with a hook nose. The man sat between Wilbur and the woman, so he was unable to clearly see the woman's face. Closing his eyes again, Wilbur returned to his private thoughts.

"I missed you this morning at breakfast," Wilbur heard the man next to him say to the woman.

"Walt Marlow spoke at the library this morning, and we thought you'd want someone there," she told him.

Wilbur barely opened his eyes and glanced over to the pair. *They know Walt Marlow?* Wilbur asked himself, closing his eyes again, pretending to be asleep.

"Why wasn't I told?" the man demanded.

"We didn't know what would come of it. And we figured you'd already be upset about the bag washing up on shore."

"That's an understatement. What did you find out?" he asked.

"According to Walt Marlow, there is no diary—no letters. He claims events in *Moon Runners* are a product of his imagination, and he only researched the era and this general area for inspiration and background," she said.

"That's a lie," he grumbled.

"I agree. It's too big of a coincidence," she said.

"July Fourth is in four days," he began. "And on the fourth, you can get into Marlow House without breaking in and look for it again."

"How do you figure that?" she asked.

"They're having a fundraiser. It includes a tour of the house. A perfect time to look for it."

"With all the people around?" she asked.

"If someone catches you looking in a drawer, what's the worst that can happen? They'll think you're nosy," he said.

"But what if we can't find it?"

"If we can't find it in Marlow House, there's one other place we need to look," he said.

"Where?" she asked.

"Jon Altar hooked Marlow up with his agent. And Altar lives across the street from him. Reportedly, they're close friends. I'm wondering if Marlow collaborated with Altar. After all, it was Marlow's first book. From everything we've learned about the man, before he showed up in Frederickport two years ago, he was a real estate agent, and I've read a couple of articles where they interviewed people who knew Marlow back when he lived in California."

What is he talking about? Wilbur wondered. *I don't think Marlow ever lived in California.*

"From what I've read on Marlow, according to those people they interviewed, before moving to Oregon, he was never much of a reader and expressed no interest in writing. That's why there must be a diary or letters. And I'm wondering if Marlow found them and took them to Altar."

"Are you suggesting Altar wrote that book, not Marlow?" she asked.

"It's possible."

"Maybe. But today, when someone asked Marlow about the book he's currently writing, he wouldn't say much. In fact, he mentioned that when he wrote *Moon Runners,* he didn't let anyone read it until he finished it, not even Jon Altar, whom he credited for helping him get the book published."

"And he could be lying. He lied about the diary or letters," the man reminded her.

"And what if we don't find them at Altar's house either?" she asked.

"I've already decided one thing we'll have to do. I don't see any way around it."

"You're not suggesting…" she began.

"I told you before, if we can't find it, we burn down Marlow House."

"But someone could get hurt."

"Someone will," he said.

"What are you talking about?" she asked.

"Marlow is writing a second book. What do you imagine it's about?" he asked.

"Yeah, that thought crossed my mind when I heard him talking about it today."

"If it comes to burning down the house, we might as well do it right. Think about it. If Marlow dies, the rest of the story dies—remains untold. And the best time to set a fire is when they're sleeping."

"You want them dead?" she asked.

Wilbur froze. He needed to stay quiet, pretend to be asleep. These insane people were talking murder and so carelessly discussing their plans while he sat next to them. If he was to stand up now and walk away, the man would undoubtably try silencing him.

"What about Altar's house?" she asked.

"When we're there on the fourth, I'm sure the Altars will be there—or more accurately, the Bartleys. If I feel Altar didn't write any of *Moon Runners*, and Marlow hasn't shared the research with him, then there's no reason to do more than take down Marlow and his house."

"What about Danielle Marlow?" she asked.

"Collateral damage."

When the plotting couple sitting next to him finally stood to leave, Wilbur remained frozen on the bench, refusing to open his eyes. He continued to feign sleep, even faking a snore. He assumed they had forgotten he was sitting next to them when they started talking, and once they stood up to leave the bench, they would see him and wonder if he had overheard their deadly conversation. But if he could convince them he had been asleep the entire time, perhaps they would not bother him. Were they now standing nearby, watching him?

After a considerable amount of time elapsed, he opened his eyes and looked around. Relief washed over him; he was alone. Many of those on the pier when he had first arrived had left. The sun was setting. Wearily, he stood up and walked to the side of the pier and looked over its edge. He watched the foamy water slosh around the wood pilings.

He remembered the gunnysack. Where had it gone? he asked himself. Surely it had not washed back to sea. The sea had tucked it under some rocks the last time he saw it. He remembered thinking it was in a safe place until he could retrieve it. Wilbur frowned. Had he picked it up and taken it with him? Perhaps he forgot.

Wilbur asked himself why he had become so forgetful lately. Why did the world seem out of kilter? When had it all changed for him?

Closing his eyes again, he thought back to when everything began spinning out of control. He should never have come to Frederickport. But Beau had agreed to his terms for a reduced price. Perhaps Wilbur was being punished for taking the money that he should have shared with his sister.

He then remembered the opium. It wasn't until after Beau had given it to him he was told what it was. After that, everything went sideways. He pondered the opium, and a thought came to him. Wilbur's eyes flew open. "That's why I keep forgetting things. I wonder...did I take it with me? Is that why I can't find it?" Wilbur said aloud. "I took it with me and left it in the house. I bet it's in the closet, I probably hid it in that box of toys. That's why I can't find it on the beach. I picked it up and took it with me. I never would have left it out in the open, where anyone could find it. That damn opium muddled my brain."

Wilbur took off in a run and raced down the pier. When he reached the sidewalk, he continued north, heading to the house he had taken refuge in. Hopefully, the redhead had not returned. He needed to get inside the house again and find the bag he had stashed there, before returning to Portland.

He was about three doors down from his destination when he spied four people walking across the street from where he had been hiding earlier. Halting, he stared at the four people. He had seen them before. One was Walt Marlow. He watched as they got to the other side of the street. The redhead with the baby walked out of the house across the street and began talking to the four people. After a moment, they all turned and walked up to the house the redhead had come from. Once they were all inside, he spun around and made his way to the beach, taking a shortcut through two houses. This was his chance to find the gunnysack before she returned.

When Wilbur reached the house a few minutes later, he didn't stop to open the door but walked right inside. Not for a moment did he consider it odd that he didn't need to first open the door. He had grown accustomed to the oddities of life since his brush with death.

Once inside, he headed to the nursery, where he searched through the closet and toy box. But it wasn't there. He stepped out of the closet into the nursery. After a few minutes of searching the room, he heard a door open and close. He stood silently in the middle of the room and listened, wondering if he needed to hide in the closet again. Abruptly the nursery door opened, and he ducked behind the rocking chair. The man who had been there earlier looked in the room briefly and then left, shutting the door behind him. A moment later Wilbur heard the man shout, "Lily, are you here?"

The next moment he heard a dog barking. Wilbur raced for the closet and tucked himself into the far corner. Although again trapped, he was for the moment safe.

TEN

If one looked into the old theater and could see the woman sitting in the front row, they might assume she was an actress preparing for her role as the Gibson Girl, a pen and ink illustration created by artist Charles Dana Gibson in the late 1800s, considering her manner of dress, style of hair and delicate facial features. Despite the uncanny resemblance, it was not a drawing come to life, but the silent screen star Eva Thorndike, in death. Eva sat with her friend, a fellow thespian and recently deceased, discussing the previous night's performance. All the seats in the theater except for theirs were empty.

The only other person—or more accurately, ghost—in the theater was Marie Nichols. Marie, who appeared as an elderly woman wearing a floral-patterned sundress, stood a distance from the pair, in the hallway leading to the restrooms, looking up at the clock. It was almost five a.m.

A moment later Marie moved from the clock to the front row and interrupted her friends' conversation when she announced, "I think I'll pop over to Frederickport and say hello to Walt and Danielle. They're back from their trip, and I'd love to see how they enjoyed Hawaii."

"Don't you think it's a little early to be popping in on them?" Eva asked with a mischievous grin. "Or is it really Connor you're dying to see?"

"I'm already dead," Marie reminded them smugly.

Eva's male friend chuckled.

Marie shrugged. "I admit, I'll probably stop in Connor's nursery first, visit him this morning so his parents can sleep in. And then a little later I'll drop in on Walt and Danielle and head back here for the next performance."

"To be honest, dear, I'm surprised you haven't gone before now. It requires little energy to travel from Astoria to Frederickport," Eva said.

"I didn't realize how much I'd miss that little stinker," Marie said. "I don't think I could love him more if he were my own grandson."

Eva smiled. "He is a sweet child."

"And I wonder, when do you suppose Walt and Danielle will give Connor a playmate? If they wait much longer, there'll be too big an age difference for them to be best friends."

"Have you given up on Adam giving you a great-grandchild?" Eva asked.

"Even if he and Melony get married, I don't hold out much promise for those two having children. Melony seems determined not to be a mother, and I have to admit Adam sincerely does not seem to want children."

Eva shrugged. "One never knows how these things will work out. But please say hello to Walt and Danielle for me, and if you decide not to hurry back, I understand."

MARIE ARRIVED in Frederickport at sunrise on Sunday morning. She stood on the middle of Beach Drive and looked over at Marlow House and watched the sun peeking over its rooftop. The street was quiet, and while she could not feel the cool crisp morning breeze, she could smell the salty scent of the ocean, and for that she was grateful.

She turned from Marlow House and made her way to Ian and Lily's, heading for the wall leading into Connor's bedroom. A moment later she stood inside the nursery, next to the window, looking at the crib, and startled to find a young thirty-something man standing over it, staring down at the sleeping child.

"Who are you!" Marie demanded. To her surprise, he looked up at her, his eyes wide.

"Alexa?" the man asked hesitantly.

Marie frowned at his comment. While he could see and hear her, she wasn't convinced he was a ghost. A medium perhaps? And if he was a medium, was he a friend of Ian and Lily's? Did they realize this man was alone with Connor in the nursery?

Focusing her energy, Marie wondered if this was a living man or spirit. She willed him to float up to the ceiling. The next moment— nothing happened. Nothing at all. He remained standing at the crib, looking at her.

"Alexa?" the man repeated.

"Do Lily and Ian know you're in here?" Marie demanded.

"Who?" he asked.

Marie gasped. Realizing he definitely should not be in the nursery and not a hundred percent certain he was a ghost, she willed one of Connor's stuffed animals to fly off the dresser. It hit him squarely in the chest and continued on, flying through his body. Relief washed over her, especially since Eva had assured her the universe would never allow a spirit to harm an innocent.

The man jumped back, startled, and looked down at the stuffed animal now on the floor. As if in slow motion, he looked back to Marie, his wide eyes now terror filled. "You're a demon," he muttered. He looked down at the sleeping baby and back to Marie. "I won't let you hurt this child!"

"Oh, settle down." She chuckled, moving to the rocking chair and sitting down. "And while you're at it, keep your voice down, you don't want to wake up Connor."

"What do you want, Alexa?" he demanded.

"First, why in the world do you keep calling me that?" she asked.

"Isn't that who you are?"

She rolled her eyes. "Obviously not if I asked why you keep calling me that. And please, come over here away from the baby so we can talk without waking him. I have to assume he can hear you since he can hear me and Eva."

He turned from the crib and walked to her as she sat calmly in the rocking chair, studying him. "What are you talking about?" he asked.

"Oh my, you really don't know, do you?"

"What are you talking about?" he repeated.

"That you're dead," Marie told him.

"What an insane thing to say!" he said.

"Says the man who accused me of being a demon and started calling me by some random name."

"Who are you?" he asked.

"My name is Marie Nichols. When I was a baby, I lived in this very house. In fact, this used to be my nursery," she said.

Both curious and confused, the man took a hesitant step toward Marie and then stopped. "Why did you say I was dead?"

"Because you are. Just like me. We're ghosts. In my case, it involved murder. In my bed. Although it wasn't my bed exactly; it took place in a bed in one of those horrid nursing homes. But either way, I'm still dead. I was in my nineties, so I had a decent run. You, on the other hand, look to be rather young. Unless you're assuming the likeness of a younger version of yourself."

"I don't understand what you're saying." Wilbur frowned.

"I wonder how old you were when you died. And how long ago it happened. But considering you haven't come to terms with your death, I doubt you could answer."

"You're saying I'm dead?"

"You're a slow one, aren't you?"

"And you're dead too?" he asked.

"I entered through the front wall; in case you didn't notice. That's not something I could do when alive. Now, please tell me, who are you, and why are you here?"

He took several steps closer to Marie before plopping down on the floor, pulling his knees to his chest, and wrapping his arms around them. For a moment she thought he might start crying.

"Oh dear, I am sorry. Truly. It is rather annoying to discover one is dead, isn't it? I wasn't thrilled when Danielle told me," Marie sympathized.

He looked up to Marie. "Who is Danielle?"

"Danielle Marlow."

"Any relation to Walt Marlow?" he asked.

"His wife," Marie said.

He frowned. "Someone is planning to kill Walt Marlow and his wife."

Marie sat up straight in the chair and stopped rocking. "Where did you hear this?"

"I overheard someone when I was down at the pier. They sat

next to me on a bench. I wondered why they talked so freely about it; I was sitting right next to them. I pretended to be sleeping, so I guess they assumed I wouldn't hear. But still, I could have woken up any minute."

"They didn't think you were sleeping," Marie said.

"They didn't?" he asked.

"Of course not. They couldn't see you. You're a ghost."

He considered her words a moment and glanced to the crib and back to Marie. "The baby can see me."

"Yes, and he can see me too. Often babies can see spirits. It's when they get older, they typically lose the ability."

"But some people have seen me in the last day or so. One looked at me and said hello," he insisted.

"Perhaps you've run into one of the mediums on Beach Drive. We have a few of them in this neighborhood."

"And the people who couldn't see me...are you saying they weren't ghosts?" he asked.

Marie smiled. "You thought they were ghosts?"

"Yes, I walked right through them, and they didn't see me."

Marie chuckled. "No. They walked through you..." Marie considered what she had just said and shrugged. "And I suppose you walked through them. But it's because you're the ghost, not them."

"It does explain a lot," he muttered.

"Have you been feeling confused recently?" she asked.

He nodded. "Yes. But things seem a little clearer now."

"It works that way. But please, you need to tell me about this person threatening to hurt Walt and Danielle, and why."

"It sounded like they're looking for some diary or letters belonging to Walt Marlow."

"Which Walt Marlow?" Marie asked.

"What do you mean?"

She shook her head. "Never mind, I don't have the time to explain now. Continue, please."

"It has something to do with a book Walt wrote," he began.

58

ELEVEN

T he purring woke Danielle, but she didn't open her eyes. Wanting more sleep, she rolled over, her back to Walt, as she clutched a pillow in her arms and curled up in a fetal position. She felt Max's soft forehead gently butt her bare shoulder, and the purring grew louder. Still not opening her eyes, she gently nudged the cat with one hand, trying to push him off the bed. Max side-stepped Danielle's attempt and jumped on her legs.

With a groan Danielle sat up, opened her eyes, intending to scold her cat, when she spied an elderly woman sitting cross-legged at the foot of her bed, staring up at her and Walt. Danielle screeched in surprise and jerked to a fully sitting position, waking Walt.

"What?" Walt asked groggily, now sitting up and rubbing his eyes. It only took him a moment to notice Marie, who wore white slacks, a Hawaiian shirt, and a cockily placed straw hat, sitting with them on the bed.

"Good morning," Marie said.

"Sheesh, Marie, you scared the crap out of me," Danielle grumbled.

"That's not a ladylike word, Danielle," Marie scolded.

"I have to assume there's a reason for this sunrise visit?" Walt asked.

"I don't make a habit of popping into your bedroom—unless it's of the utmost importance." Marie frowned and pointed to Walt. "You don't have a shirt on. Cover up. Certainly you have some pajama pants on under that blanket?"

"Sorry, I wasn't expecting guests." Walt tugged the top edge of the sheet, covering the lower half of his chest.

"I hadn't planned to come to your room, but I intended to stop over a little later, which is why I'm wearing what I have on." Marie pointed to her Hawaiian blouse. "You just came back from Hawaii and all," Marie explained, as if it should make sense. It didn't to Danielle. "It has been decades since I could sit cross-legged!"

"Why are you here?" Danielle asked.

"To warn you." Marie's tone turned somber.

"About what?" Walt asked.

"Someone intends to kill you."

They said nothing, but simply stared.

"And I don't want to explain all this twice, so why don't we do this right, and you call Chris and Heather and get them over here. Unless you think I should wake them up?" Marie suggested. "We need to inform the mediums, except for Evan."

"Who intends to kill us?" Danielle asked.

"Unfortunately, I don't have that information. It's one reason you need to get Chris and Heather over here. I considered getting Eva, but I think I can handle this myself," Marie said.

"Can you please give us a little more information?" Danielle pleaded.

Marie looked at Danielle sympathetically. "I think you need some coffee, dear. You're not fully awake yet. I'll pop downstairs, start some, and you call Chris and Heather. I'll meet you all in the kitchen." Marie vanished. Max let out a meow, jumped off the bed, and sauntered out of the room.

Danielle looked over to Walt.

Walt picked his cellphone up from his nightstand and turned to Danielle. He nodded to her phone sitting on the table on her side of the bed. It floated up on its way to her. "I'll call Chris; you call Heather," he suggested.

"No way! You call Heather. She made an enormous deal about not jogging this morning and sleeping in and how no one had better wake her up. I'll call Chris!" She grabbed for her cellphone as it hung in midair, but Walt willed it away from her reach for a moment, giving him the time to make the first call.

When she finally grabbed ahold of her cellphone, she glowered Walt's way and muttered, "Rat." He was already talking to Chris.

––––––––

PEARL OPENED her bedroom blinds and looked outside. What a lovely day, she thought. Unfortunately, it was almost the fourth, which meant cars would line the street in a few days for the Marlow fundraiser. She was half tempted to buy a ticket and attend. It wasn't that she particularly wanted to support the fundraiser, but she was curious to have a look inside Marlow House. As much as she hated to admit it, she had grown increasingly curious to get a closer look inside the old house, especially since practically everyone in town had traipsed through it at one time or another, and she always felt foolish admitting she never had, when the subject came up. After all, she lived right next door.

Looking down at the street, she spied her neighbor to the south walking by her house—Heather Donovan. While she was used to seeing Heather out and about at this time of day, as the woman regularly jogged in the mornings, Pearl was not used to seeing her dressed in what looked like pajamas and fuzzy slippers. Heather wore her black hair in one high ponytail and carried what looked like a pillow tucked under one arm. Pearl frowned at the sight.

She then noticed one of her other neighbors, Chris Johnson, walking down the street. He was a distance away, so she grabbed her binoculars from the dresser to look closer. Like Heather, he appeared to be wearing pajamas—at least pajama bottoms, with a wrinkled gray T-shirt and a pair of flip-flops. His pit bull Hunny walked by his side.

Pearl continued to watch as Chris met Heather by the front gate leading to the Marlows' side yard. Chris opened the gate, holding it while Heather entered the yard with Hunny, and followed them in. The three walked to the Marlows' side door and walked in the house without knocking.

"What's going on over there?" Pearl muttered. "Who wears pajamas to the neighbor's house? And who takes a pillow with them?"

––––––––

"THE ONE DAY I plan to sleep in," Heather grumbled as she and Chris walked in the house. They found Danielle and Walt sitting at the kitchen table with Marie. Danielle wore a robe over her night-gown, while Walt wore plaid pajama bottoms and a T-shirt. Hunny trotted to Danielle first, accepted a pat, and then nosed Walt and said hello before curling up on the floor under the table.

Marie sat in an invisible chair, leaving two of the four kitchen chairs to Chris and Heather. Cups of coffee floated toward the kitchen table.

"What's this about?" Chris asked as he sat at the table, snatching a cup of coffee from the air as it floated to him. Heather snagged the second cup for herself and sat down. Still clutching her pillow, Heather set it on her lap. In the center of the table, Old Salts cinnamon rolls filled a rose-patterned platter.

Heather helped herself to one of the sticky sweet rolls and muttered under her breath, "These are why I have to jog."

"I'm not sure what's going on," Danielle told Chris. She looked at Marie and said, "Okay, we're all here."

"Someone intends to burn down Marlow House," Marie began, "with Walt and Danielle inside."

MARIE WAS a good fifteen minutes into her story when Chris interrupted by asking, "Who was this ghost?"

"He didn't tell me his name," Marie said. "Connor woke up, started crying. I was about to pick him up, but Ian came into the nursery. It scared the ghost away, and I figured I needed to get right over here and tell you what I learned. Ian and Lily don't even realize I was over there this morning—much less about a strange ghost in the nursery."

"Not exactly," Heather said. "Yesterday Sadie found your ghost hiding in Connor's closet. She started barking—seemingly at noth-ing. So Lily brought Sadie over here to have a chat with Walt, and we all looked for him over at Lily's. But he wasn't there."

"He's back," Marie said.

"This has to have something to do with whoever broke in here the other day," Danielle told them.

"Someone already broke in?" Marie asked.

"Yes," Walt told her. "The day we got home from Hawaii.

Joanne walked in on them, but they left without being seen. We naturally couldn't tell her Max told us. They were looking through the desk in our bedroom. After she arrived, they slipped out through the hidden staircase."

"Which makes sense they would search your desk if they were looking for some diary or letters," Danielle said.

"And one of them was at the library yesterday?" Walt asked.

"Yes. According to the ghost, the woman claimed to have been there. Said something about you insisting the story was pure fiction, but that you lied."

Walt and Danielle exchanged quick glances. "The woman you said looked familiar, she asked you that question," Danielle said.

"You don't have a diary, do you?" Heather asked.

Walt shook his head. "No. But obviously they assume my former self kept a diary, which inspired the story."

Danielle looked at Marie. "Did he describe the woman or man he saw?"

Marie shook her head. "No."

"He didn't mention if she was black, did he?" Danielle asked.

"No, why?" Marie asked.

"Yesterday, at Walt's presentation, two of the women who asked about Walt's inspiration for the story, they were black. I just thought, if the ghost mentioned that, we could narrow our search. They were the only black women at the talk."

"This must have something to do with *Moon Runners*," Chris said.

"While real-life events from Walt's first life inspired *Moon Runners*, most of those events never made the news back then," Danielle said. "So this can't be about something that actually happened, because who would know about any of it?"

"Unless there was another diary," Walt said.

They all looked to him. "What do you mean?" Heather asked.

"If one of my readers recognized something in my book, then someone from my first life might have kept a diary or shared the events in a letter. While much of what I wrote about never became public knowledge, the people the ghost overheard must have read it somewhere. They recognized the similarities with *Moon Runners*. Is there something that happened back then they don't want to come out now?"

"Perhaps they fear you have the same information written in a diary and letters, with the actual names of the people involved?" Chris suggested.

"Why would they even care? Even if you gave the actual names," Heather asked. "What would it matter now?"

"It matters to someone; they're willing to kill Walt and Danielle over it." Chris then looked at Walt and asked, "Can you think of anything that happened back then that's tied into any of the events you used in *Moon Runners* that someone today would not want to come out?"

Walt considered the question before saying, "Off the top of my head, I can't think of anything."

"I have an idea!" Heather piped up.

"What?" Chris and Walt asked at the same time.

"According to what the ghost overheard, the man and woman will be here on the fourth," Heather began.

"With a bazillion other people," Danielle said.

"I seriously doubt a bazillion will show," Heather said dryly.

"So, what's your idea?" Chris asked.

"Give them what they want. If they find a diary and it doesn't include more than what was in *Moon Runners*, there would be no reason to come after you," Heather said.

"But there is no diary," Walt reminded her.

"Well, duh. But you can write one. How hard can that be? And leave it somewhere where they'll find it on the fourth," Heather said.

"I can't write the diary," Walt said.

"Why not?" Heather asked.

"I'm not even sure how I would write something like that—to make it believable. And much of *Moon Runners* came from my imagination. It's been over a hundred years. There's much I don't remember."

"You'd better start remembering," Chris told Walt, "so we can figure out who's trying to kill you and why."

TWELVE

P earl stood at her bedroom window late Sunday morning, looking up the street at her neighbor's house. She wondered what was going on over there. Were they having a party? When she had stepped out on her front porch to bring in her newspaper earlier that day, she had spied Heather returning to her house, pillow in hand, while Chris Johnson walked in the opposite direction, heading up the street to his house. He didn't have his dog with him, and Pearl assumed he had left Hunny with the Marlows.

But now she watched as Heather parked her car in front of the Marlows', with Chris in the passenger seat. They got out of the vehicle. Chris carried two large paper sacks. If she wasn't mistaken, they were to-go sacks from Beach Taco. Pearl then noticed the Bartleys hurrying across the street with their baby and dog, and then the police chief pulled up in his car, parking behind Heather's.

"What is going on over there?" she wondered.

HEATHER AND CHRIS had gone home to get dressed. Before returning, they picked up breakfast burritos. Heather drove, and Chris paid. They pulled up in front of Marlow House at the same time as Ian, Lily and the chief arrived. Once again, they circled the wagons.

65

They all gathered in the library. Walt had set up a large bulletin board on an easel, reminding Danielle of evidence boards she had seen on police television shows. While they all ate burritos, Danielle and Walt filled the non-mediums in on what Marie had told them.

Marie quietly listened to the retelling as she walked Connor around the room. To the chief, Ian and Lily, it looked as if the baby had taken flight. Danielle stood by the bulletin board, a stack of blank index cards and a pen in her hands. Walt sat in a nearby chair, facing the group. Their plan included dissecting *Moon Runners* to determine which real-life-inspired character or incident might have triggered a potential killer's interest.

For about twenty minutes they discussed elements of the book; then Danielle said, "Should we start with the characters, the ones inspired by actual people?"

"That might make the most sense," Walt said. The others agreed.

"What about the character Seraphina was to play?" Lily suggested before looking at Chris and asking, "Have you heard from Seraphina lately?"

"Not for a couple of weeks. She landed a minor role in a movie and has been working every day," Chris said.

"What was the name of the real-life person who inspired Seraphina's role?" Heather asked.

"That would be Desiree Davis," Walt told her.

Danielle jotted her name on an index card, and Walt said, "You might as well put her sister up there too, Charlene." Danielle gave him a nod and jotted Charlene's name on another card. She put both on the bulletin board, stepped back, and looked at them.

"If I understand correctly, we're thinking someone recognized one of Walt's characters as some relative of theirs. Maybe the would-be killer is a grandchild. And for whatever reason, there is something that happened back then they don't want made public?" Chris asked.

"They could be afraid Walt has even more information detrimental to their family," Danielle said.

"Okay, either way, if we're talking family members, wouldn't the most logical ones to start with be the black women who asked Walt the questions at the library?" Heather asked. "Are they related to the Davis sisters, granddaughters or something?"

Walt considered the suggestion for a moment and shook his

head. "I really don't see why anyone from Desiree and Charlene's family would care about anything in that book, much less want to kill me over it."

"Discount nothing," the chief urged. "Tell us what you remember about them."

"Desiree was a talented jazz singer. I frequented the club she played at. We were friends. The part in *Moon Runners* where the character I based her on gets involved with the club manager and he rips off a local bootlegger and almost gets her killed, that's true. But even if the moonshiner's family heard that story, all the players have to be dead by now."

"And you saved her," Danielle said with a grin.

Walt shrugged. "Yes, I got her out of there, and she always said I saved her life. But in my book, it was Hunter Rage."

"So you really based his character on you?" Heather asked.

"No, I didn't," Walt insisted. "I wasn't that colorful."

"What happened to Desiree?" Lily asked.

"She got married about a year before I did, to a musician. They left the area around the same time that I got married."

"What about her sister?" Lily asked.

"Eva knew Charlene better than I did. I had seen her in several local plays and met her backstage. Eva introduced us. In fact, I didn't realize she was part black until I discovered she was Desiree's sister. Charlene, like Eva, had been in some movies, but she never had Eva's success. At least not while I was alive."

"What happened to her?" Ian asked.

"I heard Charlene accepted an offer in Tinseltown and moved to California," Walt said.

"Tinseltown?" Heather smirked.

"It's what they called Hollywood back then," Danielle said.

"This was before I met Angela, about six years after Eva died. When I was researching for *Moon Runners*, I tried looking her up to discover what happened to her, but I couldn't find anything. I assume she changed her stage name," Walt explained.

"Did you ever ask Eva what happened to Charlene? If she made it big in Hollywood? Eva seems to keep up with that sort of thing," Heather asked.

"I did," Walt said. "But spirits don't necessarily know what happens to other people. She heard Charlene had left for Hollywood, but she didn't know if she became successful under another name."

"You killed the poor girl off in your book," Heather said.

"It was fiction," Walt reminded her. "I told you I got ideas from real-life events, but the story was my own."

"Kinda brutal, killing off poor Charlene because her lover's family found out she was black," Heather said.

"I didn't kill off Charlene. I killed the character based on her. As you well know, there was considerable Klan activity back then," Walt reminded her. "When I heard Charlene was black—"

"She was also half white," Heather interrupted.

"Yes, I know," Walt said patiently. "But that didn't matter. If a person had even a drop of black blood, society considered them black. And Charlene was playing a dangerous game. She was beautiful like Eva and surrounded by men professing their devotion. Some of those men were Klan members. Trust me, had any of them found out she was Desiree's sister, it could have been deadly. Especially if she married one. It was for the best that she took off to California."

"What about the bootlegger you mentioned?" Ian asked. "The one Desiree tried stealing from."

"I based that character on Beauregard Porter. He moved to the area not long after my grandfather founded Frederickport. Like in the book, he had two sons. The oldest was Beauregard Junior; he wasn't a bad fella, nothing like his younger brother, Ambrose. He was a bully."

"Can you blame him?" Lily asked.

"What do you mean?" Walt frowned.

"They named the poor kid Ambrose," Lily said.

"Perhaps, but I suspect it had more to do with his dad, Beau Senior."

"Hold on," Danielle said, hurriedly writing on more cards. "So we have two Beaus and an Ambrose?" After she wrote their names on cards, she added them to the bulletin board.

"The character in the book who cries on Hunter's shoulder over some Sheba after she left him for another man, that was Beau Junior," Walt explained.

"What were you going to say about Beau Senior and making his son a bully?" Ian asked.

"Beau senior was thick with the Klan, and he was a brutal man.

He saw nothing wrong with giving one of his sons or his grandson the back of his hand—or fist."

"Grandson?" Lily asked.

"Yes. Ambrose was a few years older than me. He had a son who was around eleven or twelve. Ambrose had gotten his girlfriend, Dolly, pregnant, when he was seventeen. She was about fifteen at the time. Her parents had died, and she was living with an uncle who I suspect was abusive. Her and Ambrose married and moved in with Beau Senior and Junior. But Dolly couldn't take the physical abuse, probably from her father-in-law and her husband. They were men who believed a woman needed a fist to remind them who was boss. One night she upped and ran away. She left her son behind."

"That's so sad," Lily said. "But I can't understand how a mother could desert her child like that."

"I imagine she had no choice, not if she wanted to get out alive. And if she had tried to take off with Ambrose's son, I don't even want to think what they would have done to her. My grandfather once told me Beau Senior had fought for the Confederacy. He was only a kid himself at the time. And when the war was over, his family was gone, and he ended up in Frederickport about five years later. I believe being in that war, at such a young age, experiencing unimaginable horrors for a boy, shaped him into the twisted hate filled man I remember."

"Bizarre to imagine you met someone who actually fought in the Civil War," Heather said.

"There's a lot of bizarre that goes on around here," the chief muttered.

"What else do you remember about the family?" Ian asked. "I'm thinking they might be an excellent place to start. See if any of the Porters are still around."

"They used to say being named Beauregard was bad luck," Walt said.

"Why is that?" Lily asked.

"Beau Senior and his wife had ten children, four were boys. Only two of their children survived to adulthood. They named their first son Beauregard. He died in infancy. A few years later, they had another son. They named him Beauregard. According to my grandfather, he died before his fifth birthday. The next Beauregard was the one I knew, and their last child was Ambrose. When Ambrose was born, his mother died in childbirth; their father never remarried."

"How much you want to bet that poor wife was happy to move on, if her husband was as bad as Walt says," Heather said.

"Perhaps. But I can't imagine the heartbreak of losing that many children," Lily said.

"Does this Porter have family in Frederickport?" Chris asked. "I remember in the book, his character belonged to the Klan. It's possible they've passed down some unsavory stories within the family, and someone may have read *Moon Runners* and recognize their ancestor?"

"Chris has a point," Lily said. "Look what some museum board members did trying to cover up the Klan members on their family trees."

"At least they didn't try killing us," Danielle said.

"So is it possible?" Chris asked.

"I can't think of any Porters in town," the chief said.

"When Walt was researching for his book, we found one Porter in the phone book," Danielle said. "They had moved here fairly recently."

"I think you need to check a little deeper," Ian suggested.

"We will," Walt said.

"Who else to add?" Ian asked.

Walt looked at the board for a minute. "The other characters in the book are composites of people from my life, or pure fiction. But honestly, I can't imagine how any of this has to do with whoever wants my diary."

"They don't just want your diary," Marie reminded him. "They want you dead."

"Danielle will need to help me come up with something," the chief said a moment later. They all looked at him.

"What do you mean?" Danielle asked.

"According to what Marie was told, the person threatening you will be at your fundraiser on the fourth. I think we should have a couple of officers here undercover. But I'm trying to decide how best to explain my concern. I can't very well say a ghost overheard a conversation—which he retold to another ghost."

"Not sure how I feel about you guys always insinuating I'm some skilled liar," Danielle grumbled.

"It's not that you're a liar exactly…" the chief said.

70

THIRTEEN

"What sort of favor?" Adam asked Danielle on Monday morning.

She stood in his office alone while Walt waited outside in the Packard.

"Can you install surveillance cameras in Marlow House?" she asked. "Before Wednesday."

"Um…how many are we talking about, and why?" he asked.

"I'm not sure how many. Chris is picking them up. He said he'd help you."

Adam frowned. "That's sneaky of you."

"Sneaky how?"

"I can't say no to Chris." Adam wasn't exactly kidding. While he considered Chris a friend, he was also one of his best and more lucrative clients. There was no way he could deny a favor to his best client.

"Sure you can. The person you can't say no to is me."

"Why is that?" Adam asked.

"Because this is something your grandma would want you to do for me."

Adam rolled his eyes. "Well, you did make me that divinity. I assume you want the cameras installed so you can monitor the people coming through your house on Wednesday?"

"Yeah." Danielle smiled sweetly.

"Whatever happened to the cameras you used to have installed in the house?"

Danielle understood Adam believed she had already installed hidden cameras in Marlow House. How else could she have known when he and Bill had broken in not long after she had moved to Frederickport?

"They all died," she lied.

"Okay, but you owe me," he said.

"Consider this a favor for Chris."

Adam chuckled. "Yeah, right."

"One more thing," she added.

"What?"

"Please don't mention this to anyone. And I mean not to anyone."

"Not even Mel?" he asked.

"Okay, you can tell Mel. One more thing…"

"What's that?"

"You need to make sure that when you install the cameras, no one will know they're there."

TEN MINUTES LATER, Danielle opened the passenger side of the Packard.

"I assume by that smile he said yes?" Walt asked as Danielle got into the car.

"He did. Now let's see what we can find out at the museum." Danielle slammed the car door closed.

Walt started down the street and said, "I'm glad Marie offered to stay at the house while we're running errands. She had planned to return to Astoria."

"Me too. And if we're lucky, when we get home, we'll find the culprits tied up, and I can stop playing Nancy Drew," Danielle said.

"Don't count on it. If they meant what the ghost overheard, they don't plan to come back until Wednesday."

"Which is one reason I'm glad Adam agreed to install the cameras. If we can record everyone who comes to Marlow House, maybe we'll catch one of them trying to find the nonexistent diary. Marie can't exactly monitor everyone. And if they notice the

72

cameras and don't search for the diary, at least we'll have a record of everyone who shows up. That will be something to work with."

"We'll figure this out," Walt promised.

"I hope you're right. Because, if we don't soon, it will be nerve-racking being vigil for someone who wants to kill us while we sleep."

Walt reached his hand over and patted Danielle's knee. "Don't worry, love. It will be okay. It won't get that far."

"And what about Ian and Lily? Our mystery killer suggested they might break into their house if they can't find what they're looking for," Danielle reminded him.

"Ian is taking precautions, as we all are. And trust me, Marie will let no one get near Connor."

MILLIE SAMSON, one of the elderly docents and a historical society board member, welcomed Walt and Danielle when they walked into the museum late Monday morning. In the gift store another docent stood behind the counter ringing up books and post-cards for one museum visitor, while two couples and a family of four toured the displays.

"It's been so busy today," Millie chirped.

Before Walt or Danielle could ask a question, two more people walked in the door. Since they didn't belong to the historical society, Millie scurried from Walt and Danielle to sell the recent arrivals admission tickets.

"They look busy," Danielle whispered.

"We might as well look through the old newspapers," Walt suggested.

"You know their collection isn't complete," Danielle reminded him.

"Won't hurt to look."

Together Walt and Danielle walked to the back of the museum and sat at the table with the books of old newspapers. They searched through them for about thirty minutes, and as Danielle predicted, they kept coming up empty.

"Looking for anything in particular?" Millie asked when she eventually walked up to the table.

Danielle closed the book and looked up to Millie. "Actually, we were wondering, do you know anything about a family who used to live in Frederickport named Porter? Beauregard Porter?"

"Certainly," Millie said. "They still have family in town. In fact, Earl recently moved into the same care home Marie was in."

"Earl Porter?" Danielle asked.

Millie shook her head. "No. His mother was a Porter. His last name is Barr. He's younger than I am. I heard he has Alzheimer's."

"Is he married?"

"He's a widower. His wife died a few years back. To be honest, we were casual acquaintances at best. Family always kept to themselves. Very private. I believe the Beauregard Porter you mentioned was his great-great-grandfather."

Danielle's evil-self resisted the temptation to ask Millie if she knew who Beauregard was because her Klan ancestors used to night ride with him. But to be fair, Danielle told herself, other than wanting to cover up her family's racist history, Millie had seemed sincerely ashamed of that branch in her family tree.

"Does he have any children?" Walt asked.

"Yes," Millie said. "Two girls, but they aren't exactly girls anymore. They married and left Frederickport years ago. They rarely visit their father. Although, they were in town recently to move Earl into a nursing home. Why do you ask?"

"Marie mentioned Beauregard Porter once," Danielle lied. "Said he fought in the Civil War—for the Confederacy. I found that fascinating."

"Did she now?" Millie frowned. "I wonder where she heard that?"

"AND YOU ASK why we talk about your uncanny ability to spin a yarn at a moment's notice?" Walt teased as they got into the Packard fifteen minutes later.

"A yarn? What are you, from a hundred years ago or something?" she teased back.

Walt chuckled.

A moment later they sat quietly in the parked car, in front of the museum, the doors shut. "Well, that was a bust," Walt said.

"I don't see a guy with Alzheimer's coming after us," Danielle said.

"And according to the ghost, it was a man and woman."

"I suppose it could be one of Earl's daughters and her husband," Danielle suggested.

"The way Millie was talking, I don't think the daughters are in town."

"She did say they came to help their dad move. Maybe they're still here. Also, creepy that they put the poor guy in that place." Danielle shivered.

"The person responsible for Marie's death is no longer there. Hopefully, they now have better staff."

WHEN WALT and Danielle returned to Marlow House, they told Marie what they had learned at the museum.

"Earl Barr?" Marie said. "Unpleasant man. A few years back, one neighbor had him arrested, but they dropped the charges. Never heard why he'd been arrested, and the neighbor refused to talk about it."

"I wonder what happened," Danielle muttered.

Marie shrugged. "I didn't remember his mother was a Porter, but now that I think about it, that sounds familiar. I liked his wife, though. She was a sweet thing. I used to see her at church sometimes."

"I don't remember you going to church," Walt teased.

"I did sometimes," Marie said primly. "And how would you know? You never left this house."

"Did you know the daughters?" Danielle asked.

"Not really. But I don't recall them ever getting in trouble. I used to think Earl smacked Lizzy around. Lizzy was his wife."

"Pleasant man," Danielle said. "And I was feeling bad about them putting him in the same nursing home as you were in."

"Perfect place for a man like him," Marie said. "While the family used to keep to themselves, I would occasionally see Lizzy at church and run into her at the grocery store. A few times I noticed what I was sure was a black eye under makeup. She was a timid thing and rather jumpy. But when I'd see her with her daughters, she seemed like quite the doting mother. From what I recall, those girls left town when they turned eighteen. But I heard they used to come back to visit their mother. You say they were here to put Earl in a home?"

"That's what Millie says."

"Well, there is one thing I can do," Marie said.

"What's that?" Danielle asked.

"I'll pop over to the home, see if I can find out if the daughters are still in town. If they aren't, then I suspect this is a dead end," Marie said.

Danielle was about to ask Marie how she intended to find out about the daughters, but the ghost vanished before she had a chance.

"I think Marie rather enjoys the freedom of being a spirit," Walt said.

"Yes, I noticed that," Danielle agreed.

"Someone who spent almost a hundred years as a spirit confined to one location, and only able to harness energy the last couple of years, might be jealous of Marie," Walt said.

"But you aren't?"

"No. I'm exceedingly grateful how it all worked out."

Danielle stood on her tiptoes and brushed a kiss over Walt's mouth.

After the brief kiss Walt said, "Why don't we go make some sandwiches?"

WALT AND DANIELLE sat at the kitchen table, eating tuna sandwiches, potato chips, and sweet pickles, when Marie materialized in the room.

"I'm back!" the ghost announced.

"So I see. That was quick," Danielle said, taking a bite of her sandwich. "Did you learn anything?"

"I did," Marie said as she took a seat at the table with them. "I don't believe Earl or his family are who you're looking for."

"Why do you say that?" Walt asked.

"I met a friendly man there, Fred," Marie began.

"Fred?" Danielle cocked her brow.

"He had the room before Earl. Good thing I got there when I did. He was just getting ready to pass over to the other side. But fortunately, he stuck around, and we had a brief chat," Marie explained.

"I assume you're talking about a ghost?" Danielle asked.

"Didn't I say that?" Marie asked.

"So what did he tell you?" Walt asked.

"Fred saw the daughters when Earl first moved in. Said they were very cool toward him. Not rude or cruel, but there was no sign of affection. He overheard some discussion about how they were selling the father's home, and that money was paying for his care. The day they left, Fred overheard them tell the nurse they were leaving town, going back home. Wherever that is. The nurse asked if they would be visiting soon, and the girls didn't answer. But he overheard one sister whisper to the other, right after the nurse walked away, 'When *hell freezes over.*' Fred assumed that was in response to the question about visiting their father."

"Any idea how long ago that was?" Walt asked.

"From my calculations, a couple of weeks ago," Marie said.

Danielle looked at Walt, who had just finished his last bite of tuna sandwich. With a sigh she said, "Marie is right, sounds like that's a dead end. What do we do now?"

"I think there is only one thing we can do," Walt said in a serious tone.

"What's that?" Danielle asked.

"I think we should split that last piece of double fudge chocolate cake."

FOURTEEN

Hunny stayed behind at Marlow House while Chris shopped for security cameras in Portland on Monday. She spent the morning inside with Marie while Walt and Danielle went off to run errands and stop at the museum. When they returned, the pit bull headed outside to enjoy the afternoon sunshine and romp in the backyard while Max napped on one branch that arched overhead some twelve feet above the ground.

Marie planned to visit Connor while Walt and Danielle ate their chocolate cake. After moving through the north-facing kitchen wall into the side yard, Marie paused when she didn't see Hunny. Where was the dog? To get a better view, she moved upward, as if riding an invisible elevator in the middle of the yard.

The unusual sight caught Max's attention, and he lazily lifted his head from where it had been resting on his front paws. He looked Marie in the eyes and meowed.

"Why am I up here?" Marie repeated Max's question. "I'm looking for Hunny. Have you seen her? Did she go back in the house, and I missed her?"

The cat meowed again.

"What do you mean she's next door? Next door where?"

Max looked toward Pearl's yard.

Marie gasped, and the next moment she stood in Pearl Huckabee's backyard, only a fence separating it from Marlow House property. To her astonishment she found Pearl sitting on a patio chair, the pit bull's chin resting on her lap as the normally cranky woman affectionately rubbed the dog's head and ears, whispering baby talk.

"Who is a good baby girl?" Pearl cooed. "Who loves her Hunny?"

Pearl then did something Marie never imagined the woman would do—she kissed the dog's nose.

Hunny, whose back was to Marie, and whose eyes were closed, was unaware of the ghost watching them and seemed perfectly content receiving Pearl's affection. Her wagging stump of a tail attested to that fact.

"I would never have believed it if I hadn't seen it for myself," Marie said aloud.

Startled, Hunny opened her eyes, lifted her chin from Pearl's lap, and looked behind her. Upon seeing Marie, she snuggled up closer to Pearl and looked embarrassed.

"What's wrong, baby?" Pearl asked in a loving voice. "What scared you?"

"How long has this been going on?" Marie asked.

The dog looked at Marie a moment and then rested her chin on Pearl's knee while keeping one eye on Marie.

"Yes, I can see you like her," Marie said with a frown, still confused.

A meow distracted them, and they looked to the fence separating the two yards. Max stood on the fence, looking down at the three. Hunny's butt again wagged with her tail, and the dog whimpered.

Marie looked back to Pearl and noticed a brief frown cross the woman's face before disappearing.

With a sigh Pearl said, "Okay, Hunny. I still don't like that cat, but he's obviously your friend, so I'll tolerate it." She leaned down and gave the dog another pat and kissed her head. "You'd better go home now." Pearl reached into her pocket and pulled out a dog treat. She fed it to Hunny. After finishing the treat, Hunny swiped a wet tongue across Pearl's face and then trotted back home, squeezing through an opening under the fence.

Still perplexed at the sight, Marie stared at Pearl for a moment. The woman sat alone on the chair, silently watching where Hunny had just disappeared. She watched as Pearl got up from the chair and started to her house.

"Those treats…" Marie muttered, still watching Pearl as she headed to her side door. The next moment, the remaining dog treats floated up and out of Pearl's pocket, making their way to Marie. Had Pearl looked back, the sight of floating dog treats might make her suspect that medical marijuana she had vowed to never again take hadn't left her system. Marie snatched the treats from midair and examined them.

"Just to be safe, I think we should check these out," Marie said.

Deciding her trip to visit Connor would have to wait, she entered the Marlows' yard. Hunny had already gone into the house. She intended to tell Walt and Danielle what she had just witnessed and show them the treats, but her plans changed a moment later when she came face-to-face with the mystery ghost she had met in Connor's nursery.

He looked as if he would flee again, so she shouted, "Please don't leave. At least tell me your name."

He stopped and looked at her. "My name is Wilbur Jenkins. Can I ask you a question?"

"What's that?" Marie asked.

"If I'm dead, like you say, and I think you're right, does this mean my sister won't be able to see me if I find her?" he asked.

"If your sister is still alive and not a ghost, chances are she won't see you. But there are some people—it's not that common—who are mediums and can see and hear people like us."

"We're still people?" he asked.

Marie shrugged. "I use that term loosely."

"I need to find my sister and explain everything."

"Maybe I can help. I know a few mediums. If you tell me your sister's name, where we can find her, then they can pass on your message."

"Would they do that?"

"I'm sure they would," Marie said, although she wasn't sure that was accurate. It wasn't like a medium could just walk up to his sister and tell her they had a message from beyond. But she wanted to get his name, and once he felt comfortable, he might help them find the people who wanted to hurt Walt and Danielle.

"How do we do this?" he asked.

"First, tell me your full name, and about your sister."

"My full name is Wilbur James Jenkins. I live in Portland. My sister is Kimberly Kate Jenkins. She lives in Portland too and runs a little bookstore there called Kimberly Kate Books. Do you really think your friends would give her my message?"

Before Marie could answer, Walt and Danielle walked out to the side yard with Hunny. Hunny spied the new ghost and came running toward him, eager to meet someone new.

Startled by the quickly approaching dog, Wilbur vanished.

"Stop! Come back!" Marie yelled.

Walt and Danielle, who had not noticed Marie or Wilbur when they had first stepped outside, rushed to Marie's side when they realized they had scared away a ghost.

"Was that him?" Danielle asked when they reached Marie. Honey circled the yard, looking for the disappearing spirit.

"Yes. I really wish you hadn't scared him off," Marie groaned.

"I'm sorry," Danielle said.

"At least I got his name. Not that it will help us find the people threatening you, but at least Wilbur isn't a complete mystery," Marie said.

"Who's Wilbur?" Walt asked.

"The ghost you scared away." Marie handed Danielle the dog treats she had been holding.

"What's this?" Danielle asked, taking the treats from Marie.

"You might check them out. Make sure they won't make Hunny sick." Marie then told Walt and Danielle what she had witnessed at their neighbor's house.

WHEN CHRIS RETURNED from Portland late Monday afternoon with the cameras, he had Heather with him.

"I ended up going," Heather said when she plopped down on the living room sofa and watched as Chris set the full shopping bags on the floor. "We had some other errands to run for work, and Chris gets lost in Portland."

"I do not," Chris argued as he sat down on a chair.

"Actually, you do," Danielle said as she looked through the bags he had set on the floor. "How much do we owe you?"

"The receipt is in the bag. I might have offered to pay for them, but then you made that crack about me getting lost," Chris said.

"I didn't say it," Danielle reminded him, pulling one of the small boxes from the bag. "Heather did. I was just agreeing."

"Chris likes to explore original routes, and sometimes he forgets how to get back," Walt suggested.

Hunny, who had been outside, ran into the living room, her stump of a tail wagging. She greeted her human.

Danielle looked up from the bag to Walt. "You need to tell Chris about Hunny."

"What about her?" Chris asked.

They told Chris and Heather what Marie had witnessed next door.

"Did you check the treats?" Heather asked.

"There was nothing wrong with the treats," Danielle said.

"How do you know?" Heather asked.

"I had a long talk with Hunny," Walt said. "Apparently this has been going on for some time. As best as I can tell, since Pearl had that mishap with the ladder over Christmas. For the last six months Hunny sneaks over there; Pearl lavishes affection on her and gives her treats. Hunny didn't tell me because I had expressly told her to stay away from Pearl, and it seems Hunny is fond of the woman."

"That is so unlike Hunny," Chris said. "She's always obedient, and she knew we didn't want her near that house."

"Technically, she's a teenager," Danielle reminded him. "In dog years. And you know how teenagers are."

"I thought dogs were good at judging people," Heather said.

"I had noticed Pearl petting Hunny through the fence. Even overheard some of that baby talk," Chris said.

"Yeah, and I told you she was probably plotting against poor Hunny," Heather said.

"Pearl is not my favorite person. I remember how rude she was when we visited her at the hospital to give her flowers and offered to check on her house. You would have thought we were plotting to break in and steal all her worldly possessions," Danielle said.

"Exactly," Heather agreed.

"But the fact is, some people don't like people—but they love dogs," Danielle said.

"She didn't love dogs when she threw such a fit over Hunny being off a leash after Chris's house burned down," Heather reminded them.

"True. But obviously Hunny has won her over," Danielle said. "I think Pearl's initial response to Hunny stemmed from fear."

"I suspect the change has something to do with Hunny saving her life," Walt said. "From what we know, Pearl was on that cold ground for a couple of hours before Hunny found her."

"Aside from Pearl no longer making it her mission to ban pit bulls from the neighborhood," Danielle began, "from what Marie overheard, Pearl promised Hunny she would learn to tolerate Max, since they were friends. Which makes me feel better, considering she tried trapping Max at least one time that we're aware of."

"Since when are Max and Hunny friends?" Heather asked.

"Since Max realized Hunny had gotten to a dangerous size and could easily bring him down if she wanted," Walt said.

"Hunny wouldn't hurt Max," Heather scoffed.

"Perhaps not, but Max also realizes that there's an advantage to having a pit bull ally; one never knows what new dog will move into the neighborhood. And Max learned long ago how to survive," Walt said. "And you know Hunny, she just wants to be everyone's friend."

"Terrific," Heather said dryly. "With Bella's snotty attitude, if Pearl realizes how she torments Hunny, she may decide to rid the neighborhood of her."

"In other news, we discovered the name of the mystery ghost. Unfortunately, he took off again before we could get him to find our wannabe arsonists," Danielle said.

"Who is he?" Chris asked.

"He told Marie his name is Wilbur James Jenkins. He lived in Portland and has a sister who lives there too, named Kimberly Kate Jenkins. He told Marie his sister runs a bookstore called Kimberly Kate Books, so I have to assume she owns the bookstore since it has her name. Unless it is some wild coincidence."

"I've been there," Heather said. "In fact, it's right down the street from where we were today. It's kinda retro. But I seriously doubt they named it after his sister."

"Why do you say that?" Danielle asked.

"According to the sign in the store, it's been there for over a hundred years. They have some cool photos on one wall, showing what it used to look like. Unless someone photoshopped those old pictures, it was called Kimberly Kate Books when it was first established."

"Or perhaps we have been incorrectly assuming Wilbur is a spirit of a recently departed person?" Chris suggested.

FIFTEEN

After Heather and Chris left late Monday afternoon, Walt and Danielle went to the basement to take down the boxes of Fourth of July decorations. While they were heavy and stored on a top shelf, Walt didn't need a ladder or Chris's help to get them down. He only needed Danielle, and that was to remind him which boxes she wanted. Storage shelving lined one wall of the basement. Walt and Danielle stood side by side, looking up at its top shelf, and watched as the boxes Danielle pointed to floated down to the floor.

"I thought we should do this today and not wait until the morning," Danielle said after the first box landed on the concrete floor, followed by a second one, and a third. "Joanne said she'll be here first thing in the morning, and it would be a pain to get these down with her here."

"I would need to get up on a ladder," Walt said as he brought the last of the boxes down, touching none of them.

"Can you take them upstairs and put them in the hallway?" Danielle asked.

"Of course." Walt looked down at the six boxes. They rose from the basement floor and formed a line and began slowly making their way toward the stairs.

"I was wondering," Danielle began, but stopped talking when all six boxes fell to the floor.

"Damn," Walt muttered.

"What happened?"

Walt looked at Danielle and asked, "Have you ever tried to pick up more packages than you can comfortably carry and then drop them?"

"Um…yes…does this mean you can't take all six boxes upstairs at once?"

"No. It just means I can't do it while you're talking to me. I need to concentrate."

"Oh…sorry." Danielle cringed.

"That's okay. This many boxes at once requires more focus." Walt turned back to the six boxes. Once again, they floated up into the air. Danielle remained silent as Walt willed the boxes up the stairwell to the first floor.

LATER THAT AFTERNOON, Danielle walked alone down the beach, heading to Pier Café. She kicked the cool sand with her bare feet and held her flip-flops in one hand. Walt had stayed home to work on his new book and keep an eye on the house, should one of the would-be arsonists break in again before the fourth. After Walt had stacked the six boxes neatly in the hallway, she had volunteered to walk to the pier and pick up hamburgers for dinner. If they had any fresh pie, she'd bring some pie home too.

Before reaching the pier, she spied him. He stood watching her. Danielle recognized him immediately. Earlier she had gotten a good look at him right before he had disappeared. If she wasn't mistaken, he assumed she could not see him.

She thought he looked a few years older than herself, which was far too young to die. If Chris was correct, he could have died years ago, and by his clothing, she thought that might be true. He wore oddly shaped dark slacks and a rumpled white button-up shirt. She noticed several of its top buttons were missing.

Not wanting him to leave, Danielle said, "Wilbur Jenkins, please don't disappear. Talk to me."

Startled, he stared a moment before asking, "Are you dead or one of those mediums I heard about?"

"I'm a medium. My name is Danielle Marlow. And I need your help."

"You want to know who plans to kill you."

"It would be nice. I'm not ready to move over to your side," she said.

"I wasn't ready."

"How did you die?" she asked.

"I'm not sure. But I think Beau murdered me."

Danielle frowned. Beau, it was a name she rarely heard. But how many times had she heard it in the last couple of days? There was Adam's client, Beau. Two Beaus whom Walt based characters on, now a Beau who might have killed Wilbur. "Beau who?"

"Does it really matter? It won't bring me back."

"If you don't want to discuss your death, can you at least help prevent mine?" she asked.

"How can I do that?"

"One way, you could come home with me, stay a couple of days. We're having a party, and according to what you told Marie, the person you overheard will be there. You could point out who it is."

He studied her for a moment. Finally, he said, "If you help me first."

"Help you how?" Danielle asked.

"I lost something the other day, when I first got here. I put it right over there." He pointed to a pile of rocks along the ocean.

"What did you lose?"

"It was a large gunnysack," he explained.

"A…a gunnysack?" Danielle squeaked.

"Yes. Did you see it?"

"Those were your bones?" she blurted. He vanished.

"No, come back!" Danielle looked around. He was nowhere in sight. "Why did I have to say that?"

She stood on the beach for over five minutes, waiting for him to return. When he didn't, she continued on to Pier Café.

WHEN DANIELLE STEPPED into Pier Café, she wasn't surprised to find all the tables and booths taken. The town was full up for the Fourth. Fortunately, there were several empty seats at the counter. She quickly claimed one.

"Are you waiting for anyone?" Carla asked Danielle as she filled her water glass. Today red, white and blue streaks colored Carla's hair, with sprinkles of glittery blue stars. Danielle silently wondered if the stars were firmly attached to the hair, or would they be falling in some customer's food? At least with the glitter Eva occasionally tossed around, it typically vanished before hitting a surface, and was never visible to non-mediums.

"No. Just me. I want to order some takeout. I didn't feel like cooking tonight, and Walt didn't feel like going out."

"Who ever feels like cooking?" Carla asked.

"And maybe some pie, too. What do you have?"

"A fresh apple pie came out of the oven less than five minutes ago. It's still hot," Carla said.

"Oh...sounds good. I'll have the piece of pie first. With a scoop of French vanilla ice cream."

"We have vanilla, not sure it's French," Carla said.

"That's fine."

"So dessert before dinner?" Carla asked with a grin as she scratched the order for pie on her small pad of paper.

"How else? And put in a to-go order for two cheeseburgers and fries."

"Okay, I'll put that in and get you the pie."

"Oh, and a piece of pie to go for Walt."

As Carla jotted down the second piece of pie, Danielle added, "Make that two pieces of apple pie to go."

Carla looked up to Danielle and paused a moment.

"I don't want Walt to eat pie alone," Danielle explained.

"So you don't want pie and ice cream now?" Carla asked, her pen hovering over the pad of paper.

"I didn't say that."

Carla laughed, wrote something on the pad, and left to fill the order.

Fifteen minutes later, as Danielle nibbled her slice of warm apple pie and vanilla ice cream, she pondered the strangeness of the recent glut of Beaus. She was about to take another bite when Carla stopped by, leaned against the counter, and asked, "Are you really going to eat two pieces of apple pie tonight?"

Danielle shrugged and said, "I doubt it. I'll probably let Walt have them both."

"He does have a sweet tooth," Carla noted.

Danielle glanced up to Carla, thinking about the Beau Walt had once known, and his property that had recently sold. She impulsively asked, "Do you know Earl Barr?"

"In a way. He used to come in sometimes, not much of a talker. Likes to keep to himself. But I doubt he'll ever be in here again. His daughter Cindy told me he has early stages of Alzheimer's. They just put him in a home."

"You know his daughters?" Danielle asked.

"Sure, they used to come in when they'd visit their mom. But I doubt I'll see them again. I don't imagine they'll be back to Frederickport."

"Not even to visit their father?" Danielle asked.

Carla gave a snort. "Are you kidding? They couldn't stand their father. So why do you ask?"

"No reason, really. I just heard something about the Barr place…" Danielle didn't feel especially creative at the moment and couldn't think of a plausible reason to explain why she was asking the question.

"Oh, you heard about it being haunted," Carla whispered.

Danielle looked up quickly. She hadn't expected Carla to say that.

"I'd never heard about it before," Carla said. "But when Cindy stopped in here with her sister a couple of weeks ago, they said they were celebrating because the escrow on their dad's property had just closed. The main reason they wanted to sell was so there would be enough money to keep him in that nursing home. Frankly, I don't understand why they cared. I mean, if they dislike their dad so much, it's not like they're responsible for paying for his care."

"What is this about it being haunted?" Danielle asked.

"Oh, that, well, Cindy said they never talked about it before, because she figured everyone around here thought their family was weird as it was, but according to them, that place is haunted. It's one reason both those girls got the hell out of Frederickport when they turned eighteen. That and they hated their father. Although, I think they cared about their mom. Anyway, they were afraid the buyer might do a walk-through before the close of escrow and then get spooked off and cancel the deal."

"Who supposedly haunts the place?" Danielle asked.

"I've no idea. They didn't say. But they told me creepy things have been going on there for as long as they could remember. Cindy said that was one reason they never invited friends over to their house. And I guess their parents didn't really have any friends."

Motion from Danielle's right caught her attention. She glanced toward the door and noticed two women about to leave the restaurant. They were the black women who had asked Walt the question about a diary.

"Hey, Carla," Danielle whispered. "See those two women who are just leaving?"

Carla glanced briefly to the exit door. "That's Raven and her cousin. Raven is the taller one. I don't remember the cousin's name. What about them?"

"They were at a talk Walt gave at the library and asked him some questions about *Moon Runners*. I was wondering, are they from around here or tourists?"

"Little of both, I guess," Carla said.

"What do you mean?" Danielle asked.

"If you're really curious about them, ask Adam."

"Adam? Why Adam?"

"They're renting a house from him. Staying for the summer. So I guess that makes them tourists. But according to what one of them told me, they had a grandmother who used to live in Frederickport."

"Really?" Danielle looked back to the door.

SIXTEEN

Walt volunteered to pick up cinnamon rolls from Old Salts Bakery on Tuesday morning. They were out, and if they expected Adam and Chris to hook up the surveillance cameras, they needed to keep them happy. Lily, Heather, and Ian also planned to come over to help put up the decorations.

While Walt left to get the cinnamon rolls, Danielle cooked up a pan of bacon and whipped up some scrambled eggs. She figured they needed protein to go with all that sugar.

Adam arrived first and entered through the kitchen door. The moment he stepped in the house, he took a deep breath, taking in the smell of freshly cooked bacon and coffee brewing.

"Good morning," he greeted her before snatching a slice of bacon from the platter sitting on the counter. "Where's Chris and Walt?"

"Walt's picking up cinnamon rolls, and Chris called. He's running a little late. He should be here in about twenty minutes," Danielle said as she poured Adam a cup of coffee.

"So where are the cameras?" Adam asked, sitting down at the kitchen table with his coffee.

"I put everything in the dining room," Danielle said, sitting down at the table.

"What else do you need to do to get ready?" Adam asked.

"Joanne will be here in a little while to clean the house."

"Why bother? With all the people who'll be tromping through here tomorrow, why not just have Joanne clean on Thursday?"

"Seriously, Adam? Don't you clean your house before you have company?" Danielle asked.

"Um…no." Adam shrugged. "And when do I have company?"

"Such a slob," Danielle teased.

"What about the decorations? Aren't you putting them up this year?"

"Yeah. Lily, Ian and Heather are coming over a little later to do that."

"You need us to help take down the boxes first? Didn't they get shoved on that top shelf in the basement?"

"Walt and I already got them down. They're piled in the hallway."

"All of them?" Adam frowned.

"Yeah."

"Wasn't there, like, ten boxes?"

"Six."

"I hope you didn't break poor Walt's back getting them down. So what about food?" Adam asked.

"I took a shortcut this year. Pearl Cove is catering."

"Fancy schmancy."

"Hey, Adam, I wanted to ask you about one of your renters. They were at Walt's talk at the library, asked him several questions about *Moon Runners*. According to Carla, they've rented a house from you for the summer, and their grandmother used to live here."

"Are you talking about the Kings?"

"I don't know their last name. Carla called one Raven. Two women, cousins."

"Yeah, that's the Kings. A brother, sister and their cousin. Raven is the cousin. The other two are Kiara and Laken."

"What do you know about them?" Danielle asked.

"Why?" Adam asked.

"Just curious. They asked a lot of questions at the library. I wondered who they were."

"They rented the house for the summer," Adam said.

"Carla told me that. So, they're here on vacation?" Danielle asked.

"They're here on a quest."

"Quest? What do you mean?" she asked.

"They're on a quest to learn more about their family history. Or more accurately, to solve a family mystery," Adam explained.

"What kind of family mystery?" Danielle asked.

"Their grandmother used to live here. Or their great-grandmother? I don't remember. But she had a sister who went missing. And they seem to think they might figure out what really happened to her. Not sure how they plan to do that."

"When did she go missing?" Danielle asked.

Adam shrugged. "I'm not sure. The topic came up when I offhandedly asked how they decided on Frederickport for the summer. One of them said their grandmother used to live here, so I figured they used to come here to visit her. But then another one said they had never been here before. So I said something like this trip being about retracing family or something lame like that. The guy said that was an understatement, and his sister said they were here to unravel a family mystery. And then someone mentioned a missing relative. That was about it. They didn't go into any detail."

"Can I ask you another question?" Danielle asked.

"You're going to anyway. Why ask if you can ask?"

Danielle shrugged. "Habit."

"Go ahead, but I don't know much about them other than they're from California, but I don't remember offhand what city."

"No, this is a question about a real estate sale in town. Do you know anything about property that recently sold in Frederickport, owned by Earl Barr?"

"Seriously, Danielle? I talked about this the other night. I introduced you to the buyer."

Danielle looked blankly at Adam.

"At Pearl Cove. He walked right up to our table. I introduced you."

"Beau somebody?" Danielle asked.

"Beau Stewart."

"You didn't say he bought the Barr property."

Adam shrugged. "I thought I did."

"So Beau Stewart is related to Earl Barr?" Danielle asked.

"Yeah. First cousins."

"Carla said something about the property being haunted."

Adam laughed. "That sounds like something Carla would say."

"So it isn't? You've never noticed anything funny over there?"

"Are you seriously asking me if the place is haunted?" Adam asked.

"I'm just curious if there's some local legend about the place—you know, like with Presley House."

"And your house," Adam added with a smile.

"Well, is there?"

Adam considered the question for a moment. "You know, now that I think about it, I do sort of remember something that happened back when we were in high school. I'll have to ask Mel if she remembers. Personally, I've never even stepped on the property. Oh, I've driven by it lots of times. It needs a lot of work."

"You've never been there, not even when you sold it?" Danielle asked.

Adam shook his head. "No. I wasn't the listing agent. Beau called me after they listed it, told me he wanted to buy it and what he was offering. It was all done between me and the other Realtor."

"You didn't do a walk-through?"

"No reason to. Beau intends to level the place. And I assume he's been there before, since his cousin was the previous owner."

"What's this Beau like?" Danielle asked.

"You sure are nosey today." Adam laughed.

"Come on, humor me."

"He has a lot of money. Might be richer than you."

"After you introduced him the other night, Ian said Beau's father was a developer, and that's where Beau got all his money," Danielle said.

"True. But the property they developed came from Beau's mother's side of the family. The same grandparents as Earl's. I learned that when I checked out the property records. The Stewarts own a crapload of property in Oregon. It all came from Beau's maternal grandparents."

"Stalking your clients again to see how much they're worth?" Danielle teased.

Adam shrugged. "Doesn't hurt to find out how much a client can really afford. They don't say *'Buyers are liars'* for nothing."

"So poor Earl's side only inherited the property here, and his cousin's family got the rest? According to Carla, Earl's daughters needed to sell his house to pay for his long-term care."

"That's kind of what I heard too, about the money going to pay for the care home. And I don't think Earl had any other money, but it has nothing to do with Beau's side inheriting it all. What I learned when checking out those property records, half the grandparents' property went to Earl's side, the other half to Beau's. Earl's family didn't do a terrific job managing their property. From what I've heard around town, Earl had a serious gambling problem. He's been selling off his property for years—all to his cousin Beau. I suspect to pay off gambling debts. The only thing he still owned was that property he just sold to Beau."

"No wonder Earl's daughters had an issue with their father and resented selling to Beau," Danielle said.

"Yeah, he inherited all that real estate, and nothing to show for it. Unless he didn't use the money to pay off gambling debts and there are rusty coffee cans buried on the property stuffed with cash. And now that the poor guy has Alzheimer's, he doesn't remember." Adam grinned at the idea.

"A word of advice," Danielle said.

"What's that?"

"Don't sneak over there and start digging up the place, looking for buried treasure. I hear the place is haunted," Danielle teased.

Adam rolled his eyes. "Funny."

WALT ARRIVED BACK at Marlow House at the same time as Chris. After they ate the breakfast Danielle had prepared for them and half the cinnamon rolls, Chris and Adam started installing the surveillance cameras.

Unfortunately, twenty minutes into the project Chris discovered two faulty cameras. He called the company he had purchased them from in Portland, and while they had two replacements, someone would have to drive to Portland to pick them up.

"Walt and I can get them," Danielle suggested. "Lily and Ian can take care of the decorations, and this way you guys can finish installing what you have, and if you run into any more glitches, we can pick up what you need."

"I FEEL A LITTLE GUILTY, leaving everyone else to do the work while we take off," Danielle said as Walt backed out of the garage and she sat in the passenger seat.

Walt laughed. "It was your idea."

"True." She looked at Walt and added, "Adam says adding the two cameras we're bringing back will only take a couple of minutes after they hook up everything else they have. So I was wondering…"

"Where do you want to go?" Walt asked.

"I was thinking we should probably stop at the police station first. I need to tell the chief what Wilbur told me. I tried calling him last night, but his cellphone kept going to voicemail. And I seriously did not want to leave a message about a ghost. I suppose I could call and tell him, but I'd rather do it in person. And then…"

"You want to go somewhere else?"

"We're going to Portland anyway, and according to Heather, the bookstore Wilbur's sister worked for is up the street from where we're going."

"Don't you think figuring out one mystery—who wants to burn our house down—is enough to keep us busy right now? From everything we know, it looks like Wilbur has been dead for a long time. And Marie has helped him realize he's no longer alive. It's entirely possible he's already moved on by now."

"I suppose. But the Beau thing is just bugging me."

"What Beau thing?"

"It's just a name I rarely hear," Danielle said.

"I don't understand what you're getting at," Walt said.

"Since we got back from Hawaii, we met a Beau at Pearl Cove. I met a ghost who claims a Beau killed him. You told us about two Beaus, a father and son. Let me think…are there any more?"

"You aren't suggesting this Wilbur ghost is linked to the people who broke into our house?"

"Other than what he overheard at the pier, no, of course not. But even so, I'd like to learn more about him, and we'll be right down the street from the bookstore, anyway."

"Not sure what good it'll do, but I don't think it'll hurt to drop by for a few minutes."

SEVENTEEN

Chief MacDonald called Joe Morelli and Brian Henderson into his office on Tuesday morning. He was sitting behind his desk, going through the day's mail, when they walked in.

"You wanted to see us, Chief?" Joe asked. He and Brian stood before the desk. Some twenty years spanned the ages of the two men, with Joe being the youngest. In his thirties, Joe had never married, but he lived with Ian's sister, Kelly. He had dated Danielle briefly when she had first moved to town, and if he wasn't now with Kelly, he understood Danielle's social group would not regularly include him.

Brian, twice divorced, had a knack of picking the wrong woman. While he considered himself an excellent judge of character, the results hadn't proved out, especially when one looked at several women he had dated. He had disliked and distrusted Danielle after she first moved to town, yet the pair had since become unlikely friends.

MacDonald pointed to the chairs facing him and said, "Why don't you sit down so we can talk?"

They each took a seat, and Brian asked, "Is everything all right?"

"Could you work tomorrow? I know you both have the day off."

Joe groaned, but Brian said, "No problem."

"If you really need us, okay, but can you tell Kelly I can't go with her to the Fourth party at Marlow House?" Joe asked.

"Don't worry, Joe. You won't miss it. I need you and Brian to go undercover at Marlow House," the chief explained.

"Undercover?" Brian asked with a frown. He leaned back in the chair and crossed one leg over the opposing knee.

"Whoever I send, I don't want their presence drawing attention. I'd rather people assume you're off duty, and many people in town know you're friends of Walt and Danielle."

"Danielle is a friend, not sure about Walt," Joe grumbled.

Brian chuckled at Joe's comment. He looked at the chief and asked, "Why do you want someone over there?"

"While Danielle and Walt were in Hawaii, someone broke into their house," the chief began.

"I heard nothing about that," Joe said.

"I'd prefer we keep this between the three of us," the chief said.

"Are you saying Danielle didn't file a report on the break-in?" Brian asked.

"She didn't, and Joanne isn't aware of the break-in," the chief explained.

"Then how do you know someone broke in?" Joe asked.

"After Walt and Danielle got back, they noticed someone had gone through Walt's desk."

"What about Joanne?" Brian asked. "Wasn't she in the house while they were gone?"

"Danielle is adamant Joanne would not go through Walt's desk. Plus, they could tell someone had been in the secret staircase," the chief explained.

"So what does all this have to do with the Fourth party?" Brian asked.

"Um…well…I have information that someone believes Walt Marlow's diary inspired *Moon Runners*…the original Walt Marlow. They're trying to get their hands on it and intend to do anything to destroy it, even burn down Marlow House."

"Where did you get this information?" Joe asked.

"I'm not at liberty to say," the chief said.

Joe and Brian exchanged glances. Brian looked back to the chief and asked, "Have you gone through the diary to determine what they want to keep quiet?"

"There is no diary," the chief said.

"I thought you said they're looking for the diary?" Brian asked.

"They're looking for something that does not exist," the chief said.

"Why do they think there's one?" Joe asked.

"Because of what Walt wrote in his book. And please, this can't leave my office," the chief insisted.

"What do you want us to do?" Brian asked.

"I need you both to pay attention tomorrow. Look for anyone who wanders off. Watch for any suspicious behavior. I don't want you to prevent anyone from looking around; I'd just like to find out who's looking."

When Joe and Brian stepped out of the chief's office twenty minutes later and closed the door behind them, they stood in the hallway, glancing warily back to the office.

"Once again, an anonymous source," Joe said. "I don't get this."

"You have to admit, the chief's anonymous sources normally pay off."

"None of this makes any sense," Joe said.

"When does anything that has to do with Marlow House make sense?" Brian asked.

JOE AND BRIAN left the police station about ten minutes before Walt and Danielle arrived. Danielle had called ahead, to tell the chief they planned to stop by, so he was expecting them. When they arrived at the chief's office, he was no longer going through his mail and was now busy reviewing reports. After they greeted him and walked into his office, the chief updated them on what he had asked of Joe and Brian.

"So did it work? What we decided you'd say to them?" Danielle asked. She and Walt sat in the chairs facing the chief's desk.

"I suppose. Yet I have the feeling they're wondering where I keep getting this anonymous information. But they both agree to be there and keep an eye open."

"Like I mentioned on the phone, Walt and I are on the way to Portland to pick up a couple of cameras. The reason I wanted to stop by has nothing to do with whoever is looking for the nonexistent diary," Danielle said.

"Then why?" the chief asked.

"It's about those bones the dogs found. I think I know who they belong to," Danielle said.

"Who?"

"Someone named Wilbur Jenkins." Danielle told the chief what she had learned about Wilbur and then said, "I looked up that bookstore. It's down the street from where we have to go. We'll stop by, see if we can find out anything about this Wilbur."

"Until we get the test results back, we really don't know when our John Doe—or Wilbur—died. Even then, what we learn may be of little help. It's possible the murder occurred a hundred years ago, because of the bullet type. But antique guns have killed people before," the chief said.

"You said before you were running a DNA test," Danielle said.

"Yes. It's one test we're waiting on" The chief turned to his computer. "Let me check something. What did you say his name is?"

"He gave Marie his full name. Wilbur James Jenkins," Danielle said.

The chief nodded while staring at the monitor, his fingers typing on the keyboard. Danielle stood up to get a closer look at what he was doing. She and Walt quietly watched. Finally, the chief stopped typing and looked up to her and shook his head. "Nothing. No missing report on a Wilbur James Jenkins in the last ten years."

"Regardless of that bullet, I find it hard to believe those remains are of someone who died almost a hundred years ago," Walt said. He remained sitting.

Danielle sat back down and glanced to Walt. "Why?"

Walt looked at the chief. "Didn't you say that gunnysack was relatively new? That it hadn't been in the ocean for a long time?"

"What about the gunnysack?" Danielle added, looking to the chief. "You mentioned before you were tracking down who bought them."

"Yes, the bag was relatively new. And Brian is still trying to track down who purchased them. So far, we've located three buyers, and they still have them," the chief said.

"If the person attached to those bones—Wilbur or someone else —died a hundred years ago, why would anyone throw them in the ocean? That's something a killer does trying to hide evidence, not someone who just stumbled on the remains. And if he died that long ago, his killer is dead by now," Walt said.

"Which is one reason I don't believe they're that old," the chief confessed. "Initially I did, but I think I was trying to be optimistic. I'd rather deal with a hundred-year-old murder than a current one."

"If those bones don't belong to Wilbur, they belong to someone he's attached to. And if they aren't his, my bet, they belong to someone killed at the same time as he was," Danielle said. "Wilbur first showed up at Ian and Lily's a couple of hours before the dogs found the bones. He talked as if he was carrying them with him. But that can't be the case, because from everything I saw, he hasn't learned to harness his energy. I don't believe he carried that bag; he was following it."

"Which makes me think they probably are his," Walt said. "Someone killed Wilbur. Long enough ago that his body decomposed, leaving behind his skeleton."

"Which would be over a month," the chief said.

"And our killer gets rid of the evidence now that the body has decomposed. It's easier to transport a bag of bones rather than a corpse," Walt said.

"The thought gives me the creeps," Danielle said.

"We also know Wilbur was not cognizant of his death—according to Marie. But he felt connected to those bones, and when the killer moved them, he followed," Walt said.

"Makes sense," the chief agreed.

"If those remains belong to Wilbur, and it sure looks like it, we also have the killer's name. At least who I think might be the killer. Someone named Beau. Wilbur told me he thought Beau killed him."

"But he wasn't sure?" the chief asked.

"Walt's proof a ghost doesn't always know how he died, or who killed him," Danielle reminded. "But if you find Wilbur and then find a Beau he knows, you may have your killer."

The chief let out a sigh and leaned back at his desk. "Since you're going to Portland anyway, find out what you can. But be careful. No one has reported Wilbur missing. And whoever dropped that burlap bag in the ocean probably knows the police have it. They might be getting a little nervous about now. I'm serious; be careful what you ask. And if you run into a Beau at that bookstore, smile and leave and let me take care of it."

Danielle stood up. "Don't worry, Chief. Walt and I have enough problems. We don't need to give someone else a reason to bump us off. All we'll do is go in the bookstore and see if Wilbur's sister still works there. If she does, well, then you'll want to talk to her. I imagine you'll want to get some DNA to match, and from how Wilbur talked, it didn't sound like his sister killed him."

EIGHTEEN

Danielle gave Walt credit; he had no problem driving in traffic despite the fact when he had learned to drive, few roads had pavement or many cars on them. Leaning back in the passenger seat, she watched him effortlessly maneuver holiday traffic. It had been over two years since his transformation, yet some mornings she still woke up terrified it had all been a dream and she would discover the man she loved still haunted Marlow House.

He had quickly adapted to the technology of her era. Of course, she had introduced him to email back when he was still in the spirit realm. While grateful he hadn't continued smoking his cigars when he stepped over to her side, she had to admit she missed the sweet scent of his favorite brand. He didn't seem to miss smoking—he was far too busy eating, especially her double fudge chocolate cake and Old Salts cinnamon rolls. She quietly smiled to herself over Walt's enthusiasm for the flavors and textures of the food he had been denied for almost a hundred years. Plus, he was always making her feel like the most talented baker in the world. If one listened to Walt, Danielle should be a star of a Food Network show.

He still abhorred tattoos, especially on women. She would occasionally overhear him mumbling under his breath about circus people when someone covered with tats passed him. It annoyed him when men wore baseball caps backwards, and while he owned some denim pants, he rarely wore them.

Danielle glanced in the back seat and spied Walt's fedora. She had never seen him wear a hat when he had been a ghost, something she once mentioned to him. He had reminded her it was rude for a man to wear a hat inside, and when he had been a ghost, she had only seen him inside the house.

She looked back to Walt, who hummed along to jazz music playing on the radio. That was another thing that hadn't changed. Walt preferred music from his era. While she had never been an enormous jazz fan, she had come to appreciate it after listening with Walt. She figured he had adapted to so many things from her era, that if she loved him, she should appreciate what he enjoyed from his era. And she did love him.

When they arrived in Portland, they stopped first at the electronic store. After exchanging the cameras and checking with Chris to see if he needed them to pick up anything else, they headed to the bookstore.

THE BOOKSTORE WAS LARGER than Danielle had expected. It wasn't as large as a Powell's; although what bookstore was? Nor was it as large as a Barnes and Noble; it was bigger than many of the family owned independent bookstores she had visited over the years. Despite its size, there didn't seem to be many customers. Danielle wondered if the day before July Fourth was typically a slow day for book sales.

Instead of heading for the shelves of books, Walt and Danielle lingered along the walls by the front entrance, looking for the history display Heather had mentioned.

They had only been looking for a minute when a voice asked, "Can I help you find something?"

Danielle and Walt turn toward the voice and found a pleasant-looking forty-something woman looking at them. She wore a store name tag that said Betty.

Before they could respond, she gasped, "Are you Walt Marlow?"

Surprised at her greeting, Walt smiled softly and said, "Yes, I am."

"Oh my goodness," the woman gushed. "I'm an enormous fan. I was disappointed when I read they weren't making the movie. I understand why. That's horrible what happened, but please tell me someone else will make the movie?"

"At the moment, there are no plans," Walt said.

Betty glanced over to Danielle, who stood silently listening. "Oh, I'm sorry. You're Danielle Marlow, aren't you? I've seen your picture."

"Yes, I am," Danielle said with a smile.

"I'm Betty White. I work here and—"

"Betty White?" Danielle blurted out before thinking, unable to suppress a giggle.

Betty grinned. "Yeah, I told my husband I should take back my maiden name."

"I'm sorry, I didn't mean to laugh," Danielle said. "We have a friend named Joe Morelli."

"I love Stephanie Plum!" Betty said.

"Our friend Joe Morelli is also a cop," Danielle explained.

Betty laughed. "Sharing a name with a famous person—real or imaginary—leads to some interesting conversations. And I really am an enormous fan of your husband." She looked at Walt and said, "If you would ever be interested in doing a book signing here, I would love to arrange it."

"Thank you," Walt said. "I'll seriously consider your offer."

"So what did you come in for today?" she asked. "What can I help you find?"

"We're in the neighborhood, picking up something at a store down the street, and we noticed your sign. Walt and I love bookstores." It was partially true. Walt and Danielle did love bookstores.

"How long has this store been here?" Walt asked.

"In two years, we'll be celebrating our hundredth anniversary," Betty said proudly.

"How long have you worked here?" Danielle asked.

"Since I was twelve." Betty grinned. "My mother owns the store, but I've been managing it since I got out of college. Her grandmother started it. There are some pictures of the early days over there." Betty pointed to the wall behind them.

Walt and Danielle walked to the wall with Betty. Danielle was fairly certain this was what Heather had talked about when she mentioned a collage of photographs showcasing the bookstore in its early days.

There were about a dozen framed photographs and news clippings hanging on the wall. In the center was the largest, a black-and-white with four people standing in front of the store, grinning proudly into the camera. By the vehicles in the photograph, Danielle guessed someone had taken the picture during Walt's first lifetime.

She looked closer and recognized one person in the photograph. It was Wilbur.

Danielle pointed to the framed photograph and asked, "Who are the people in the picture?"

Betty looked. She pointed to the first person on the right. "That was my mother's grandmother, Kimberly Kate Jones."

"Um…was Jones her married name?" Danielle asked.

"Why, yes, it was. She wasn't married yet in that picture. So technically, in that photograph she was Kimberly Kate Jenkins," Betty said.

"And next to her?" Danielle asked.

"That's her brother, Wilbur Jenkins. And next to him are two of her first employees in the store. But I don't remember their names."

"I notice the store is named for her. Was her brother part owner?" Danielle asked, trying to figure out a way to find out what had happened to Wilbur without it sounding like an odd question.

"Oh, no." Betty looked at Walt and said, "If you're ever looking for a story idea for one of your books, Wilbur and Kate's father would make a good subject."

"How so?" Danielle asked.

"Jerome Jenkins, that was my great-grandmother's father, made a fortune during the California gold rush," Betty began. "He settled in Oregon and bought up a ton of property. He married several times. One ran off with his partner; another died. His last wife was the mother to Kimberly and Wilbur. They were his only children. He was in his seventies when he married his last wife. She was in her thirties. But the old coot outlived her. He was in his nineties when he died."

"I guess his two kids inherited all his money?" Danielle asked.

Betty let out a sigh. "Yes, but as you can see, I'm still working in the bookstore, so the fortune didn't make it this far."

"What happened?" Walt asked.

"As the story goes, Kimberly started the bookstore using her allowance. She was trying to show her father she was responsible, whereas her brother, Wilbur, he was a party boy, not especially ambitious, and loved having a good time."

"So who did he leave his money to?" Danielle asked.

"Old Jerome didn't believe a woman could handle her own finances. A significant portion of this estate included the land he owned, which he left to his son, but he put any cash he had in stocks, and left that and the family home to the daughter. But she couldn't do what she wanted with it, not without her brother's approval."

"This was the brother who just wanted to have a good time?" Danielle asked.

Betty nodded. "Exactly. After the father died, Wilbur wanted cash instead of land, so he sold off all his father's property, liquidated everything and then took off, doing what he always wanted to do, travel. With him gone, it tied his sister to the terms of their father's will, and when the stock market crash of 1929 came, she lost everything except for this store."

"What happened to Wilbur?" Walt asked.

"His sister never saw him again after he took off on his grand adventure. But she always felt he probably lost his fortune and was too ashamed to come home."

"Wow. Poor Kimberly," Danielle said.

"Don't feel too sorry for her. Mom told me her grandmother was always happy, loved the bookstore. Her biggest regret wasn't losing her father's fortune, it was losing her brother."

"Do you know what happened to him?" Danielle asked.

"No. Once my grandmother tried to find him. Unfortunately, back then, that was difficult to do. But when DNA testing started being a thing, I had mine done and registered on a genealogy website. I figure if one of old Wilbur's descendants gets tested, we'll get a match. Wouldn't that be neat to find him after all this time?"

"BETTY WHITE WILL PROBABLY GET that DNA match any day now, but I don't think she'll get any cousins out of it," Danielle said to Walt after they started back to Frederickport.

"So that was him in the photograph?" Walt asked.

"Yeah, I recognized him right away. Unless he's assuming a

younger image of himself, I think he died not long after that photo was taken."

"If those are his remains, it would lead one to believe he died here. Perhaps he never left Oregon," Walt suggested.

"If that's true, what happened to all his property?"

"According to Betty, he sold it all before he left. He must have. I'm sure if he disappeared before he sold the property, his sister would've known," Walt said.

"Did he stay in Oregon with all that money? I wonder how much it was and what happened to it."

"Good question."

Danielle opened her purse and retrieved her cellphone. "I should probably call the chief and tell him what we found out. I imagine he'll be relieved that whoever killed poor Wilbur is no longer a threat."

"But there is still another disturbing question," Walt said.

Danielle paused a moment, phone in hand, and looked at him. "What question is that?"

"Why would someone put his remains in a gunnysack and toss them in the ocean?"

NINETEEN

Both Danielle and Walt rose before daybreak on Wednesday, July 4. Walt wore a three-piece pin-striped suit Danielle had purchased online, similar to the blue one he had worn when in the spirit realm. She thought he looked like a dapper author from an earlier era.

The red dress Danielle wore came from a local dress shop. While Walt looked as if he had stepped out of the twenties in his suit, she looked as if she had come from the forties in her dress, with its fitted waist, full skirt, white collar, and blue star buttons. When Lily first saw the dress after Danielle tried it on in the dress shop, she had said, "That's adorable, but I guess this means you won't be wearing the Missing Thorndike this year."

AN HOUR after Danielle and Walt were up and dressed, Lily opened Connor's bedroom blinds, looked outside and across the street. Her son was in the kitchen with Ian having breakfast. She wanted to tidy the nursery before they left to help Walt and Danielle.

Standing silently at the window for a moment, she thought about the first time she had set eyes on Marlow House, over four years ago. At the time she never imagined she would move to Frederickport, making it her home. She had expected to just spend the summer here, helping Danielle open the bed-and-breakfast, and then she would return to California, back to her teaching job. While she had returned to California after the summer, fate intervened.

When she first saw the house, Danielle had told her the Victorian was actually a Second Empire mansard style. Lily had later looked it up online and read French architecture from the Napoleon era had initially inspired the design. Four years earlier, Lily had compared its overgrown grounds to a jungle. Today its many trees no longer branched off wildly in all directions, and the manicured grounds provided a parklike setting.

There had been no summer showers the night before, and all the decorations they had put up yesterday remained intact, which pleased Lily. Red, white and blue bunting hung from the eaves, a stars and stripes pendant banner wrapped around the top of the fence railing, and a patriotic wreath with bursts of shiny red, white and blue stars hung from the front door.

She was about to turn from the window when she noticed someone across the street putting up the American flags. It was Walt, and she could see he wore the blue suit Danielle had bought him.

Lily turned from the window and began straightening the nursery. When she finished, she needed to get dressed for the day. She would wear her new white pedal pushers and a red and blue short sleeveless blouse. She also planned to wear her hair up in a high ponytail.

JOANNE ARRIVED at Marlow House first. The housekeeper wanted to be there when Pearl Cove's catering department delivered the food. While she waited, she arranged the tables.

The next to arrive was Melony, who had volunteered to be in charge of ticket sales. While the gate would not open for a couple of hours, she wanted to get there early and see if there was anything Danielle needed her to do before people began arriving.

"I really appreciate your help today," Danielle told Melony as she showed her the table at the side gate for admissions. "Everything is under control. We're just waiting for the food now, and it won't be here for a couple of hours. I tried to help Joanne set up for the food, but that woman is on a mission, and I think I was in her way."

"I suppose Joanne has done several of these already; she has her system," Melony said.

"Yeah. If I had prepared most of the food, like I have before, then I would be in helping her. But when I decided to let Pearl Cove cater, I went over the menu with Joanne, and she had some definite ideas, so I'm letting her do her thing," Danielle explained.

"She seemed to be enjoying herself in there," Melony noted.

"Since we have some time, and everything is under control, why don't we have a cup of coffee and a cinnamon roll on the front swing?" Danielle suggested. "Once this thing gets started, I don't imagine we'll have much time for ourselves."

DANIELLE AND MELONY sat on the front swing, each holding a cup of coffee. They ended up splitting a cinnamon roll, but that quickly disappeared.

Before taking a sip of her coffee, Danielle said, "Yesterday Adam and I discussed the property Beau Stewart purchased."

"The Barr place?" Melony asked.

"Yeah. Carla said something about it being haunted, and I asked Adam if he ever heard any stories about it. At first, he didn't remember, but then he said there was something, but he couldn't recall what it was and said he thought you might know."

"That's because Adam wasn't there when it happened. He was home sick with the flu. I don't think he ever believed me when I told him about it."

"So something did happen?" Danielle asked.

Melony shrugged and took a sip of her coffee. She said, "Not sure I believe the place is haunted, but something weird happened back then. When I think about it now, how I remember it probably isn't what happened. Just scared teenagers and overactive imaginations."

"What do you remember?" Danielle asked.

Melony stopped the gentle rocking of the porch swing with the toe of her right shoe, leaned down, and set her now empty coffee cup on the ground. She resumed rocking before saying, "It was a Friday night. Adam was supposed to go to the party with us, but he got the flu and had to stay home. The party was down the street from the Barr place. Three of us got bored, so we got the bright idea to go TP the house."

"Did the place look like it does now?" Danielle asked.

"It did. That place has always been a dump. Old red barn that needs painting, outbuildings that need bulldozing, and the house, which looks like it does today. Little more weathered. I don't think they've painted it in the last fifty years."

"I understand the new owners are tearing everything down," Danielle said.

Melony nodded. "That's what Adam tells me. Did you know the Stewarts were friends of my parents?"

"I thought they never lived here?" Danielle asked.

"They never have. Dad used to do some legal work for Beau. The guy owns property everywhere. Apartment buildings, commercial property."

"I understand he inherited most of it from his parents," Danielle noted.

"That's what I was told. Family money. And frankly, it surprised me when he started getting involved in politics. I remember my mother always saying they were very private people."

"If you want to preserve your privacy, I'd think you'd avoid politics," Danielle said.

"No kidding. Also, what I find weird, Beau has been trying to buy that property from his cousin for years."

"He has?"

"Yep. When I was going through my dad's old files, I remember coming across several copies of old purchase offers for the place. Looked like he made an offer on the property about every year."

"Was Adam aware of all this when he made the offer for Beau?" Danielle asked.

"No. I didn't realize he was working with Beau until I ran into him in Adam's office right before escrow closed."

"So what was that strange thing you think happened back when you were in high school, but might not have happened?" Danielle asked.

"Me and two of my friends each swiped a roll of toilet paper from the house that was having the party. We walked over to the Barr place. Everything was dark, and there were no cars around. We didn't think anyone was home. We were going to TP the house, but right when we started, the rolls of toilet paper flew out of our hands. Each of us was holding a roll, and it happened exactly at the same time."

"Was it windy?" Danielle asked.

Melony looked at her. "For a minute, I guess. It must have been. What else could it be? But it was odd. I remember that night being so still. It was unusually hot for Frederickport in July, and I remember us talking about it while we walked over to the Barr place in the dark, and how a breeze would cool things down. And then this gust of wind comes up out of nowhere, knocks those rolls of TP out of our hands, and blew them all the way to the barn."

"Maybe it was one of those little dirt devils?" Danielle suggested.

"I'm sure it was. But back then, well, it's not how I remember it. It didn't feel like wind. It…" Melony looked off in the distance, not finishing her sentence.

"What did it feel like?"

"It felt like someone literally ripped that roll out of my hand. And there was the laugh."

"Laugh?" Danielle frowned.

"We all heard it. Laughter. Like someone ripped those rolls from us and then laughed about it. But now, I realize it had to be the wind. But back then, well, it was freaky."

"Did you leave?"

Melony shook her head. "No. But we should have. We almost did, but one of my friends did that nervous laugh, you know the laugh, when someone is afraid of something and feels stupid about it. He convinced us it was just wind, and we were acting like a bunch of chickens. We all laughed along with him and decided to get the TP and finish the job. By the time we got to the barn, its door was wide open, and all three rolls had blown inside. We could see them. The moon had come up, and I remember how it was just at the right angle, the moonlight was like a spotlight shining right inside the open doorway, landing on those three rolls of toilet paper. It was like the moon was telling us, go on, go get them. And being stupid teenagers, we followed them inside."

"The way you say stupid teenagers, I assume something else happened."

"Yep. The moment we got in the barn the door slammed shut. We couldn't get it open. Then we heard what sounded like crying.

Not sure which was creepier, the sound of laughter or crying. More like sobs, pleading. Scared the crap out of us. We finally got the door open and ran like hell. Left the toilet paper in the barn."

"What do you think it was?" Danielle asked.

"It must have been the wind. Wind blowing through those old buildings can make some weird sounds. I imagine that's all it was, being on edge, lurking around a creepy place in the dark. Wind knocked the rolls of TP out of our hands, made the creepy sounds, slammed the barn door shut. That's probably what it was. But honestly, back then it sure as hell didn't feel like it. And don't tell Adam, but when I think about that evening, I still get the chills. Silly, huh?"

Danielle shook her head. "No. It's not silly."

"And you know what else was strange?" Melony asked.

"What?"

"Normally, if you throw a roll of toilet paper, it unwinds, leaving a trail of TP," Melony said.

"Yes."

"Well, those three rolls, they made it all the way from the house into the barn. And none of them had unrolled. Not even an inch."

TWENTY

They opened the gates at noon. The cars already lined Beach Drive. The volunteers took their positions. Chris moved primarily from the second floor to the attic, while Heather helped Joanne and monitored the first floor and basement. Lily stayed outside, pushing Connor around in a stroller, chatting with the people and looking for anyone suspicious. Ian and Walt led home tours, while Marie watched anyone who might wander off.

Walt had locked the front walk gate earlier that morning, to prevent anyone from using the front door. They directed all incoming and outgoing traffic for home tours through the side yard and kitchen door. Melony and Adam manned the admission table by the front gate into the side yard.

Before going to the kitchen to help Joanne with the food, Danielle checked on Melony and Adam, and discovered they had everything under control. She was about to go to the house when she spied Pearl walking down the street toward the gate. Danielle inwardly groaned, preparing herself for Pearl's inevitable ranting in protest of the charity event. She glanced around for Brian, knowing he was used to handling Pearl, but he stood on the other side of the yard, his back to her.

When Pearl walked through the open gate a moment later, she handed Adam her ticket—one she had purchased prior to the event, surprising Danielle. Pearl said nothing to Danielle as she walked past her, toward the crowd of people gathering on the back patio.

"Was that your neighbor?" Melony whispered to Danielle after Pearl was out of earshot.

"Yes. I can't believe she came," Danielle said.

"Well, it is for a good cause," Melony reminded her.

OFFICER BRIAN HENDERSON stood on the back patio of Marlow House, drinking a beer. The chief said he was undercover, so he figured he would blend in better with a beer in hand. At least, that was the excuse he intended to go with. So far, he had seen nothing suspicious, mostly locals and a few tourists.

About to take a sip of beer, Brian looked toward the road and saw Pearl Huckabee coming his way. Taking a deep breath, he braced for the woman, and once again cursed himself for ever giving her his business card and telling her to call him if she needed his help.

"Officer Henderson," Pearl said primly when she reached him.

"Mrs. Huckabee, I told you before, the Marlows are within their rights to have a fundraiser, and they have a permit, and—"

"Whatever are you talking about?" Pearl asked. "I'm here to support the Humane Society. A very worthy cause."

He frowned. "You are?"

"Yes. I purchased a ticket at the hardware store. Do you know where I can go for the tour? I'm here anyway; I might as well see what the inside of this place looks like. Everyone is always making such a fuss about it being a historical landmark. I've seen the photographs online, of course."

Brian pointed to the house and said, "I believe Walt and Ian are giving tours. You can go through that door."

She gave him a nod and started for the house. He watched her walk away, still not quite believing what he was seeing.

JOANNE HAD ARRANGED the refreshments on the patio's picnic table. After leaving Adam and Melony, Danielle headed to the table to see if it needed replenishing. As she stood by it, surveying the spread, a male voice whispered in her ear, "You always win them over, don't you?"

Startled at the voice and words, Danielle spun around and looked up into Brian's eyes, a silly grin on his face.

"What are you talking about?" she asked.

He nodded toward the house and said, "Pearl. She's in there taking a tour. Finally won her over, I see."

"I'm not sure about that." She glanced briefly to the house and back to Brian. "I was shocked to see her come in. I thought for sure she was here to bitch at me. But she had a ticket. She didn't say hi or anything. And now that I think about it, I didn't greet her. I was in too much shock."

Brian shrugged. "Maybe she's coming around."

"I think it's that she prefers animals to people. This *is* a fundraiser for the local Humane Society."

"Even pit bulls?" Brian asked, remembering all the times Pearl went apoplectic over Hunny.

"Especially pit bulls. Apparently, she has become quite fond of Hunny. I suspect it was what happened at Christmas."

Brian was about to respond but stopped when four people walked up to Danielle, wanting to say hello.

DANIELLE TURNED from Brian and found Beau Stewart standing there with his wife and a younger couple. She smiled at them and said, "Mr. and Mrs. Stewart, glad you could make it."

"Please, it's Beau and Francine," Beau told her. "I'd like you to meet our son and daughter, Brad and Kathy."

"Nice to meet you," Danielle said. She guessed they were about her age and found it interesting how both son and daughter favored the mother. They exchanged a few words, and Danielle turned to introduce them to Brian, but he was no longer there. Glancing around, she didn't see him.

Turning back to the family, she gave them a smile and motioned to the food on the table. "Please help yourself to any of the food. You'll find beverages in the tubs of ice around the yard. We have a croquet set over there…" Danielle briefly pointed the way. "And if you would like a tour of the house, my husband and Ian are giving tours."

"That wouldn't be Ian, as in Jon Altar?" Francine asked excitedly.

WHEN BRIAN ENTERED THE KITCHEN, he found Heather helping Joanne fill pitchers of ice with freshly brewed tea. He said hello to the women and continued on through the house. Once in the entry hall, he spied Ian heading upstairs with a group of people, including Pearl. He didn't see anyone else on the first floor. All the guests inside appeared to be going with Ian on a tour.

Brian glanced in the library, dining room, and then the living room. They were empty, as was the downstairs bedroom. He imagined more people would come inside shortly. He continued on to the parlor and noticed they had rearranged the furniture since the last time he had been in the house. Stepping into the parlor, he glanced around. He spied Danielle's cat, Max, napping soundly on the windowsill. If the cat rolled over, he would fall off.

They had moved the small sofa to the opposite side of the room, now facing the inside wall. Behind the sofa was a collage of framed black-and-white photographs. One frame tilted to the right. He walked to the sofa, stepped behind it, and reached out his hand to straighten the picture. To his annoyance, the framed picture and the nail it had been hanging on fell to the floor. He reached down to pick it up and search for the nail when he heard a male voice say, "Max, here you are."

Brian peeked around the sofa, concealed from view, and watched as Walt stepped into the room and closed the door behind him, as if he wanted privacy. He was about to stand up and reveal himself but stopped when he heard Walt say, "Max, wake up. I need to talk to you."

Crouched behind the furniture, Brian watched as the cat lifted his head and meowed at Walt.

"Come here, Max," Walt ordered. Max jumped down from the windowsill, walked to the desk, leapt up on it, sat down, and faced Walt, his tail swishing.

"Yes, I know you wanted to sleep," he heard Walt say. "We need your help."

Still crouching behind the sofa, Brian frowned and listened.

"According to the ghost, they're supposed to be here today. You need to listen. See if you can recognize their voices."

Max meowed again.

"I know all human voices sound the same to you. But that's not entirely true."

Another meow.

"If you recognize them, tell me or Marie. Whoever you see first. Do you understand?"

Max meowed and jumped off the desk. Walt walked to the parlor door and opened it. Together Walt and Max left the room.

Brian slumped down on the floor behind the sofa, the framed photograph he had been holding moments earlier abandoned on the floor. He sat in silence, thinking. After a few moments, he laughed.

"That son of a bitch saw me come in here. He's messing with me." Brian's laughter stopped a moment later, and he remained sitting on the floor. "At least I sure as hell hope he was messing with me."

THE STEWART FAMILY helped themselves to refreshments before going inside to take a tour. As they filled their plates, Heather came outside from the kitchen, carrying several pitchers of iced tea. Kathy Stewart moved out of the way, allowing Heather to set the pitchers on the table. As she stepped aside, she curiously looked Heather up and down. When Heather left and returned to the house, Kathy asked her father, "Who was that?"

Beau glanced to the kitchen door Heather had just entered and back to his daughter. "I've met her. I think her name is Heather. She works for the Glandon Foundation."

"Does she think she's a witch or something?" Kathy asked.

Beau laughed. "She dresses like it."

"Think she's part of that witches' coven in Frederickport?" Kathy asked seriously.

"I told you, don't be silly. There is no such thing as witches," Beau told his daughter.

"I didn't say I believe they're really witches. But some people imagine they're all sorts of things, like Elvis, Napoleon, Jesus, and even witches. By the way that woman dresses, I'd say it's a good bet she thinks she's a witch." Kathy finished filling her plate, unaware that Marie had come outside minutes earlier and had overheard the conversation.

Finding the speculation amusing, Marie hurried back inside to share what she had overheard with Heather.

TOURS OF MARLOW HOUSE continued to attract curious guests well into the late afternoon. To Danielle's surprise, Pearl hadn't left after her tour with Ian, but lingered outside, chatting with townspeople and munching on food from Pearl Cove. While she appeared to be enjoying herself, she didn't spare Danielle a smile, even when given one. When Danielle stopped by Pearl's group, she asked, "I hope you're all enjoying yourselves." Most assured Danielle they were and complimented the food and lovely surroundings, while Pearl suggested the iced tea might be rancid.

THE OTHERS in their tour had just followed Walt into the closet off the second-floor master bedroom, to explore the hidden staircase. They stayed behind, lingering in the bedroom. There was no reason to go in the secret staircase. They had seen enough of that when breaking into the house.

"You need to come see this," she whispered to her brother. They were the only two people in the bedroom. He walked over to her and watched as she pushed aside a painting from the wall. It concealed a safe.

"How did you find that?" he asked.

"Pure chance. I was looking at the painting. I don't think Marlow saw me touching it," she said, arranging the painting as it had been before she moved it to one side.

"You think that's where it is?" he asked.

"It could be. But burning the house down is a really stupid idea now. Can you imagine, we torch the freaking house, and that stupid safe remains, they get in it and see what's written in the diary? We risk going to prison, and we don't even destroy the damn thing."

He glanced toward the closet where everyone had gone. "Let's check the rest of this room until they come back."

TWENTY-ONE

Someone might mistake Brian Henderson for a marine—albeit an older one—as opposed to a member of the Frederickport police force. He stood at the refreshment table, filling a paper plate with food, his gray hair shorter than he normally wore it, after a recent trip to the barber. His husky physique stretched out the snug-fitting golf shirt. Brian wasn't trying to show off his abs, the ones he cultivated by regular trips to the gym, but he was single, and when doing laundry the last time, he had shrunk a load of clothes, and he had no other clean shirt to wear today. Plus, it was blue, a fitting color for a July Fourth party.

He had stepped away from the table and took a bite, still standing, when he heard Joe Morelli's voice say, "I think the chief's anonymous source was off this time." Brian turned to the fellow officer now standing by his side. He glanced briefly over Joe's shoulder and spied Kelly, Joe's girlfriend, some distance away, holding her nephew, Connor, while talking to her sister-in-law, Lily.

After swallowing his bite of food, Brian said, "I think you're right. I haven't noticed anyone straying away from the tours inside. And it's mostly familiar faces. Except for her." He nodded to a black woman about to go into the house.

"Adam introduced us earlier," Joe said. "She and her cousins are renting a house here for the summer."

They chatted for a few minutes about the crowd before Brian

nodded toward Kelly in the distance. "Kelly looks natural holding a baby."

Joe glanced over to his girlfriend. "Connor's not really a baby anymore. He's been walking for a few weeks now."

"When are you going to give her one of her own to hold?" Brian teased.

"It would probably be a good thing if we got married first," Joe said.

"No one waits anymore," Brian said.

Joe let out a snort and said, "Have you met my mom? She's not thrilled we're living together. If I told her we were having a baby out of wedlock, I don't even want to imagine her reaction."

"So you don't want kids?" Brian asked.

"I didn't say that. Just said Kelly and I need to get married first."

With a plate of food in one hand and a plastic fork in the other, Brian arched his brow. "So you two getting married?"

Joe glanced over to Kelly but said nothing.

MARIE HAD SPENT the last thirty minutes following a couple around who had wandered away from Walt's tour. A nosey couple, they peeked in drawers and opened cabinets, but by their conversation, Marie doubted they were the couple contemplating arson. After following them downstairs, she watched as they finally left the house for the side yard. She was about to go upstairs when she spied a black couple coming down the staircase. She had seen them earlier taking a tour with Walt. As they reached the first-floor landing, they paused a moment and looked toward the doorway leading to the kitchen. Today everyone had been coming and going via the kitchen, entering and exiting through the back door into the side yard.

A moment later a young woman stepped out from the kitchen into the hallway and hurried in the couple's direction; they met her halfway.

"Did you find anything?" the new arrival asked in a whisper.

Marie barely heard what she had said and moved closer.

"Where have you been, Raven?" the man asked.

"I was talking to the woman who's married to Jon Altar, or

whatever his name is," Raven said. "According to her, he wrote no part of *Moon Runners*. Did you guys find anything?"

"We looked everywhere upstairs. We even found a safe in one bedroom. It's locked, so if it's in there, we can't get to it," the man said.

"I think we have a winner!" Marie announced.

"Did you check the library yet?" Raven asked.

"We tried to earlier, but there were people in there," the other woman said. "So we took the tour with Walt Marlow instead."

"Let's go see if anyone is in there now," Raven suggested.

Marie followed the three down the entry hall and to the library. When they arrived in the room, there were two people checking out the portraits while Max sat nearby on the sofa, watching them. The three people Marie had followed into the room said hello to the couple and assumed the pretext of checking out the titles on the shelves.

When the couple left, the three began hurrying around the room, opening drawers, looking on the shelves, and examining books. After about ten minutes of looking, the one named Raven took a seat on the sofa and began petting Max.

"Raven, come on," the man urged.

"We're not going to find anything," Raven said, reaching out and picking up Max, setting him on her lap. "This is stupid."

The other woman looked to Raven and said, "You'll get cat hair all over your pants."

Raven shrugged. "He's a sweet cat. Can you hear that purr?" She laughed.

MARIE WENT UPSTAIRS to tell Walt what she had overheard. When she found him, he was with a group of people, and while she could convey her message, he could not respond. Not unless he wanted to look crazy.

She found Ian by the stairwell leading to the attic bedroom, chatting with several people, but there was no reason to tell him what she had overheard. He could neither see nor hear her. By the closed bathroom door and the light slipping out, Marie suspected Chris was using the bathroom, and she didn't imagine he would appreciate her barging in the room with him.

Marie headed back downstairs and found Heather in the kitchen, helping Joanne. She almost shared with Heather what she had overheard but decided to find Danielle instead. Earlier, Heather hadn't found Marie's witch story amusing, and she seemed a tad annoyed with her for sharing.

A moment later, Marie stood outside on the back patio, looking for Danielle. More people crowded in the yard than in the house. She credited the sunny weather for keeping the guests outside. Those who ventured inside took one of the tours and then returned to the patio for another trip around the refreshment table.

Toward the rear of the yard, where Heather had set up the vintage croquet set that morning, a number of guests gathered, some playing the game, others watching. By the gate entrance, Adam and Melony sat at the table, chatting with Susan Mitchell from the bank and her husband. But still Marie did not see Danielle.

The sound of the back door opening caught Marie's attention, and she turned around. The three people from the library stepped outside.

"Let's get out of here," the one called Raven said.

"I want to get something to eat," the man said.

"Okay, then we leave," Raven said.

"Oh dear," Marie muttered. "I need to tell someone before they leave."

Marie looked around again. While she couldn't find Danielle, she spied Police Chief MacDonald standing in the yard under a shade tree, talking with Brian Henderson. Taking another quick glance around the patio and yard, she spied the chief's youngest son, Evan MacDonald, standing alone by the refreshment table.

She suspected Evan was getting ready to snatch a chocolate cupcake, the way his long-lashed big brown eyes stared at one, and the tip of his tongue absently licked a corner of his mouth. Marie didn't imagine a cupcake would hurt him. He looked thinner than she remembered, yet she assumed that had something to do with how fast he had grown, shooting up in height. *Was he eight now?* she wondered. He looked much older.

Evan was the only medium in sight, the only one who could tell the chief what she had learned about the three people.

"I need your help, Evan," Marie said when she materialized next to the boy a moment later.

He looked up at her and grinned but said nothing.

123

"I need you to tell your father something for me," she explained, glancing over to where the police chief stood talking to Brian Henderson.

Evan nodded and turned, running to his father.

"Dad—" Evan began when he reached the chief a moment later.

The chief glanced down at his son and said, "I told you, no more cupcakes."

"But, Dad," Evan continued.

"Evan, no," the chief snapped.

"I need to talk to you," Evan said.

"What is it?" Edward asked, looking at his son.

"Can we go over there?" Evan asked, pointing some distance away where he could have privacy to talk to his father.

"In a minute, Evan, you interrupted a conversation."

"But, Dad—" Evan said. Again, the chief silenced his son.

"Edward, you can be so stubborn sometimes!" Marie snapped. She reached over and grabbed hold of the police chief's right earlobe, giving it a firm tug.

Evan's eyes widened as he watched the ghost tweak his father's ear. He failed to suppress a giggle when the chief made a yelping sound and grabbed his sore lobe.

Edward frowned down at his smiling son, who only shrugged, while Brian asked, "What's wrong, Chief?"

"I think something bit me," Edward grumbled, still rubbing his ear. "Excuse me. I need to talk to my son." He reached down, grabbed hold of Evan's hand, and led him away to a private section of the yard while his other hand rubbed the injured ear.

"Marie is trying to get my attention, isn't she?" the chief asked.

Evan nodded.

"If you weren't so doggone stubborn, I wouldn't have to take such harsh measures," Marie snapped.

"What is she trying to tell me?" the chief asked.

"She said if you weren't so doggone stubborn, she wouldn't have to take such harsh measures," Evan repeated.

The chief couldn't help but smile. "I suppose she's right. What else did she want to tell me?"

MARIE HAD FINISHED RELAYING the message to Evan, who repeated it to his father, when Danielle came walking outside with Walt. MacDonald asked Marie if she would bring the couple to him while he waited with Evan.

A few minutes later, Danielle and Walt joined the chief and his son. The four stood in the middle of the yard, whispering amongst themselves. Five, if you counted Marie. After Marie filled them in, they looked toward the three suspects, who now sat at a picnic table on the side patio, finishing their food.

They silently watched the suspects, deciding how to handle the situation, when Max suddenly appeared, jumping up on the picnic table and trying to sniff the food on one plate. The woman whose plate Max inspected did not seem overly concerned and gently pushed him away while scratching under his chin.

"I have an idea," Walt told his small group. "Stay here."

Silently Danielle, MacDonald, Marie and Evan watched as Walt walked over to the picnic table.

WHEN WALT REACHED THE TABLE, he snatched up Max, holding him in his arms. He smiled down at the three. "Sorry about Max."

The woman who had been petting Max returned the smile. "It's okay. I love cats."

Still holding Max firmly in his arms, Walt looked down at him.

Everyone else is eating, Max conveyed.

I don't care about that, Walt silently returned. *Their voices? Are any of them the same as the ones who broke in the other night?*

Max looked up to Walt and meowed.

TWENTY-TWO

The previous day Police Chief MacDonald had allowed the Kings to leave Marlow House without questioning them. According to Max, none of their voices matched the people who had broken into Marlow House. For a cat, Max was emphatic they were not the burglars. While Danielle wanted to believe him, she kept thinking about Hunny and how she had recently gone to the dark side by befriending Pearl. Was it possible an artful scratch behind the ear or crab appetizer from Pearl Cove had swayed Max? There had been crab appetizer on that woman's plate. Raven, Danielle reminded herself. The woman's name was Raven.

While they let the Kings leave without the police confronting them, it didn't mean they would let it slide. Walt and Danielle decided they would visit the Kings today and question them. But first, Chris searched through the previous day's surveillance footage to prepare a video for the Kings. The chief reluctantly agreed to the plan after Danielle reminded him Walt could easily protect them both.

It was almost ten a.m. on Thursday morning when Chris showed up at Marlow House. He found Walt and Danielle sitting at the kitchen table, talking. When he walked in the back door, Danielle asked, "Is it done?"

"Yes. No way can they deny they practically ransacked your house. The camera even got them looking behind the painting at the safe. They weren't the only ones," Chris said as he helped himself to a cup of coffee and joined Walt and Danielle at the table.

"What do you mean?" Danielle asked.

"One thing I learned from watching those videos, people are damn nosey. It was especially interesting watching it at top speed. People running around like some Laurel and Hardy movie, opening and closing drawers and closets," he said with a laugh.

"I'm surprised people still behave like that. It seems everyone has security cameras up these days," Danielle said.

Chris looked at Walt with a grin and said, "There was a great one of you having a conversation with Max in the parlor. Unfortunately, we didn't record any of the sound. What were you two discussing?"

"I forgot about the camera," Walt said.

With a shrug Danielle said, "I guess that answers my question. People forget about cameras."

"We could ask Brian what you said," Chris added with a snicker.

"What do you mean?" Danielle asked.

"Another thing that camera caught, Brian Henderson going behind the sofa, I assume to look at the pictures on the wall. One of them fell. He reached down to pick it up, and Walt walked into the room."

Walt stared blankly at Chris. "Are you telling me Brian was in the parlor when I was talking to Max?"

Chris nodded with a wide grin and took a drink of coffee.

Danielle groaned.

WALT PARKED in front of the rental house and glanced over at Danielle, who sat in the passenger seat, talking on her cellphone.

"Yes, Chief, I promise. I'll call you as soon as we leave." A moment later she hung up and looked over to Walt.

"You ready?" Walt asked.

"Yeah, but I also feel awkward. I mean, if they were just being snoopy, I kinda feel embarrassed for them."

"From what Marie overheard, sounds like they were being more than just nosy."

"I know. And I hope Max knows what he's talking about." Danielle reached for the car door.

"Unless they're working with someone, and that's who broke in," Walt suggested.

"I sure didn't see them talking with anyone yesterday, aside from Adam and Mel." Danielle let out a sigh and added, "Wish Marie was with us." Marie had stayed back at Marlow House as a security measure, assuming someone other than the Kings was threatening Walt and Danielle.

"We don't have to do this," Walt reminded her.

"Yeah, we do," Danielle said, opening the car door.

WALT AND DANIELLE stood on the front porch of the beach rental. In Danielle's right hand she held her cellphone, while her purse strap hung over her left shoulder. Walt rang the doorbell.

When the door opened a few minutes later, the woman Danielle remembered as Raven stood in the open doorway, looking at them. By her expression, it surprised her to find them standing on her front porch.

"Walt and Danielle Marlow? Why are you here? Did we leave something at your house?" Raven asked with a frown.

Danielle held up her cellphone and began playing the video. "We want to talk to you and your cousins about this."

Raven stared at the video playing on the iPhone. It showed her and her cousins searching various rooms at Marlow House. Expressionless, she watched the video for a minute. She let out a sigh, threw the door open wider, and said, "This is probably for the best. Come on in. This is how I wanted to do it, anyway."

Raven turned her back to them and headed into the house, leaving the door open. When she was about six feet inside and realized they were not following her, she glanced back and waved them in. "Come on. The others are on the back patio."

WALT AND DANIELLE followed Raven to the patio off the dining room. There they found Laken and Kiara sitting at a wicker and glass table, each reading a section of the morning newspaper. Raven put out her hand to Danielle, silently asking for her phone. Danielle handed it to her after opening the screen with the video.

Laken started to stand up to greet them, although he, like his sister, looked perplexed to see them. Before he got completely to his feet, Raven shoved the phone in his face and turned it on. With a frown, he took hold of the phone and absently sat back down, his eyes on the now playing video.

Curious, Kiara leaned over to her brother to see what he was watching. After a moment she looked up to Danielle and Walt and with a gasp said, "You were recording us?"

Danielle reached out and took her phone from Laken, who didn't attempt to keep it. He stared blankly at her.

"Not exactly. We weren't recording you per se. But we were trying to catch the people who broke into Marlow House last week."

"We didn't break into Marlow House!" Laken blurted.

"But you were looking for something," Walt said. "What?"

The siblings exchanged quick glances and looked back to Walt and Danielle.

"We were looking for Walt Marlow's diary," Raven announced.

Walt and Danielle turned to Raven, and Walt said, "Supposedly that's what the people who broke into Marlow House last week were looking for."

Instead of making another denial, Laken let out a low whistle and said, "So we aren't the only ones looking for the diary."

"But there is no diary," Danielle said.

"There has to be," Kiara insisted.

"Perhaps you could explain what this is all about?" Walt asked.

IT WASN'T that Danielle thought they might try to poison them and toss their bodies in the ocean. But she didn't think it a terrific idea to accept a beverage from anyone possibly connected to the wannabe arsonist. They were alone with them on their back patio, and a drugged Walt could not use his telekinesis powers. Danielle politely declined the offer for iced tea—for both her and Walt, which earned her a frown from her thirsty husband. But he said nothing. Instead, they joined the Kings at the patio table to discuss Walt's sought-after, imaginary diary.

"Our great-grandmother was Desiree Davis," Raven began.

If that announcement surprised Walt or Danielle, their expressions did not show it. They both sat silently, listening.

Raven took in their nonresponse and rolled her eyes. "Oh, come on, you know who she is."

"I'm afraid I don't," Walt lied.

"I told you," Laken snapped at his cousin. "He won't say anything that besmirches the sacred memory of his namesake."

"What do you think Walt did?" Danielle asked. They all turned to her. "I mean the original Walt Marlow?"

"Okay. We'll play your game." Laken did not mask his contempt. He looked at Walt and said, "You clearly based two of your characters in your book on our great-grandmother, Desiree Davis, and her sister, Charlene Davis."

"Even if my cousin left a diary, which he didn't, and I based my story on those two people, why is it so important to find the diary?" Walt asked.

"Because we want to solve a family mystery," Raven said. "We want to find out who murdered my great-grandmother's sister."

"Charlene was murdered?" Walt frowned.

"You wrote about it in your book. How she had been dating a white man and his family killed her. We'd like to discover who that was," Kiara said.

"I made that all up," Walt insisted. "Honestly, that was pure fiction. Are you saying someone murdered your grandmother's sister?"

"Great-grandmother," Kiara corrected. "But we weren't sure until we read your book."

"I sincerely do not understand," Walt said.

Laken started to say something, but Raven stopped him. She took a deep breath and looked at Walt. "According to the story our grandmother told us, her aunt, like the character in your book, passed for white. She was an actress, and our grandmother's mother was a jazz singer. They were at odds, because Charlene was passing as white and Desiree did not approve, especially considering some men she was running around with. Like in your book."

"And she was murdered?" Danielle asked.

"My grandmother's mother didn't think so at first," Raven said. "She was told Charlene went off to Hollywood, to pursue her career, that she had some offer. But she never contacted Desiree again. She simply disappeared. None of her friends heard from her. And Desiree could find nothing that showed she had an offer in Hollywood, like she had been led to believe."

"I would assume if Charlene was passing for white, considering how it was back then, she probably changed her name when she got to Hollywood," Walt suggested.

"That's what Desiree thought at first," Kiara said. "But then she started hearing stories about how Charlene had never left Frederickport. That someone had lied to Desiree about Charlene getting offered a job in California. And later, Desiree heard Walt Marlow knew what happened to her. But by then, he was dead, and she couldn't ask him."

"Why would Walt Marlow know what happened to her?" Walt asked.

Laken looked Walt in the eyes and said, "That's why we wanted the diary."

"I wish there was a diary," Walt said. "I would happily let you see it. But honestly, what I wrote, about the murder of the actress, that truly was a work of fiction."

"You can ask the museum," Danielle told them. "I've been very open with the museum in sharing anything I found at Marlow House. And if I had come across a diary, it would have been long before Walt ever came to Frederickport. Why would I hide it?"

As the Kings silently considered her suggestion, a thought popped into Danielle's head. "Although, now that I think about it, I can explain this misunderstanding about a diary."

Walt glanced questioningly at Danielle.

Danielle flashed him a smile and turned her attention to the Kings. "I had a friend. She died a while back. Marie Nichols."

Walt arched a brow and silently listened.

"Marie was ninety-one when she died. Her father was a close friend of Walt Marlow—the original Walt Marlow. In fact, they lived in the house across the street when Walt was murdered."

"What does she have to do with our family?" Raven asked.

"Marie understood I was interested in Marlow history. She often shared stories her father had told her. Marie told me how Walt Marlow dabbled in bootlegging, and a jewel heist, and how he had been in love with the silent screen star Eva Thorndike."

Walt rolled his eyes at Danielle's last comment, but the Kings missed it.

"And I recall a story she told me about a jazz singer Walt befriended, according to her father. And her sister, who was a black actress who passed as white. But she didn't remember the names.

Apparently, the actress was a friend of Eva Thorndike. But Marie said nothing about a murder. Just that the actress left for Hollywood, according to her father. I shared many of those stories with my husband when he was researching local history for his book, so I'm sure that's where some uncanny similarities to real-life events originated. From stories Marie told me. Not a diary."

TWENTY-THREE

Danielle called ahead to let the chief know they were stopping by his office. When they stepped in the front lobby of the Frederickport police station, they ran into Joe and Brian, who were just leaving.

"We had a good time yesterday," Joe told Danielle as they stopped to say hi. "But you're slacking, having Pearl Cove cater."

"You didn't like the food?" Danielle asked.

"No, actually it was great. Almost as good as your cooking," Joe said with a grin.

"And no one was murdered, that has to be a first," Brian said dryly.

"Okay, so a few of our past July Fourth parties had issues," Danielle said.

"No kidding. I imagine that's why the chief wanted us there, considering its history," Brian said. "But it looks like this time, the chief's anonymous source was off."

Joe flashed Brian a frown. Brian returned with a shrug and said, "Obviously Danielle and Walt are aware the chief asked us to be there yesterday and why." He turned back to the pair and asked, "Am I right?"

"Yes," Danielle said.

"I want to apologize, Brian. It was good of you to come over yesterday and help. I know it was your day off," Walt began. "I shouldn't have played that joke on you. But I couldn't resist."

"Joke? What joke?" Joe asked. "What's he talking about?"

"But I wondered why you were hiding behind the couch," Walt said jokingly.

"I wasn't hiding. I was picking up something that fell off the wall behind the couch," Brian said without a smile, eyeing Walt suspiciously.

"So that's why you were hiding." Walt grinned.

"I would have stood up," Brian said impatiently. "But when you started having a conversation with your cat, I thought I'd spare you the embarrassment and stay where I was."

"Which I feel bad about," Walt lied. "I was being a jerk, and you were probably thinking I was acting crazy."

"Yeah, well, you could say that," Brian said.

Walt held out his hand to Brian. "No hard feelings?"

Brian hesitantly shook Walt's hand.

"BRIAN DIDN'T LOOK like he believed your story," Danielle said after Brian and Joe left the building.

"No, he didn't. I think Brian has seen far too much over the last few years not to question one of my explanations," Walt said as they walked toward the chief's office.

"Like what?" Danielle asked.

Walt stopped in the middle of the hallway and looked at his wife. "Like the time I slugged him."

"Yeah, but that was before you ever came to Frederickport." Danielle made a hand gesture to Walt's body to emphasize the word "you."

"And there was the time I handed him a towel—my former self he could not see handed him a towel. I believe that was at Ian's bachelor party."

"Again, before you ever came to Frederickport."

"What about what the chief told us? How Brian compared my handwriting—and fingerprints to—"

"Okay, okay, I get it. Which probably explains why I sometimes catch him watching you in that creepy way of his."

"I wouldn't describe it as creepy," Walt argued. "And I might add, it seems Joe is still a little sweet on you."

Danielle frowned at Walt. "What are you talking about?"

"Pearl Cove's food was *almost* as good as yours."

"How does that have anything to do with him being sweet on me?"

"A man can tell, Danielle."

"He's living with Kelly," Danielle said.

"So? I don't see a ring on her finger."

———

THIRTY MINUTES LATER, after recounting their morning conversation with the Kings, the chief sat behind his desk, considering what he had just been told. Finally, he said, "I really don't see why they would be so desperate to destroy your diary they'd be willing to kill you. In fact, none of that gives them a reason to want to destroy the diary. It sounds to me like they just wanted to read it."

"We agree with you," Walt said. "Danielle and I discussed that on the way over here. I think Max was right. It's not them."

"But there is something in that diary that someone does not want to come out," the chief said.

"There is no diary," Walt reminded him.

"You know what I mean," the chief said.

"Let's say it's the murder," Danielle began.

"What murder?" Walt asked.

"Charlene's murder," Danielle explained.

"Charlene wasn't murdered," Walt argued.

"Maybe she was. Think about what they told you. After you died, Desiree came to believe someone killed her sister. And she wondered if you knew something about it. Why? What happened back then to raise those questions?" Danielle asked.

"Are you suggesting I made up a murder that actually happened?" Walt asked.

"Stranger things have happened," Danielle said.

"Even if that is true, why would anyone be willing to kill to keep it quiet?" the chief asked. "That happened almost a hundred years ago. And while there are no statutes of limitations on murder, whoever killed Charlene—if anyone did—has been dead for years."

"Are they trying to protect their family's honor?" Danielle

suggested. "Like the board members from the historical society didn't want everyone learning they had parents who liked running around in white sheets and burning crosses on people's front yards."

"I think it has to be something else," the chief said.

"I agree with Edward," Walt said.

"What else is in your book that might concern someone today?" Danielle asked.

Walt shook his head. "I have absolutely no idea."

BEFORE GOING HOME ON THURSDAY, Walt and Danielle stopped at Pier Café for lunch. When they walked in, they spied Adam and Melony sitting at a booth. Adam waved them over.

"Looks like you made beaucoup bucks for the Humane Society," Adam said when they reached their booth.

"You mean we all did. I really appreciate you manning the ticket table," Danielle said.

"I handed out a lot of my business cards yesterday, so it's not just the Humane Society that won," Adam said with a grin.

"Come, sit with us," Melony said as Danielle chuckled at Adam's comment. "We haven't ordered yet. And my treat." Not waiting for an answer, Melony moved from her seat to sit next to Adam, leaving the bench facing them free for Walt and Danielle.

The next moment Carla walked up. As she turned the clean water glasses right side up and filled them, she said, "I wish I could have gone to your fundraiser yesterday. I heard you had Pearl Cove cater. I didn't particularly like working for them, but they put out great food."

"Did you have to work?" Danielle asked Carla.

The waitress stood by their table, hand on one hip while the other hand held the half-filled pitcher of water. "Yeah, and we got slammed yesterday." Carla looked at Adam and said, "One of your clients came in for breakfast this morning and told me all about it. I didn't know it was one of your clients who bought the Barr house."

"Yes, and I understand you told Danielle it's haunted," Adam teased.

Carla shrugged. "Just what I heard. But I have to say, your client sure seems a lot nicer than old Earl that used to own that place. They're cousins, right?"

"That's what I was told," Adam said.

"Well, let me know if he sees any ghosts," Carla said with a laugh as she left the table.

Danielle watched Carla walk away, and she began thinking about Walt's book. The moonshiner Walt had mentioned in *Moon Runners*, the one who had almost killed the character based on Desiree Davis, had been Beau Stewart's ancestor. Beau, the name that kept coming up since all this started.

Danielle turned to Adam and asked, "Where exactly did you say Beau's family got their money?"

"Beau's father built his fortune by developing land his wife inherited," Adam said.

"Passed down from the Klan grand wizard," Melony said with a chuckle.

"Not something he wants to broadcast, considering his run for the senate," Adam said.

"Who was this exactly?" Danielle asked, although she was fairly certain it was Beauregard Porter.

"Old Beauregard Porter," Melony said. "My mother told me about him. Not that she had ever met him, he was years before her time, but she had heard stories about the family."

"I assume over time, Beauregard Porter's descendants accumulated the land that Beau Stewart's father built the family fortune on?" Walt asked.

"Nope," Melony said. "It was old Beauregard himself. According to the old stories Mom's grandfather told her, he'd fought for the Confederacy and moved to Frederickport a few years after the war. He was active with the local Klan. And the land Stewart owns now all started with Beauregard."

"When I checked out Beau Stewart—and you didn't hear me say that—I discovered he owned a crap load of land in Oregon. Almost half of it he bought from his cousin Earl, the same one who sold him that property recently. But all the land owned by the cousins, it came down through the family, originating with Beauregard Porter," Adam said.

"Who owned it before Beauregard Porter?" Danielle asked.

"That's another thing I found interesting, it was all purchased from the same person, at the same time. Someone named Jenkins. Back then it was a lot of money, what he paid for it. But I did some checking, and Porter got a deal. Looks like he paid about sixty cents on the dollar for it. Now those properties are worth millions. Most are developed, not vacant land. Apartment buildings, commercial property. I have to give it to Stewart; he has done a good job keeping the family fortune in the family. At least in his immediate family," Adam said.

"DO you want to know what I don't understand," Walt said as they drove away from the pier after lunch.

"What is that?" Danielle asked.

"Beauregard Porter never did an honest day's work in his life. How could he afford to buy all that property, even if he got a deal on it, and paid sixty cents on the dollar?" Walt asked.

"Didn't you tell me he was a moonshiner?" Danielle asked. "I've heard a lot of people got rich that way. Many say that's how the Kennedys made their fortune, bootlegging."

"He wasn't that good at it. Hell, Desiree's boss wasn't the only one who tried stealing from him—and many got away with it. How I portrayed him in *Moon Runners* was fairly accurate. And when they made some money, those sons of his spent it. Their place was a dump, and from how I've heard people describe it now, sounds like it hasn't changed much."

"I don't know, Walt. After all this talk about Beauregard, I'm wondering if we need to look at another client of Adam's."

"You think Stewart is responsible for the break-in?"

"He was there yesterday, and according to Wilbur, whoever he overheard said they would be there. And there is another thing I find unsettling."

"What's that?"

"What was the name of the landowner Beauregard Porter purchased the land from?" Danielle asked.

"Jenkins, the same name as Wilbur," Walt said.

Danielle nodded. "Exactly. And according to Betty, Wilbur sold off the land his father had left him before he took off. Did he sell it to Beauregard Porter? Is that the Beau Wilbur claimed killed him?"

TWENTY-FOUR

D anielle expected to see Joanne's car parked in front of Marlow House when they arrived home on Thursday afternoon. Joanne planned to come over to clean the house and hadn't yet arrived when Walt and Danielle left to see the Kings. She assumed Joanne could not make it over. But when she stepped inside, she realized Joanne had already come and gone. The housekeeper had left a note for them on the kitchen table. Danielle picked it up and read it after she walked in and tossed her purse on the kitchen counter.

"She's done already," Danielle told Walt.

Walt, who had wandered to the refrigerator and opened the door, looked inside and said, "She's quick."

Tossing the note back on the table, Danielle looked at Walt and asked, "What are you looking for? We just finished lunch."

"Where are the Pearl Cove leftovers?" Walt asked, still looking through the refrigerator shelves.

"I told Joanne she could have any of the leftovers. She must have taken them. Surely you're not still hungry?"

Walt shut the refrigerator and shrugged. "No, I'm not hungry, but..."

Danielle chuckled. "Yeah, well, you might consider joining Heather in her morning jogs if you keep eating like you do."

Hands on hips, Walt faced Danielle and asked with a faux pout, "Are you calling me fat?"

"I never use the F word." Danielle giggled. She walked to Walt and wrapped her arms around his waist. "I prefer cuddly."

Walt returned the hug and kissed her nose. He asked in a whisper, "You think I'm getting chubby?"

"I'm teasing. I think you're perfect. But you are starting to sound like a girl," Danielle said.

Walt chuckled and kissed Danielle when a female voice said, "Ew, get a room, would you?"

Moving apart from each other, they turned to the intruder and found Heather entering through the back door, followed by Chris.

"This is our house," Danielle reminded her.

Heather shrugged, and Chris said, "You two need to save that for later. We came over to find out what you learned at the Kings."

"Don't you two ever work? It is a Thursday," Walt asked.

"We took the rest of the week off for the Fourth," Heather told him.

AFTER JOANNE HAD ARRIVED to clean Marlow House, Marie went to spend time with Connor while regularly checking across the street, watching for any arsonists or another break-in. But now that Walt and Danielle had come home, and Heather and Chris had just arrived, she followed Ian and Lily over to Marlow House with Connor and Sadie.

The Beach Drive friends gathered in Marlow House's living room. Lily placed a quilt on the floor for Connor, where Marie sat with the baby, keeping him occupied while she listened in to the conversation.

Danielle and Walt shared what they had learned at the Kings, along with their lunch conversation with Adam and Melony.

"If it's not the Kings, then my vote would be for Beau Stewart," Heather said.

"That's just because his daughter thinks you're a witch," Chris teased.

"Oh, shut up," Heather snapped.

"I talked to him and his wife for quite a while yesterday," Lily said. "They seemed nice. The wife is a huge fan of Ian's work."

"And according to what Wilbur's ghost told Marie, those people he overheard claimed they would be here yesterday. Is there anyone else who was here yesterday that has some connection to anything that happened in *Moon Runners*? According to Walt, the Klanny moonshiner was based on Stewart's ancestor. Heck, they even named him after the old racist!" Heather said.

"She has a point," Marie said.

"See, Marie agrees with me!" Heather chimed.

Lily glanced over to the quilt and watched as Connor played with wooden blocks. She understood Marie sat with him, yet she could not see the ghost.

"If it's Stewart, what is his motivation?" Chris asked.

"It can't be to cover up his ancestor's dubious Klan past," Danielle said. "While it's not common knowledge, I suspect it wouldn't be hard for any of his opponents to dig up that information from old newspapers. Plus, Mel heard about it from her mother, and I'm sure Mel wasn't the only one Jolene told."

"What do they always say, follow the money?" Ian said.

They all turned to Ian.

"What are you thinking?" Walt asked.

"From my prior research on Stewart, I learned everything he has today began with his family's inheritance," Ian said. "Think about it, what would threaten a man like Stewart? I don't think it's the embarrassment of some racist ancestor. I think everyone has someone like that in their family tree."

They all sat quietly for a few minutes, considering scenarios. Finally, Danielle spoke up. "I have to agree with Ian. Money is a huge motivator. According to what Adam told us, Stewart's fortune comes from the land they bought from someone named Jenkins. Is Wilbur that Jenkins? Wilbur is from Porter's era. Was he the one who sold him that land? Was there something hinky about the purchase? Maybe Porter forced him to sign the land over and then murdered him—buried his body in his own backyard. Wilbur did say someone named Beau may have murdered him. And Stewart found the remains—we know he is having the property cleaned up —and they dumped the bones in the ocean, Wilbur's spirit followed. Maybe that's it!"

They all looked to Danielle, considering her suggestion for a moment. Finally, Chris said, "That's an interesting possibility. Unfortunately, several sizable holes there."

"Such as?" Danielle asked.

"First, are you suggesting Stewart knew who the remains belonged to when they were found—if they were found—on his property, before dumping them in the ocean?" Chris asked.

"Does it matter?" Danielle asked.

"Well, yeah," Chris said. "First, if he knew who the bones belonged to, that would suggest Stewart knew about the murder. What was the first Beau to him? Like his great-great-grandfather? While some families like to pass stories down to the next generation, I find passing down something like, '*Old gramps once murdered a man and buried his bones in the backyard. They're still there,*' far-fetched, and *I* believe in ghosts."

Walt chuckled. He looked at Danielle and said, "I'm sorry, love. Chris has a point."

"But if Wilbur Jenkins was the Jenkins who sold Porter that property, don't you think it's more than a coincidence that he washes up on shore with his bones at the same time as Beau Stewart moves to town? Not to mention the rest of it—Porter being in your book, his great-great-grandson showing up yesterday, and someone who shares those two things wants to torch our house. And us," Danielle said.

Before anyone could respond to Danielle's comment, feathers began floating down from the ceiling above Connor. They landed on the quilt and disappeared. Connor looked upwards and giggled; his chubby arms outstretched as his hands tried unsuccessfully to snatch an elusive feather from the air. Only Lily and Ian could not see the feathers, and they wondered what sort of game Marie was playing with their son.

"I believe Eva is arriving," Chris announced.

"I hope it's Eva and not some molting angel," Heather muttered, eyeing the rain of feathers.

The next moment Eva stood in the middle of the living room, dressed in a blue and white striped dress, its narrow waist accentuating her trim figure while its full skirt fluttered around her ankles.

"So this is where you all are!" Eva said gaily as the feathers disappeared. She looked at Marie and said, "I rather expected you would eventually return. I hope everything is all right."

"I'm sorry, dear, but they needed me here," Marie said.

"Do you have to go back?" Heather asked Eva.

"No. Last night was the final performance," Eva said. "It went beautifully. Now tell me, what have I missed?"

They spent the next twenty minutes updating Eva with all that had gone on while she had been in Astoria at the theater. When they concluded, Eva looked at Walt and asked, "Do you really believe someone murdered Charlene?"

Walt shrugged. "The Kings believe it. Do you know anything about her during her last days in Frederickport?"

Eva considered his question a moment and then said, "After I died, I ran across her many times over the years. Normally at the theater. But now that I think about it, the last time I saw her was probably a year or two before you died. I'll be honest, I didn't give her much thought."

"And you heard nothing about her death?" Chris asked.

Eva shook her head, "No. Not that I recall."

Danielle repeated for Lily and Ian what Eva had said.

"Maybe no one killed her," Ian said. "She very well could have changed her name after she moved, and disappeared, yet not by criminal or malicious means."

"That's what I suggested," Walt said.

"As for the other person you mentioned, Beauregard Porter, I remember him. And those dreadful sons of his. Although, as I recall, young Beau was not so bad. I think he had a good heart. But the poor lad didn't have much of a chance. Not with that family of his," Eva said. "I avoided the old Porter place in life and in death."

Danielle repeated Eva's words for the non-mediums.

Lily stood up and announced, "I think I'll take Connor home. It's getting to be his naptime. And now with Eva here, maybe it would be better if you all put your heads together and see what you can work out. Eva might know more than she realizes about back then, to help you figure this out. Dani can fill us in later."

Ian stood up. "I'll go with Lily and do a little online sleuthing, see what I can find out about Stewart and Jenkins. And maybe I can find a lead on Charlene."

AFTER LILY, Ian, Connor, and Sadie left, Eva said, "I hope I didn't chase them off."

"No," Danielle said. "It just drives Lily crazy when she has to listen to one side of a conversation. And I think she feels funny when I repeat everything for her, like it's annoying for everyone else."

"What were you saying about Porter, before Lily left?" Chris asked.

"His old place is one part of town I avoid, in the same way I avoid the old site of the Marymoor Sanatorium," Eva said.

"That place is haunted, big time," Heather said, meaning the site of the Marymoor Sanatorium.

"No kidding," Danielle agreed.

Heather looked at Eva and asked, "What I don't understand, why would a ghost avoid someplace like the Marymoor Sanatorium site? I mean, yeah, sure, it's haunted. But you're a ghost. Don't ghosts like to hang out at haunted places, like graveyards?"

"Heather, you have a lot to learn. Not all spirits are amicable. There are evil spirits."

"But I thought you said the Universe—whatever that is— wouldn't let a spirit hurt an innocent," Heather asked.

"True. But I have a question for you. Are there any horror movies you don't like to watch?" Eva asked.

"Sure, why?" Heather asked.

"Why don't you watch them?" Eva asked.

Heather considered the question for a moment. "I don't know. I guess they're just too creepy and scary."

"Do you think those movies can actually hurt you?" Eva asked.

"No. They're just movies," Heather said.

"Then you have your answer. I avoid places like the Marymoor Sanatorium site and the old Porter place for the same reason you don't watch certain horror movies."

TWENTY-FIVE

D anielle and Walt moved to the parlor after everyone left late Thursday afternoon. Eva promised to return, but she wanted to go to the cemetery and check with her contacts there to see if anyone might know what secrets from the past *Moon Runners* had disturbed. Marie went with her after Walt and Danielle insisted there was no reason to babysit in the daytime. The wannabe arsonist had made it clear they would strike at night, after everyone was in bed, sleeping.

In the parlor, Walt picked up the book he had been reading earlier and made himself comfortable on one chair, while Danielle stretched out on the sofa, shoving a throw pillow under her head. She snatched a magazine from the coffee table to read. But instead of opening it, she rested it on her lap as she looked up at the ceiling, contemplating their puzzle.

"I still think this has something to do with Wilbur. Beauregard Porter murdered him for the land. You said yourself Porter didn't have that much money. And according to Wilbur, someone named Beau may have murdered him." Danielle paused a moment and rubbed her forehead with one thumb.

"Do you have a headache?" Walt closed his book and set it on one knee.

"Too much thinking." She winced from the dull pain.

"And you believe Stewart somehow knew Grandpappy Beau

murdered Jenkins, and he recently dug up the remains and tossed them in the ocean?" Walt asked.

"Yes. It's the only thing that makes sense. If he stole that land from Jenkins, murdered him and buried his body on the property, it could mean they never purchased the land, and Stewart risks losing everything."

"I'm sorry, but I have to agree with Chris. That's far-fetched," Walt said. "Not that it happened, or even that Stewart knew it happened. But Stewart knowing about the remains and removing them, that seems implausible to me."

Danielle let out a sigh. "But why else would Jenkins's bones wash up on shore in Frederickport now? Why now? Because someone found them, dug them up, and threw them in the ocean. And like Heather said, Stewart is the only one remotely connected to any of the stories in *Moon Runners* who showed yesterday. And Wilbur over-heard them say they would be here. It has to be them."

"That is not entirely true," Walt said.

Danielle sat up on the sofa and looked over at Walt. "What? You think it might have been the Kings after all? I thought we agreed they wouldn't want to destroy the diary; they would want to read it."

"I'm not talking about the Kings. When writing *Moon Runners*, many actual events from my first life inspired the story, and some people involved back then have family still living in Frederickport, some who were here yesterday."

"Why didn't you mention this before?" Danielle asked.

"We discussed it when it first came out. But I never imagined any of those retellings would trigger someone. I couldn't imagine anyone alive now would know about any of them. For example, in the scene where the boys are cutting up the hemp whips to smoke, I'd shared that story with you before," Walt reminded her.

"And I don't imagine someone is plotting to kill us to keep the world from finding out Grandpa smoked buggy whips," Danielle said with a snort.

"Exactly. I can't see any grandchild or great-grandchild compelled to destroy a diary because they don't want someone to learn it's true."

"It's not just destroying a diary; they want to kill us," Danielle said.

"It could be something like Charlene's death. That came from my imagination. Did someone recognize a true event in the story, something passed down in their family, and then something I made up got too close to a truth they don't want to come out?"

Danielle groaned. "If that's the case, then we really are screwed."

"If we're lucky, perhaps you already figured it out—even though it seems far-fetched. Maybe it is about Wilbur's murder and a stolen fortune."

"But we have to wait for that DNA to come back on Wilbur's bones. Unfortunately, the chief can't identify the remains based on testimony from their ghost." Danielle rubbed her forehead again and grimaced.

Walt stood up. "How about I get you a couple of aspirin?"

The doorbell rang.

"How about you get the door instead?" she said.

Walt tossed his book on the end table, walked over to Danielle, and gave her forehead a quick kiss before going to answer the door.

Several minutes later, Police Chief MacDonald walked into the parlor with Walt.

"Hey, Chief," Danielle greeted him. "What brings you over here? Please tell me you figured out who Wilbur overheard at the pier."

"Sorry, Danielle, nothing new on that front. But I wanted to stop by and tell you something I do know. The bones the dogs found, they weren't Wilbur's."

Danielle sat up straight on the sofa, putting her feet on the floor. "You got the DNA test back?"

"No. That hasn't come back yet."

Danielle pointed to the chair across from her. "Why don't you sit down?"

The chief nodded and sat down on the chair while Walt took a seat on the sofa next to Danielle.

"If you don't have the DNA test back, then how do you know it isn't Wilbur Jenkins?"

"After you told me about him and seemed fairly certain the DNA test would prove those were his remains, I did a little digging on our ghost. I came across several photographs of him online, in old newspapers. One was of him and his sister and a couple of employees in front of her bookstore."

"We saw that picture. At least, I assume it's the same one. Betty has a framed picture like that on her wall in the bookstore."

"How would you describe Wilbur?" he asked. "You saw his spirit, not just his picture."

"What do you mean?" She frowned.

"For example, was he a very tall man?"

Danielle considered the question for a moment. "No."

"He didn't look very tall in the photographs I found. One was taken next to a well-known boxer from that era. Apparently, Wilbur was a boxing fan."

"What does a photo of the boxer have to do with the bones?" Danielle asked.

"While I couldn't find Wilbur's height online, I found stats for the boxer he posed with. Wilbur was a good head shorter. As for the remains found, according to the coroner, the deceased was about six foot three. Wilbur was much shorter."

"So those remains aren't Wilbur's?" Danielle asked.

The chief shook his head. "No. Definitely not."

"Why was he with them? He wanted me to help him find the gunnysack," Danielle asked.

"You would know more about things like that than I would," the chief reminded her.

"This could also mean no one murdered Wilbur," Walt said.

Danielle frowned. "But he said Beau might have murdered him."

"*Might*, Danielle," Walt reminded her.

WALT WALKED the chief to the front door fifteen minutes later, to see him out. When he returned to the parlor, he found Danielle sitting up on the sofa, resting her forehead in her open palms.

"I'm getting you some aspirin," he announced.

"We're out," Danielle said. "I gave Susan Mitchell the last two yesterday."

"Then I'll run down to the store and get some," he told her.

Danielle looked up from her hands. "I hate to make you do that."

"You're not making me do anything. I want you to lie down, close your eyes, and rest. I won't be long," Walt told her.

DANIELLE CONSIDERED GOING UPSTAIRS and climbing into bed, but she didn't have the energy to walk up two flights of stairs. Stretched out on the parlor sofa, staring up at the ceiling, she wondered if Walt could levitate her up to their bedroom when he got home. She imagined herself floating up the two flights of steps. But then the memory of Walt dropping the boxes when he had lost focus popped into her head, and she cringed. "That would hurt," she muttered.

Closing her eyes, she let out a deep breath and tried to fall asleep, anything to keep her from dwelling on her now throbbing head. But then she heard footsteps.

Sitting up, she looked to the open parlor door and called out, "Walt? That was fast."

It wasn't Walt who appeared in the doorway a moment later, but two masked people dressed all in black. One pointed a revolver in her direction.

"Stand up," he said gruffly, attempting to conceal his or her voice. "If you don't want me to shoot you, come here."

Slowly, Danielle stood and reluctantly obeyed the gunman. Both people wore ski masks, covering their heads, gloves concealing the color of their skin, along with sunglasses, concealing their eyes. She didn't imagine it made it easy for them to see.

"You're going upstairs with us and opening your safe. Do you understand?"

Danielle nodded.

"Get going. Move!"

Some guests had discovered the safe behind the painting in her old bedroom when they had lingered behind the tour and snooped around. Chris had mentioned it after reviewing some of the footage. Danielle told herself that if she survived this encounter, they would need to review the video again for a list of suspects. She also regretted turning the cameras off, which meant this encounter would not be captured on video.

Once they reached the second floor, Danielle obediently walked toward the safe. She had initially installed it to protect the Missing Thorndike, for those rare occasions she brought it home from the bank to wear.

She wondered what they would do when they discovered an empty safe. They kept nothing of value in the safe except for the necklace and…the letters. Danielle had forgotten about the letters.

They were the letters from Walt to Marie's father. Marie had given them to Danielle long ago. After the chief told her of Brian's obsession with the similarity of the handwriting of the original Walt Marlow and her husband, she decided it best to lock the old letters away. She didn't want to destroy them, but she didn't want anyone to happen across the letters—such as Adam or Joe or Mel or Kelly or anyone who wasn't aware the original Walt Marlow was in fact her husband. Walt had distinctive handwriting, and it hadn't changed in the last hundred years. Holding her breath, she opened the safe and stood back, allowing them to see inside.

The one holding the gun reached in and snatched the stack of letters. Holding them in one hand and the gun in the other, the masked intruder asked, "What is this?"

"They're letters from Walt Marlow to his neighbor," Danielle explained. "The neighbor's daughter gave them to me before she died. But they aren't of any value. Only to my husband. That's where he's gotten ideas for his book. Sort of like a diary, but Walt Marlow never left a diary. I'm sorry, we keep nothing of value here."

TWENTY-SIX

The motorcycle woke Max. Racing down Beach Drive, it was already out of sight by the time Max opened his eyes. Yawning, the cat leapt down from the porch swing and started for the side yard and the pet door. He didn't know how long he had been sleeping, but he was hungry. By the position of the sun hovering over the houses across the street, Max surmised it would soon be nightfall.

A few minutes later he stood in the kitchen, sniffing his food bowl. It was empty. Max started out the open doorway into the hall, looking for someone to fill it. He strolled through all the rooms on the first floor, meowing as he went. When he found no one, he headed for the stairs. Once on the second-floor landing a few minutes later, he made his way to the staircase leading to the attic. He was passing one open doorway when he heard something. Stopping, he paused for a moment. It was the room where Danielle used to sleep until she moved to the attic with Walt. Someone was in the room. He meowed again and went to inspect, wanting food.

Max entered the bedroom, but no one was there. He was about to turn around and continue on his way to the attic when he heard the sound again. It came from the closet. Suspecting a mouse might have found its way into the room and now hid in the closet, Max went to investigate and found its door slightly ajar. Stealthily, he moved into the unlit space and heard it again, rattling. Someone was inside the stairwell. He meowed. The rattling stopped. He meowed again.

"Max? Max, are you there?" Max heard Danielle's voice. He recognized his name, but the rest of the words were meaningless.

"Max! Go get Walt! Hurry, get Walt!"

Max sat at the door and listened. Again, he recognized his name. He also recognized Walt's name. But what Danielle was trying to tell him, he did not understand. He just knew he was hungry. Max meowed again.

"Max, I'm locked in here. Get help!"

Like a feline boxer, Max raised his paws and began batting away on the panel door. He couldn't understand the meaning of her words, but surely, she would understand he wanted her to open the door. Sitting before the panel door, he pounded away with his front paws in a steady knocking.

"No, Max, I can't open the door! Get help!"

Max boxed the door for another minute and then stopped.

"What am I doing?" Danielle grumbled from the stairwell. "He's a cat, not Lassie."

Confused and hungry, Max turned from the closet. He needed to find Walt. Danielle would not come out of the closet and feed him. He loved Danielle, but sometimes humans were not very bright.

AS WALT ENTERED the house through the side door into the kitchen, Max walked into the room from the hallway. He looked at Walt and meowed.

"You're hungry?" Walt asked, tossing the paper sack with the aspirin on the table.

Max sat on the floor and watched as Walt walked to the pantry and grabbed a can of food. He meowed again.

Walt looked at the cat and said, "Danielle has a headache." The cat meowed again. "I was hoping she might take a nap."

Walt opened the can of food and began dumping it in the bowl as Max nosed his hand. He looked down to the cat and frowned.

"She's upstairs? She can sleep more comfortably in our bedroom."

Max positioned himself in front of the bowl and began to eat, yet not before conveying, *If she's trying to sleep, she's doing it on the stairs, not the bed.*

"What do you mean she's sleeping on the stairs?"

Max looked up from his food and conveyed another thought.

MAX WASN'T MAKING any sense, Walt thought. But he was a cat, he reminded himself. Walt quickly filled a clean glass with water, grabbed the small paper sack from the table, and hurried first to the parlor where he had left her.

As Max had said, she was no longer there. He continued up the stairs, grateful he didn't find her sitting on a step. That would indicate something worse than a headache if she couldn't make it to the second floor. Obviously, he misunderstood whatever Max had been trying to tell him.

A minute later he discovered she was also not on the attic staircase leading to their bedroom. Hurrying up the stairs to his wife, medicine and water in hand, he expected to find her sleeping in their bed, but when he got there, she wasn't. In fact, the bed looked undisturbed. That morning they had made the bed after getting up. It looked as it had the last time he was in the room.

Glancing toward the bathroom, he called out, "Danielle?" He set the glass of water and sack with the aspirin on the nightstand.

Instead of a response from the master bath, he heard a faint, "Walt," coming from the panel leading into the hidden staircase. He found it locked, which was odd, as they had kept it open for yesterday's tour.

Unlocking the door, he slid open the panel. Danielle flew into his arms, doing her best to stifle her sobs.

NOTEBOOK AND PEN IN HAND, Brian Henderson stood in the middle of the living room at Marlow House. Danielle sat quietly on the sofa, Walt by her side as he wrapped one arm protectively over her shoulder, and she absently rubbed the heel of her right hand over her forehead.

According to Lily, none of them had been there when the intruders had broken in, or when Walt found Danielle locked in the hidden staircase. But they all showed up before he arrived: Lily, Ian, Connor, Heather and Chris. Brian wondered if Walt had called them before or after he had called the police.

"Are you sure you didn't recognize them?" Brian asked Danielle.

She glanced up to him. "I told you, they both wore ski masks and sunglasses."

"How did they keep the glasses on with their ears covered?" Brian asked.

"I don't know," Danielle snapped. "I was too busy looking at the gun he had pointed at me."

"So it was a man?" Brian asked.

"I'm fairly sure the one holding the gun was a man. He tried to disguise his voice, making it all raspy. Didn't sound natural. It could have been a woman, yet it sounded more like a guy. But the other one said nothing," Danielle explained.

"And all they took were Walt Marlow's letters?" Brian asked.

Danielle nodded. "That's how I know it has to be the ones the chief got a tip on. Someone who wants Walt's diary—a diary that does not exist."

"Why exactly do you keep old letters in the safe?" Brian asked.

Danielle looked up to him and frowned. "What does that have to do with anything?"

Brian shrugged. "Just curious. I find it odd you'd keep old letters in a safe. If that's what they came for, and that's what they ended up taking, then what was in those letters that they would risk arrest? We need to know that if we intend to catch whoever this is."

"I explained. They believe Walt used a diary or letters of Walt Marlow to write his book. There is no diary. But I had some letters. Which they took."

"But what was in the letters? Why would they want them? Danielle, if you want us to catch these people, you need to tell me everything."

"You're not listening," Lily snapped from the sidelines.

Brian looked her way.

"Marie gave Danielle some letters ages ago that Walt had sent Marie's dad. I read them. The only thing Walt wrote in those letters was about his travels. Nothing that Walt used in *Moon Runners*. Those jerks just think something is in those letters. Now do you get it?"

"Not really," Brian mumbled, jotting something down on the paper.

PEARL HUCKABEE HAD JUST OPENED her refrigerator door when she heard the doorbell. Letting out a sigh of annoyance, she closed the refrigerator and made her way to the front door. When she opened it, she found Officer Brian Henderson standing on her front porch.

"Officer Henderson, is something wrong?" She glanced over to the Marlows'. Whenever something was wrong in the neighborhood, it typically originated at her neighbor's house.

"Did you see anyone around Marlow House in the last hour?" Brian asked.

Pearl stepped out onto the front porch with Brian and closed the door behind her. Standing on her tiptoes, she looked over to her neighbor's again and asked, "What did they do now?"

"Someone broke into Marlow House."

She looked back to Brian, her eyes wide. "Really? What did they take?"

"Did you see anyone?"

"You know, if they wouldn't be so free with opening their home for just anyone to poke around, these things would not happen. I bet it was someone who was there yesterday, casing the place," Pearl said.

"Did you see anyone?" he repeated.

Pearl considered the question for a moment and said, "I saw Walt Marlow. He left and then returned about thirty minutes ago. I think he was gone about twenty minutes. And there was that motorcycle that flew by here about ten minutes before he got back. You really need to do something about that. Someone will get hurt the way they race around here."

"Did the motorcycle stop at the Marlows'?"

Pearl frowned at Brian. "No. Why would you think that? I just said it flew down the street."

Brian glanced at the open notepad in his hands, took a deep breath, looked back at Pearl, and asked, "Did you see anyone else?"

"Yes. I was just about to tell you. Two on bicycles. I saw them leaving out the back door at the same time that motorcycle raced by."

"Can you identify them?" he asked.

"They were wearing dark clothes, and each wore one of those

hoodie jackets. But I wasn't able to see their faces, and I'm not sure if they were men or women. Before I got a good look, that motorcycle raced by, and when I looked back, I saw them riding off on two bicycles."

"DID SHE SEE ANYTHING?" Joe asked when Brian got into the squad car five minutes later. He had stayed in the vehicle to take a phone call while Brian had talked to Pearl.

"She saw two people leave the house right before Walt got back from the store. She couldn't identify them other than they wore dark clothes and hoodies. They left out the kitchen door. Sounds like they took off down the alley on two ten-speeds, the way she described them. She told me people wouldn't be breaking into their house if they didn't keep opening it to the public so anyone could case the place."

"I have to agree with Pearl," Joe said.

TWENTY-SEVEN

The pair raced into the driveway, almost plowing him down with the bicycles. He jumped out of their way and let out a curse as they slammed the brakes to a sudden stop, the tires making a squealing sound and leaving behind two black streaks on the driveway. They hastily tossed the bikes into the bushes, concealing them from view.

"What happened to you two? And where did you get those bikes?" He looked them up and down with a disapproving frown.

The taller one glanced over his shoulder to the street and said, "We can't talk out here."

"You don't expect to come into my house like that?"

"We got into the safe at Marlow House," the shorter one said in a quiet voice.

The man studied the pair through narrowed eyes. "Okay, but wash up first. I'll meet you in the dining room. And take your shoes off before you go in the house."

Fifteen minutes later, the pair joined him in the dining room. He sat at the table, waiting.

"Where did you get those bikes?" he asked.

"Stole them," the taller one said with a grin.

"I hope no one saw you," he snapped.

"No one saw us take them. And you didn't want us to take our car—or yours. We weren't going to risk parking by their house again."

"And you got in the safe?" he asked.

"We did," the taller one said with a grin.

"How did you do that?"

The taller one pulled a gun from his pocket and set it on the table. The man's eyes widened at the sight of the gun. "Tell me you didn't shoot someone? Rather defeats the purpose."

"We didn't have to. Danielle Marlow was most cooperative," the shorter one said.

"And the diary?" the man asked.

"It was just as we thought, it was in the safe, but it wasn't a diary," the taller one said.

"What do you mean?"

The shorter one set a bundle of envelopes on the table.

The man hadn't noticed them before. He frowned at the crumpled stack and asked, "What's that?"

"Letters. Letters written by the original Walt Marlow."

"What happened to them?" he asked.

"That's another story…"

ON FRIDAY MORNING, Chris sat with Walt and Danielle in Police Chief MacDonald's office. Chris had stayed up late Thursday night, going through the videos captured by the security cameras during the open house charity event.

"When putting together the video to take to the Kings, I just looked for clips of them. Once I'd found them, I moved on to the footage from another room. Last night I looked through all the security footage taken in the room with the safe."

"Did you find anyone else who looked at the safe behind the painting?" MacDonald asked.

"I did," Chris said.

"Who was it?" MacDonald asked.

"Practically everyone," Chris answered.

The chief frowned. "Excuse me?"

"It seems the safe is no longer a secret—like the hidden staircase," Danielle said.

The chief looked questioningly to Danielle but did not comment.

"My guess," Chris began, "someone noticed that safe early on and must have told someone and the word spread. When people came up for the later tours, they were looking to see the safe, like they wanted to see the hidden staircase and the entrance to the tunnels."

"People lingered in that room, but I didn't realize they were looking for the safe," Walt said.

"I thought Marie was helping to keep an eye on people when they were alone in a room?" the chief asked.

"She didn't stay in one place, and we figured our burglars would focus more on our bedroom, where Walt has his desk, or the library or parlor. Places where they might think we'd keep the diary. To be honest, I didn't give the safe much thought. We rarely open it. And frankly, when that person had a gun on me, I was praying I would remember the safe's combination," Danielle confessed.

"Whoever it is, they will be back," Walt said. "Once they read those letters and realize there's nothing in them."

"I did make a point about how you used those letters when writing your book, and how Walt hadn't kept a diary," Danielle said.

Walt looked at his wife and said, "I don't remember what was in the letters, but considering when I wrote them, I don't imagine they'll find anything that was in *Moon Runners*. They'll be back. Maybe they'll believe there's no diary, but I imagine after they read the letters, they'll assume there are more letters—some that I didn't return to the safe."

Danielle groaned. "I didn't consider that. But I did think about something else."

"What's that?" Walt asked.

"I was hoping they would take the letters and just go away. But what happens if they're caught with them?" she asked.

"Isn't that what we want?" MacDonald asked.

"When that gun was pointed at me and I remembered what was in the safe, I thought maybe those letters might be an unexpected blessing. But then, after they took them, I thought, what if they're caught and the wrong person sees them and recognizes how similar the handwriting is to Walt's."

Walt studied his wife a moment, smiled, and then said, "You're overthinking everything. I could always say I copied the original letters for some reason or wrote them in the first place."

Danielle frowned at Walt. "Why didn't I think of that?"

"You would have," Walt said.

"But we didn't tell Brian and Joe the burglars took copies," Danielle argued.

"Let's worry about that later," the chief said. "Brian talked with your neighbor, Pearl. She saw two people leaving out your back door and out through the alley. They got on a pair of bicycles, a red one and a blue one."

"While I find it disturbing Pearl's looking in our side yard—she must stand upstairs and peep, probably with binoculars—it might help catch these guys," Danielle suggested.

"I don't think it will help," the chief said, "Her description of the pair wasn't much different from yours. Except they had hoodies instead of ski masks, and she didn't see their faces."

"But the bikes. That could be a good lead," Danielle said.

"We got a call last night about two bikes being stolen—a red one and a blue one," the chief said.

"Then you need to catch them with the stolen bikes before they dump them," Danielle insisted.

"Too late. We found them this morning, abandoned in some bushes," the chief told her.

"Any chance someone's security camera caught someone dumping them?"

The chief shook his head. "We've already checked. Nothing."

DANIELLE SAT in the passenger seat of the Packard with Walt in front of the police station. Chris had just driven away in his car, heading home. She looked at Walt and asked, "If you were so concerned about a diary someone had written decades earlier, where would you look?"

"With their family, I suppose. Why?"

"Where else?" Danielle said. "If you're a historian and coming to Frederickport to write about this area or a person from this area, where would you go?"

"Are you suggesting the people who broke in are historians?" he teased.

Danielle rolled her eyes and said, "Please, just humor me."

He considered the question a moment and said, "The local library, the museum, if they have a genealogy society…"

"And if there was already a display at the local museum, wouldn't you go there first?"

"What are you getting at?" Walt asked.

"I was just thinking. These people—whoever they are—why would they assume the information you drew from was a diary or letters you had in your possession? Wouldn't it make more sense that they would first assume you found this information when you were doing research? And if you can't find it online, then at the local museum—especially since that person whose diary you want is featured at the museum with his family. Hell, his portrait is even there."

"His portrait? You are talking about me, you know," he said with a grin.

"Come on, Walt, you know what I mean," she said impatiently.

Walt reached out and gently brushed his fingertips along the side of her face. "Settle down, love. I'm teasing. We need to keep our sense of humor."

"It didn't feel hilarious yesterday, with a gun pointed at me," she grumbled.

Walt leaned over and kissed her nose. "I'm sorry. I hate to see you so upset. But I'm taking this seriously. Go on."

Danielle let out a sigh and said, "I know you are. My point being —and I suppose I should have gotten to it instead of wanting you to figure out what I'm thinking."

"Yes, that would be nice," he said with a chuckle.

"If I'm looking for a diary written almost a hundred years ago, one of the first places I would look would be the museum. As far as they know, you arrived in town a couple of years ago, and I've only lived in Marlow House for a little over four years. Why assume Walt Marlow's diary would be in our possession, or any letters?"

"You think they asked at the museum?"

"Yes! Exactly. I think we should go to the museum, see if anyone has been down there in the last few months, asking about any diary or letters they have from Walt Marlow. It's common knowledge there's an entire storage room filled with documents and memorabilia from the area not on display," Danielle said.

DOCENT MILLIE SAMSON greeted Walt and Danielle when they walked into the museum late Friday morning. The elderly woman told them both how much she had enjoyed her time at Marlow House on Wednesday.

"I'm glad you could make it," Danielle said. "I was wondering if I could ask you a question."

"Why, certainly," Millie said. She stood with them in the museum's entry hall.

"A while back someone asked me if we had any letters or a diary that Walt Marlow left behind." She glanced briefly at her husband and then to Millie and smiled. "The original Walt Marlow, of course. They said they had checked the museum first, but you didn't have any. I'm trying to remember who that was, but I'm drawing a blank. Do you remember anyone asking?"

"Actually, I do. Several people. A couple of young women came in here about a month ago." Millie glanced around and whispered, "They were black."

"Anyone else?" Danielle asked.

"There was Ruby," Millie said.

"Ruby Crabtree, from the Seahorse Motel?" Danielle asked.

"Yes. I think it was for some historical display." Millie lowered her voice again and said, "I think you gave her that idea when you had the B and B. Your website and brochures you'd hand out on local history, I think she's trying to do something like that for the motel."

"Anyone else?" Danielle asked.

"None of those rings a bell yet?" Millie asked.

Danielle shook her head. "No, I'm afraid not."

"That's all who asked me. But someone might have asked one of the other docents."

Danielle glanced briefly to Walt, who flashed her a sympathetic smile.

"Oh, wait, there was someone else. The Barr girls," Millie said.

"Barr girls?" Danielle asked.

"I believe we discussed them the last time you were in the museum. They were in town recently to put their father in a nursing home and, while in town, stopped by the museum."

"And they asked about a Marlow diary?" Danielle asked.

TWENTY-EIGHT

W alt and Danielle followed Millie Samson into the museum gift store as they talked to her. She made her way behind the counter so she could finish affixing price tags to a stack of new souvenir coloring books while she answered their question.

"It wasn't as if they came in the museum and asked if we had Walt Marlow's diary," Millie explained, now standing behind the counter, facing Walt and Danielle. "They had just finished reading *Moon Runners*, and they wondered if Walt based his story on true events. So they came here, asking what reference material Walt used when writing his book. I'm the one who suggested it was possible Walt used some information Danielle had gathered on local history. Considering the discoveries over at Marlow House since you arrived —the Missing Thorndike, the staircase and tunnel, it would be entirely possible you came across some old Marlow diary or ledger."

"Was there anything in particular about my book they were curious about?" Walt asked.

Millie considered the question and said, "Yes, there was." Millie looked at Danielle and asked, "You don't know Earl, do you?"

Danielle shook her head. "No, why?"

"He was always a private man," Millie explained. "Kept to himself. When his daughters were here, asking about any of the reference material we had on hand, they told me Earl never talked about his family or past. As you know, Earl has Alzheimer's; that's why they put him in that place. It's not uncommon for someone who has Alzheimer's forgetting people around them yet remembering things from the distant past. Apparently, Earl began talking about his childhood and how his grandfather had been a bootlegger. It made the girls curious about local moonshining in the area, especially after reading Walt's book."

"I wonder if they were close to their Stewart cousins," Danielle asked, speaking more to herself than expecting an answer from Millie.

"Why do you wonder that?" Millie asked.

Danielle shrugged. "Colorful stories of grandparents typically get passed around in families. If Earl's daughters never heard those stories, either Beau or his parents didn't retell them either, or the cousins weren't close. Even though my cousin Cheryl and I had our issues, as kids growing up, we talked about our families."

"I have no idea what stories Beau Stewart knows," Millie said. "But they weren't close. In fact, according to Earl's oldest, they had only met him once over the years, never his children or wife, although he kept in regular contact with Earl. She said her father didn't hide the fact he wasn't fond of his cousin and didn't want them associating with him or his family. Which is why the girls were so resistant to Earl selling the property to him and insisted they list it. They figured, if Earl had been in his right mind, he would never have sold the land to Beau."

"I wonder why he had such an issue with his cousin?" Walt asked.

"Frankly, I think it was Earl. I told you he is an odd man, and not very nice to his wife. I give those daughters of his credit for trying to do the right thing, especially since it's clear they have issues with him. In my opinion, any concern they're showing Earl comes from a sense of obligation, not love. I also think it's such a shame Earl discouraged them from getting to know their cousins."

"Do you know them?" Danielle asked.

"I can't say we're friends or that I really know them, at least not well. But I met them at your house on Wednesday. Had a lovely conversation with Beau and his wife. Such friendly people. So different from Earl. I also talked a bit with their son and daughter. Polite and intelligent young people. A wonderful addition to our community."

"I understand Frederickport will just be their vacation home," Danielle said.

Millie nodded. "Yes, they mentioned that. But, who knows, they could end up moving here full time. He promised to come in and join the historical society. Did you know fixing up the old Barr place is a family project?"

"What do you mean?" Danielle asked.

"The Stewarts can easily afford to have someone come in and renovate that place. But they're making it a DIY family project. That's why they've rented a house here for the summer. They're removing the old buildings themselves, not hiring anyone. And their son and daughter are both rolling up their sleeves and pitching right in."

"Wow. They're doing everything themselves?" Danielle said.

"Not everything. They're hiring an architect and builder. But not until the family clears the land. Although, I got the impression the wife won't be helping. I suspect she would prefer they hire someone to do the work. Not that she said that, mind you. But I have to give her husband and children credit; they all three seemed enthusiastic about the project."

"Seems like a lot of work," Danielle muttered.

"Yes, but think of the family bonding, a project they will remember for years. Beau Stewart and his wife have true family values. I think he will make an excellent senator for our state. I'm voting for him."

BACK HOME AN HOUR LATER, Walt sat on the porch swing in front of the house, a pen and pad of paper in his hands. That was where Danielle found him after she got off the phone with Chief MacDonald.

"What are you doing?" Danielle asked when she took a seat next to Walt, looking down at the blank pad of paper in his hand.

"I'm trying to jot down some ideas for my book, but I can't stop thinking of who locked you in the stairwell, and when they'll be back."

"So you're sitting out here, standing guard?" she asked, leaning closer.

"Something like that." Tossing the pen and paper to the ground, he draped one arm around Danielle's shoulders, pulled her closer and leaned back, using one foot to start a gentle swinging motion.

"I just got off the phone with the chief. He checked on Earl's daughters. Apparently, not long after they settled their father in the home, the two sisters went to Europe with their husbands. According to whoever he talked to, they had been planning the trip for a long time. Which might be why they were eager to get their father settled. They haven't returned yet. So they couldn't be the ones who broke in here," Danielle told him.

"None of it makes any sense."

"I keep thinking, if only Wilbur would come back so we could ask him more questions. But now that we know those remains aren't his, he probably has absolutely nothing to do with this. Although, it is a bizarre coincidence, him showing up when all this is going on. If we didn't know about his connection to the Porter family, I'd assume he has since moved on, and not given him another thought."

"It could very well be nothing but a coincidence," Walt said.

"And I thought of another reason you and Chris were probably right about my theory being far-fetched."

"Why is that?" he asked.

"Whoever those remains belong to, I doubt they came from the Barr property," Danielle said.

"Why do you say that?" Walt asked.

"Because if Wilbur has been following them, I have to assume he was there when they put them in the gunnysack. The Stewarts have been working on that property, and if they found the remains and threw them in the ocean, certainly Wilbur witnessed at least part of it."

"I understand where you're going with this," Walt said. "Wilbur didn't recognize the couple he overheard on the pier."

"Exactly. And if it was one of the Stewarts, at the very least he would've told Marie they looked familiar. Or that they were the same ones who had the gunnysack he was following. It's still possible, but like you and Chris said, far-fetched."

"It was a good theory," Walt said.

"But I'm still curious. Who do those remains belong to?"

"While learning the answer to that question probably won't help us, I have to admit I'm also curious," Walt confessed.

A vehicle pulled up in front of the house and parked, interrupting their conversation. Both Danielle and Walt watched to see who it was, since neither of them recognized the car. A minute later its driver got out. It was Raven King, and she was alone. After closing the car door behind her, Raven headed to the walk leading to the front door of Marlow House, a large purse in hand.

TWENTY-NINE

R aven sat with Walt and Danielle in the parlor.
"My cousins don't know I'm here," she confessed. "Laken is convinced you have Walt Marlow's diary but won't let us see it because you don't want people to discover most of *Moon Runners* came from the diary and not your own story. And he also suspects there are things about Walt Marlow that you would rather people not find out."

"Even if Walt had a diary—which he doesn't—there would be no reason to keep it from you. It's not uncommon for a writer to use real-life events in their fiction," Danielle said.

"I understand that. But you won't convince Kiara and Laken. From the very beginning, I wanted to come and ask you what you had."

Walt studied Raven for a minute, noting how she fidgeted nervously with the purse on her lap. Finally, he asked, "If your cousins didn't want to just come and ask, what did they want to do?"

She looked up at Walt, shifting uneasily in the chair. "We did sort of snoop around when we were here the other day."

"So why are you here now?" Danielle asked.

"I started thinking about what you said when you came over the other day. How that friend of yours told you stories her father told her. And I thought she might have told you other things, things you forgot, but might remember if something triggers your memory," Raven explained.

"Like what?" Danielle asked.

Raven smiled and opened her purse. She pulled out a portable cassette tape player. "Before my grandmother passed away, I interviewed her. I wanted to preserve our family history. This is the tape where she discusses her aunt. I was wondering if you would listen to it. I'm hoping there might be something in this interview that triggers a memory—something your friend might have told you. It's a long shot, but we've come this far. I don't want to give up. I want to solve this family mystery."

Danielle glanced at Walt, who said, "I'd love to hear the tape."

Raven smiled. "Thank you." She stood up, set the tape player on the coffee table, and turned it on. They listened.

"GRANDMA, tell me about your aunt Charlene."

"She was my mama's little sister. They were a year apart. I never met her, but I saw pictures of her. She was beautiful, like my mama, and talented. She was an actress and appeared in several silent movies. But I've seen none of them. My mother had many regrets about the relationship with her sister. They had a falling-out a few years before my parents married. They never reconciled, and they never saw each other again."

"Why did they have a falling-out?" Raven asked.

"As you know, my grandfather was white. Charlene took after her father—she easily passed. She didn't want to spend her career playing housemaids, and there were no leading roles for black actresses back then. My mother didn't approve. Daddy said Mama felt Charlene was turning her back on her people, taking the easy way out. But Mama once told me that the actual reason she was so upset with her sister, she was afraid for her."

"Afraid why?" Raven asked.

"It was a dangerous game my aunt played. The Klan had a big presence in Oregon. Mama may have had a good reason to worry. Over the years, she came to believe someone murdered her sister."

"She didn't know for sure?"

"Not really. Charlene didn't have many close friends in the business. It was too risky. If one of them found out the truth, they could expose her. And there was a lot of competition."

"None of the actors she worked with knew she was black?"

"A few did. There was one, Eva Thorndike. She and Charlene were in a few plays together. And like my aunt, had been in silent movies. From what I understand, Eva was rather famous, yet died young, a few years before Charlene went missing."

"And she told no one?"

"I don't think Eva ever did. I imagine she kept the secret, and as I said, she died a few years before Charlene ever went missing."

"She just disappeared?"

"One of my aunt's childhood friends worked for her as a personal maid. To the outside world, it looked like the white actress and her black servant. Her name was Rosie. One day Rosie came to see my mama, told her Charlene had gotten an offer in Hollywood, and that she had already left. Mama never heard from her sister again."

"Why does she think Charlene was murdered?"

"A week or so after Rosie talked to Mama, they found her body in an alley. She had been murdered. Mama thinks someone killed her to keep her quiet."

"That's awful! They never found out who killed her?"

"I don't imagine anyone ever looked that hard. But right after they discovered the body, Rosie's brother, who worked as a dishwasher at a club, came to see Mama. He told her Rosie confided in him that Charlene had gotten involved with the wrong white man, and that Charlene's life wasn't the only one in danger. That was right before Charlene supposedly left for Hollywood."

"Did he say who the white man was?" Raven asked.

"No, and this was right after they found poor Rosie's body. It terrified the brother. According to Mama, the only reason Rosie's brother came to her, he felt she needed to know the truth. He believed this white man was responsible for both Charlene's and Rosie's deaths. And he was afraid. He wanted to leave town. He had a wife and daughter to think of, and he believed it was too dangerous to stay. He felt Mama should leave too, because if the man responsible felt Charlene had confided in her sister, they might come after her too."

"So who was the white man?" Raven asked.

"He wouldn't say. Only that the night Rosie was murdered, the man showed up at the club he worked at. Started giving him a hard time, asking him where Rosie was. He knew Rosie was his sister and that she worked for Charlene. Walt Marlow, his grandfather founded Frederickport, was in the bar that night. From what Rosie's brother said, Marlow got the man to calm down and sit with him. They talked for a long time and then left the bar together."

"Do you think they killed poor Rosie?"

"That's what her brother thought. But Mama had a hard time believing that. She had considered Walt Marlow a friend. She liked him. He used to come listen to her sing. But over the years, she wondered."

"Why?" Raven asked.

"Eva Thorndike and Walt Marlow were close friends. Eva had introduced Charlene to Walt after one of their performances, and at the time he probably was not aware Charlene was the sister of his friend Desiree Davis, the jazz singer. I'm sure he initially assumed she was white. But later, when Eva accompanied Walt to one of my mother's performances, and my aunt was there—well, it was no longer a secret. At least not from Walt Marlow. Mama assumed he had kept the secret as Eva had, but after the man was seen with Walt, and then later that night Rosie was murdered, she wondered if she had misjudged Walt Marlow all those years. Had he been responsible for telling her lover she was black?"

Walt and Danielle quietly listened to the rest of the tape. After it ended, Danielle said, "I don't believe for a minute Walt Marlow was responsible for Rosie's death or for your aunt's."

"You want to believe that. Which is why my cousins don't have a lot of faith you'll help us find the truth. But unless you have his diary, you don't know what the man was really like, what he was capable of."

Danielle glanced at Walt, who sat silently, looking off into the distance, his expression unreadable.

"For one thing," Danielle began, "what Marie has told me about Walt, from what her father told her, Walt deplored the KKK. In fact, the Klan was not fond of Frederick Marlow, Walt's grandfather, because he often hired people of color—all nationalities—and paid his employees according to their work, not the color of their skin. And when I did some research on Walt's murder, a man who tried covering it up was active in the Klan. So no, I don't see Walt being part of that group."

"I thought Walt Marlow and Desiree were friends. Did she honestly believe he had something to do with her sister's death?" Walt asked.

Raven looked up to him. "Were they friends? When we first told you she was our great-grandmother, you said you didn't know who she was?"

"We didn't recognize the name," Danielle lied. "But later, after we talked to you, I remembered Marie once telling us about one of Walt's friends, a black jazz singer. We just assumed that was Desiree."

"To answer your question," Raven said, her tone guarded, "Desiree felt Walt was her friend. In one of the interview tapes, when my grandmother is talking about her mother, she tells of an incident that is oddly similar to one in *Moon Runners*. That's one reason we thought you must have a diary or some letters of Walt Marlow. During that incident, Walt Marlow saves Desiree in the same way Hunter Rage saves the jazz singer in *Moon Runners*. Because of that, it was difficult for my great-grandmother to come to terms with the possibility Walt Marlow was involved in Charlene's death. She had liked Walt, considered him a friend. He had once saved her life."

"But she thought he killed her sister?" Walt asked angrily.

"Don't take it personally," Raven said. "It has nothing to do with you. And I don't think Desiree was ever completely convinced of his involvement, but the possibility haunted her. She had sincerely liked Walt Marlow and considered him a friend."

"And you don't know who Charlene was involved with?" Danielle asked.

"No, and neither did my grandmother, and she didn't think her mother did. Desiree didn't approve of the men her sister saw. It wasn't because they were white; their father was white. But Charlene…according to my grandmother's mother…Charlene liked to live dangerously. It was about power for her. I'm not sure I can explain."

"These white men Charlene dated, were any involved with the local Klan?" Danielle asked.

"Yes, Desiree couldn't understand. And I certainly don't," Raven admitted. "According to my grandmother, Charlene had many proposals. The men, they adored her. And I believe she rather enjoyed breaking their hearts, turning them down."

"Perhaps she liked the power," Danielle suggested. "As it was, back then a woman had little power—a black woman even less. Rather a feeling of empowerment to get one of those men to fall hopelessly in love with you, considering the circumstances."

"Exactly, which is why Desiree was so worried about her sister. But the thing was, about a month before she disappeared, Charlene told her sister she had finally fallen in love, and that he loved her. But she wouldn't tell her who it was. Charlene claimed they had things to work out. And when Desiree found out her sister had moved to Hollywood, she assumed the affair had fallen apart, and that's why Charlene moved to Hollywood so suddenly."

Raven looked at Walt. "Your book. It had everything in it. Walt saving Desiree, Charlene falling in love with the wrong man, Charlene's murder."

THIRTY

After Raven left Marlow House on Friday, Walt and Danielle went into the kitchen to make lunch. Danielle prepared chicken salad sandwiches while Walt filled two tall glasses with ice and freshly brewed tea. Fifteen minutes later, they took their lunch outside on the back porch and sat at the patio table to eat.

"Who was this belligerent man poor Rosie's brother saw you talking to in the club?" Danielle asked as she picked up her sandwich to take a bite.

"It could have been anyone. While the incident with Beau Porter —the son, not the father—inspired what I wrote in *Moon Runners*, it wasn't the first or last time something like that happened, where I ended up taking some drunk home."

"You often played bouncer?" Danielle asked as she took a bite of her sandwich.

"A friend of mine owned that speakeasy. I was one of his suppliers."

"My husband, the bootlegger," Danielle said before taking a second bite of sandwich.

"And one thing we didn't need were customers breaking up the place and getting out of hand. A speakeasy's survival depended on —to borrow Chris's reason for using another surname—flying under the radar. Not that the local cops didn't know what was going on, but they would ignore it if we paid the right person and didn't draw attention to ourselves. Brawls and out-of-hand drunks bring unwanted attention."

Danielle set her partially eaten sandwich on her plate and looked across the table to Walt. "I was thinking of all this moonshine business. Didn't you once tell me the Klan pushed prohibition?"

"Yes. It was a way to punish groups the Klan didn't like. Catholics, for example. Which included the Italians, who enjoyed a glass of wine, and Irish, who often enjoyed the pubs. While some may have sincerely disapproved of alcohol, I don't believe that was their primary motivation. And for people like old man Porter, they saw it as an opportunity to profit. He just wasn't that good at it."

"He must have improved after you died, considering the land he bought."

"According to Adam, he bought that land while I was alive, which I still don't understand how he afforded it."

"Obviously he was better at it than you thought."

Danielle's cellphone rang. She picked it up from the table where she had placed it when she had come outside. Before answering it, she looked to see who was calling.

"It's the chief," Danielle said.

When Danielle got off the phone a few minutes later, she said, "The chief's on his way over. There's something he wants to tell us."

Walt looked at the cellphone Danielle had just set on the table. He chuckled.

"What's so funny?" she asked.

"That's one thing I can't get used to," Walt said.

"What's that?"

"People today always have their phones with them. When we had our first telephone installed, I never imagined they would not only be cordless one day, but something we carried around with us. People today are tethered to their phones with an invisible cord. I can understand cellphones when we're away from the house. But we have a landline. Why do you bother carrying that thing around with you when we're home?"

"No one calls me on the landline."

175

THEY'D FINISHED their lunch by the time the chief arrived. Danielle had removed their plates, refilled their glasses with tea, and prepared a third glass for the chief. She had also filled a plate with brownies, which she had brought outside with her. The plate of brownies and extra glass of tea was already on the patio table when the chief sat down.

"Any news on who broke in here?" Walt asked the chief.

"Sorry, we don't have any leads. Whoever took the bikes wiped them down before they dumped them. There were no prints. We found a few people who saw the pair riding the bikes between Marlow House and where they ended up. But the riders wore hoodies and sunglasses, and none of the witnesses could say for sure if they were male, female, or even white. But that's not why I'm here. We got the DNA results back on the remains found on the beach."

"Were there any matches?" Danielle asked excitedly.

"Yes, but not one I expected," the chief said.

"Well?" Danielle asked.

"Whoever it was, they were related to Earl Barr," the chief said.

"Beau Stewart's cousin?" Walt asked.

"Yes," the chief said.

"What side of the family? Are the remains also related to Beau Stewart?" Danielle asked.

The chief shrugged. "I don't know, since we didn't find any DNA matches on any of the genealogy sites. It was a match to DNA from Barr, and it's possible it could have come from the other side of his family."

"How did you have Earl's DNA?" Danielle asked.

"A few years back, one of his neighbors went to his house and claimed someone attacked him from behind. They had been feuding for some time. The neighbor got knocked out, and when he woke up, he was alone, and certain Earl had attacked him. He called the police, pressed charges on Earl, who claimed he hadn't been home at the time. Earl offered to take a DNA test, said whoever beat up his neighbor probably left behind some DNA."

"I assume they didn't find Earl's DNA on the neighbor?"

"They didn't. Of course, that doesn't necessarily prove Earl didn't attack him. But they dropped the charges, not just because of the DNA tests, but someone came forward and claimed to have seen Earl around the time it took place."

"And you never found out who attacked the neighbor?" Danielle asked.

"No. But to be honest, I wouldn't have put it past the neighbor to have made the story up. He had a reputation in town. Fortunately, he moved a while back."

"Now what?" Walt asked. "Whoever he was, someone murdered him."

"I was hoping to get Beau Stewart to give a DNA test, to narrow the search," the chief said.

"And it's entirely possible that even if Stewart is related to the victim, it won't show in the DNA results, since a parent doesn't pass down a hundred percent of their DNA," Danielle noted.

"True. But at the moment it doesn't matter anyway. I stopped by their rental house, and no one was there. According to a neighbor, the entire family is in Portland for the weekend," the chief said.

"What about those burlap bags?" Danielle asked. "Someone dumped those bones in the ocean, and you said yourself, if you find out who bought one of those bags, you should be able to figure out who dumped them."

"All that bag can tell us, whoever put those bones in it did it recently. It's not something someone found sitting in an old barn, maybe even discarded without the person knowing what was inside. No. Whoever put those remains in that bag did it fairly recently. Unfortunately, we learned Toynette from the nursery bought dozens of them and gave them away in an ad promotion. She didn't keep track of who took them."

The three sat quietly at the table, each silently processing what they had just discussed. Finally, Danielle said, "That link between Wilbur and the Porters just got stronger. We suspect Wilbur was the Jenkins who sold Beau Porter all that land—which Beau Stewart now owns. And for some reason, Wilbur's ghost is following around the remains of someone related to Beau's cousin and probably to Beau too. But does any of this have anything to do with our problem?"

Walt looked at the chief and said, "Raven King stopped by earlier." Walt then told the chief about the recording they had listened to, and what Raven had said.

"You have no idea who may have murdered this Charlene?" the chief asked.

"I didn't even realize she had been murdered. Not sure I'm even convinced she was. And I'll say, I find myself somewhat offended that Desiree would entertain the thought I would ever hurt her sister. I thought we were friends," Walt said.

"Don't take it too personally. I keep thinking of *Roots*," Danielle said.

Walt looked at Danielle and frowned. "*Roots?*"

"It was a TV mini-series from the seventies based on Alex Haley's book *Roots*. My parents rented it back when people rented movies on tape, before Netflix. They called it an American family saga, a black American family. It told the story of Alex Haley's ancestor, brought to this country as a slave, and about his descendants. According to my dad, when it first aired on television, it was a huge hit. One scene I remember makes me think of Desiree and her line of thinking."

Danielle paused a moment. Walt gave her a nod and said, "Go on."

"One of the black characters grew up with the master's daughter. As children they were playmates, best friends. But as they got older and became adults, the true dynamics of their relationship became painfully clear. The white woman held the power of life and death over her childhood playmate. Friendship had been nothing more than a convenient illusion. In the scene I remember, when the white woman wasn't looking, the black woman spit in her drink."

"And you're suggesting Desiree may have seen me in the same light as the slave saw the master who she had once believed was her friend?" Walt asked.

Danielle nodded. "Pretty much."

ON FRIDAY EVENING, the Beach Drive friends gathered for a dinner of Chinese takeout, Ian and Lily's treat. Also in attendance were the spirits of Eva Thorndike and Marie Nichols. They gathered in the living room to share recent updates.

Marie held baby Connor in her arms, walking him around the room. From Ian and Lily's perspective, their son flew effortlessly around the room like a baby Superman minus the cape.

"About Wilbur..." Ian looked at Danielle. "You were right, he was the same Jenkins who sold that land to Beau Porter. I did a little digging today. I also found where a W. Jenkins booked travel to Australia during that time—and it appears he was on that ship."

"If old Wilbur really went to Australia," Heather said, "I suppose it's possible he died over there and his confused spirit tried to find his way home, so he crossed the ocean again and ended up in front of Lily and Ian's house."

"And the bag of remains he wanted to find?" Danielle asked.

Heather shrugged. "Maybe the murdered guy was an old friend of his, and he recognized him when he got back to Oregon and wanted to hang out."

Danielle rolled her eyes but did not respond.

"I hate to say this," Eva said. "I considered both Desiree and Charlene my friends, but their great-grandchildren may be the ones who broke in here and held Danielle at gunpoint. They're the only ones who have repeatedly asked about a diary."

Walt let out a sigh. "While I can't understand why they would want to destroy the diary, I'm afraid Eva has a point."

"Perhaps it wasn't so much about destroying the diary they wanted to do, but kill you," Chris suggested.

"Why kill me?" Walt asked with a frown.

"If they honestly believe you—or who they believe is your distant cousin—was responsible for the deaths of Charlene and Rosie, they could see it as avenging their deaths. Getting back at the last living known relative of Walt Marlow. The one who not only shares his name, but his looks, and someone who in their mind is profiting by those deaths by writing *Moon Runners*."

"That's a chilling thought," Danielle said.

"Then there is only one thing we can do," Marie announced, still holding Connor.

"What's that?" Danielle asked.

"If the Kings broke in here—twice—then I have to assume they'll be discussing all this amongst themselves. I need to spend time with them, see what they're saying. And if it is them, we can find out what they plan to do next," Marie said.

"Excellent idea," Eva agreed. "You go now. I'll stay here and monitor things while Walt and Danielle are sleeping, in case it's not the Kings. And in the morning, I'll go down to the cemetery, see if anyone has heard anything."

THIRTY-ONE

A wet, cold nose rubbed against her right cheek. Stray cat hair tickled her nostrils, making them twitch. Something warm and soft nudged her forehead, and then she heard the purring. Sleepily opening her eyes, Danielle looked into Max's face, inches from hers.

"Good morning to you too," she said sleepily, gently reaching up to both pet the cat and push him away so she could sit up. When she did, she glanced over and noticed Walt's side of the bed was empty.

Max jumped off the mattress and sauntered from the room in true panther fashion. Now sitting up in bed, alone in the room, Danielle reached for the nightstand and picked up her cellphone. She looked at the time. It was almost nine thirty. She had slept in.

WHEN DANIELLE WALKED into the kitchen fifteen minutes later, Walt handed her a cup of coffee.

"Did you send Max upstairs to wake me?" she asked, taking the coffee and sitting down at the kitchen table.

"Guilty. I went to wake you myself about an hour ago," Walt said as he joined Danielle at the table. "But you were sleeping so soundly, I felt you needed your rest. But I didn't think you'd want to sleep until noon, so I eventually sent up Max."

"I can't believe I slept so long." Glancing around, she asked, "Is Eva still here?"

"No, she left over an hour ago. She's checking on Marie and then going to the cemetery to see if anyone knows anything."

Danielle sipped her coffee and said, "We should conduct our own ghost interview."

Walt arched his brow. "What do you have in mind?"

"It may have absolutely nothing to do with the people looking for a diary, but I keep thinking about Wilbur and his preoccupation with those skeletal remains. Ian verified the connection between Wilbur and Beauregard Porter. So it goes to reason, that if those remains are related to Earl, it's probably from the Porter side of the family."

"According to my grandfather, Beauregard Porter lost all his family during the war, which was one reason he settled here. If true, unless an unknown cousin of his showed up later, then those remains would have to be a descendant of his," Walt said.

"And he only had two sons?" Danielle asked.

"Only two that survived to adulthood. Beau Junior and Ambrose. Beau left Frederickport before my death. As for Ambrose, I don't know what happened to him. I never came across anything when researching for *Moon Runners*. And then there is Baxter Porter."

"That was Ambrose's son?" Danielle asked.

"Yes. Which, if my calculations are correct, would be Earl Barr and Beau Stewart's grandfather," Walt said.

"And since neither one has the Porter surname, I have to assume Baxter had two daughters," Danielle said. "From what we learned, it appears they divided the Porter estate between Earl and Stewart, which leads me to think Baxter had no other children."

"Or just no surviving children," Walt suggested. "It's possible Baxter had a murdered son, one who died in adulthood leaving no heirs, and that's the owner of those remains."

"I think we should go out to the Barr place," Danielle said.

"Why would we do that?"

"According to Carla, that place is haunted. If those remains belong to a Porter, and someone murdered him, that's probably who's doing the haunting."

"Those remains are the chief's problem, not ours," Walt reminded her.

"True. But according to him, the Stewarts left for the weekend. And we know, according to Millie, they haven't hired workmen, so there shouldn't be anyone out there. What would it hurt to have a look around? And maybe we can at least solve one mystery. And you might know the ghost, and he could help solve our problem."

"Are you certain there would be no harm?" Walt asked.

"What do you mean?"

"Remember what the chief said about Barr's neighbor?" Walt reminded her. "Have you considered the attacker came from the spirit realm? Even Eva says she avoids that place."

Danielle considered Walt's suggestion for a moment before saying, "Eva never said she avoided the Porter property for fear of spirits hurting her. Remember, the universe won't allow a spirit to hurt an innocent. Plus, the chief said the neighbor could have made the entire thing up."

"Which could also mean the neighbor wasn't an innocent, and perhaps whoever haunts the place attacked him," Walt said.

"True."

"And if Ambrose was the one who got himself murdered and his spirit haunts his old home, I don't think he'll be much help. We didn't exactly get along."

"Yes, but spirits who haunt one place are typically confused and lost. And once they understand what's happening, they can be grateful and helpful. It's worth a shot."

"Fine, but I should go alone. You stay here," Walt said.

Danielle frowned. "Why would I do that?"

"Because I can't protect you from a spirit," Walt said seriously.

"Are you suggesting I'm not an innocent?"

THEY TOOK Danielle's car instead of the Packard, and Danielle drove. Once Earl Barr's property, and several generations earlier Beau Porter's, the two acres on the edge of town were surrounded primarily by pastureland.

Instead of traveling the main road leading to the front entrance of the property, Danielle took the back way. No homes lined the rarely traveled dirt road. Driving down the lane, they spied elk grazing and off in the far distance an occasional house.

Danielle parked along what had once been the west property

line near the rear section of the Porter property. They got out of the car and looked around. Other than the elk, they spied no signs of life. Overhead, the morning breeze rustled leaves from the trees lining the desolate section of road. Walt recognized the rear of the Porter property immediately, including one outbuilding some three hundred feet from the road.

"I can't believe that's still standing," Walt said as he and Danielle approached the weathered structure a few minutes later. Its siding resembled a patchwork quilt of recycled materials—warped paneling, sheets of tin, and sheetrock. A rickety wooden fence wrapped around three of the building's four sides.

"Is that a storage shed?" Danielle asked.

"It's where Porter used to keep his hogs," he told her.

"Lovely," she said dryly.

Just as they walked around the outbuilding, bringing into view its north-facing wall and the portion of fencing surrounding it, Danielle reached out and grabbed Walt's wrist, bringing him to a stop.

"We're not alone," Danielle whispered.

A woman, clad in a long blue gingham dress, sat on a portion of the outbuilding's fence, her back to Danielle and Walt, and her long yellow hair draped past her shoulders, fluttering in the breeze. Danielle assumed this was one of the Stewarts' neighbors, and she would rather the woman not tell the Stewarts they had been snooping around.

Walt backed up with Danielle when the woman turned and looked at him. It was then Danielle noticed the red handkerchief wrapped around the woman's neck. The woman cocked her head, staring intently at Walt. Without saying a word, she jumped down off the fence and slowly approached him, paying no attention to Danielle.

As the woman grew near, Danielle realized this was not a woman, more a girl, a teenager. When the stranger was about ten feet from Walt and Danielle, she broke into a smile and said, "Walt Marlow, that really is you, isn't it?"

"Dolly?" Walt choked out.

With a frown, Danielle looked from the teenager to Walt. "You know each other?"

"Um…yes…this is Dolly Porter, Ambrose's wife. Dolly, this is my wife, Danielle."

Danielle's eyes widened. No, it was not a woman, nor was it a teenager. Dolly was obviously a ghost.

Dolly glanced behind her nervously. She looked back to the pair.

"You never liked Ambrose, did you?" Dolly asked in a whisper.

"We didn't really get along," Walt confessed.

"Then help me, please!" Dolly begged.

"Help you how?" Walt asked.

"I need to get away from here before they come looking for me!" Dolly reached nervously for the scarf. Looking behind her for a moment and then back to Walt, the scarf disappeared, revealing angry red marks wrapped around Dolly's neck.

Walt started to say something, but Dolly looked behind her again, as if panicked, let out a scream, and vanished.

"Oh my," Danielle said, glancing around for any sign of the apparition. "I have a horrible feeling. I don't think poor Dolly ran away."

"One of them killed her," Walt said. "I wonder which one it was, Ambrose or his father. I wouldn't put it past either of them."

"Walt, call her back. Try. She was responding to you."

"I don't think she'll be able to help us," Walt said. "Poor girl doesn't even realize she's dead."

"That's exactly why we have to help her, because she doesn't know she's dead. The poor thing trapped all these years. She's practically a child."

Walt let out a sigh and called out, "Dolly!"

Nothing happened.

He looked at Danielle, who silently urged him to try again.

"Dolly!" Walt shouted.

Again, nothing.

"Maybe she went up to the barn or house," Danielle said, nodding to the buildings in the distance.

"Let's see." Walt reached out and took Danielle's left hand.

They walked a few more minutes before another apparition appeared before them. They both stopped.

"Wilbur!" Danielle said.

"Danielle and Walt Marlow, surprised to find you both here," Wilbur said. "Did you come looking for it too?"

"Looking for what?" Danielle asked.

"My gunnysack. You said you'd help me find it. But you didn't."

"And I asked you to stay at Marlow House and identify the man you overheard," Danielle countered.

Wilbur shrugged. "I have things to do."

"Why are you here?" Danielle asked.

"I just told you, I came looking for the gunnysack."

Danielle studied Wilbur. "But why are you looking here?"

"I thought it might have returned," Wilbur said.

"Is this where you found the bag?" Walt asked.

"I didn't find the bag; they brought it," Wilbur countered.

Danielle said something, but Wilbur cut her off. "I see you both talked to Dolly."

"Where did she go?" Walt asked.

"I imagine up to the house, trying to find Baxter. She's always looking for Baxter," Wilbur said.

"Who killed her?" Walt asked.

Wilbur looked at Walt. "How would I know? I wasn't here when it happened. But it really doesn't matter which one. They're both the same. Two peas. Poisoned peas. Evil as they come. And you should watch out because it hasn't died. It lives on."

The next moment Wilbur vanished.

"I guess Wilbur didn't move on," Walt said.

"And I have a feeling there were three bodies buried on this property before someone removed those bones and put them in a bag."

THIRTY-TWO

"Three people?" Walt asked with a raised brow. "I assume one is Dolly, the other one a Porter who was unfortunate enough to get shot and have his skeletal remains wash up on the beach across from our house, and also Wilbur? Maybe he didn't go to Australia."

"It looks that way," Danielle said. "It's not uncommon for an earthbound spirit to look for his burial site. That's why the cemetery is the first place to look if you suspect a spirit hasn't moved on."

"Do you still want to look around, or should we go home?" Walt asked.

"I don't think we can leave now. I wish Wilbur would stop popping in and out. We need to ask him more questions about who he overheard."

"Finding Wilbur on this property makes me wonder if we should take the Stewarts and Barrs off our suspect list," Walt said.

"Why do you say that?" Danielle asked.

"If you're right and Beau Porter murdered Wilbur and buried him on this property, it looks as if Wilbur has been hanging around since then. He might have only left when someone moved those bones. But the removal of the remains may have absolutely nothing to do with anything ominous. Maybe one of the Stewarts found them and did not want the negative press attention after notifying the authorities, so they dumped them in the ocean. But that also means Wilbur has seen members of both the Barr and Stewart families, and if he didn't recognize whoever he overheard on the pier, then I think for our problem, we need to look elsewhere," Walt said.

"You have a point. Hopefully, he'll stick around so we can find him again and get a better description of who he saw at the pier. But while we're here, I'd like to help poor Dolly. Bad enough she died at such a young age, not to mention murdered and trapped here for eternity." Danielle shivered at the thought.

"Everyone believed she deserted her little boy," Walt said.

"How old was he at the time?" Danielle asked.

"I think about three or four. Dolly was a couple of years younger than me. And like I told you before, her son, Baxter, was around twelve the last time I saw him."

"I'd like to help Dolly, and if Wilbur would just stick around, I'd like to tell him where those remains are so he'll stop looking. But I don't want to do that too soon, or he might leave for good before he answers our questions."

"Then let's start to the barn first," Walt suggested.

Reaching out, Danielle took Walt's hand again, and together they headed to the barn.

They were about twenty feet from their destination when the light breeze morphed into a howl, kicking up a dirt devil and, with it, bits of dry soil and brush, polluting the air around them and making Danielle cough. Wanting to shield Danielle from the unexpected assault, Walt wrapped his arms around her. As quickly as the mini-storm appeared—it vanished. It was as if someone had unplugged an invisible cord, draining the energy.

Brushing away the dry bits of foliage now lodged in her hair, Danielle glanced around. The light breeze that had been present when they had first arrived—and there before the sudden outburst —vanished with the dirt devil.

"What was that?" Danielle asked, giving her hair another swipe with a brush of one hand. Turning to Walt, she reached up and pulled a small twig from his hair and tossed it on the ground.

Before Walt answered, a burst of light filled the space before them. They stared at the bright glow and watched as it transformed itself, until no longer light, but the image of a man—albeit a transparent one, with stringy brown hair falling to his shoulders. He was not a spirit either might confuse for a living person, as they had with

Dolly, because they had a clear shot of the barn right through his body.

"I have a feeling you don't know this one," Danielle whispered to Walt while never looking away from the spirit. Had he been a living man, she would guess his age to be a few years older than herself.

"You're right," Walt whispered back, his eyes, like Danielle's, intently focused on the stranger.

"Who are you?" Danielle asked.

"You shouldn't be here," the spirit told her. "It's not safe."

"Did you make the wind blow just now?" Walt asked.

The spirit shook his head and said, "That was Dolly. You've upset her."

"Please tell us who you are. We can help you," Danielle promised.

The spirit laughed bitterly. "No one can help me now." He looked at Walt and asked, "Who is she to you?"

"My name is Walt Marlow. This is my wife, Danielle."

The spirit frowned and looked confused. "I've heard of a Walt Marlow, but he's dead. Are you dead?"

"No, we're not dead," Walt said.

The spirit looked down at his own left hand. Both Danielle and Walt noticed the wedding ring he wore. A moment later the spirit looked up at Walt and said, "You aren't now, but you will be. Beware of your wife. She may seem lovely now, but someday she might kill you." He vanished.

Danielle cringed and looked over to Walt. "Just a hunch, but I don't think he had a very happy marriage."

"I suspect it was as bad as my first marriage," Walt said and added, "And his clothes were...interesting."

"If he's dressing from his time period, he's from the sixties, considering his colorful bell-bottom pants and the even more colorful shirt."

"The beads were interesting," Walt said.

"They're love beads."

"He did remind me a little of Reverend Mike." Reverend Mike had been the aged hippy who had married Walt and Danielle when they had eloped.

"Of course, his hair wasn't as long as Reverend Mike's." Reverend Mike's gray hair had reached his waist. "And not as old as

Reverend Mike, yet older than the average hippy back in the sixties. And his hair was a little longer than a conservative person would wear back then. I've seen some pictures of my dad with a crew cut when he was about fifteen, and then down to his shoulders when he was about nineteen."

Walt looked at Danielle and smiled. "Your dad was a hippy?"

Danielle shrugged. "Mom said he went through a stage. But our ghost there. His hair was shorter than Dad's during his hippy stage, but still considered long for back then. And the clothes, stereotypical sixties."

"I wonder who he was," Walt said.

They started toward the barn again, but this time at a slower pace.

"Maybe I was wrong about three people being buried here," Danielle suggested.

"Obviously more, considering our hippy friend."

Danielle stopped walking for a moment and looked to Walt. "I didn't mean that. It's possible this place attracts spirits. It doesn't mean their bodies are necessarily here. Look at Lucas, he hung around in an old office building for over a year before figuring out he was dead. And he didn't die there." Lucas had been Danielle's first husband.

"Are you suggesting none of them died here, not even Dolly?"

Danielle considered the question. "I'm just saying I don't want to jump to any conclusions quite yet."

They started walking again, their path taking them under an apple tree. Movement overhead caught Danielle's attention. She looked up in time to see a tree limb falling down from an upper branch, aimed for the top of Walt's head.

Without hesitation, she yanked Walt away from the falling missile. It didn't miss him completely but hit his shoulder before falling the rest of the way to the ground.

Cursing, Walt grabbed hold of the injured shoulder, glaring down at the fallen limb. He glanced upwards, looking for where it had fallen from. Staring at the upper branch, he thought it looked as if someone had literally ripped it from the larger branch before hurling it in his direction.

Danielle's hand brushed his arm, and she asked, "Are you okay?"

"I think so." Walt rubbed his shoulder to make sure.

"That was freaky," Danielle said.

"Are you okay?" a voice asked.

Both Danielle and Walt turned around and faced a tall, pale-skinned man. He wasn't transparent like the last spirit, but Danielle was fairly certain that was what he was, judging by the bullet hole in the middle of the man's forehead. Walt identified him as a spirit, but it wasn't the bullet hole that gave it away. Walt recognized the man, and if he had still been alive, he would now be about 125 years old.

"Beau Porter?" Walt asked in surprise.

"Walt Marlow? What are you doing here? It's not safe."

"What happened?" Walt asked.

Beau frowned. "What are you talking about?"

"I don't think he knows," Danielle whispered to Walt.

Beau looked to Danielle and smiled. "You're a pretty thing. Are you Walt's new girlfriend?"

"This is my wife, Danielle," Walt introduced.

"Damn! You're kidding, you got yourself married?" Beau grinned. "Congratulations!"

"Do you know what happened to that tree?" Danielle asked, glancing briefly to the fallen limb.

"I suspect it's Dolly. She's upset right now. Looking for Baxter again. She won't find him. He's not here. Won't be coming back, and even if he did, it wouldn't make her happy. He's just like his father."

"Why are you here?" Danielle asked.

Beau shrugged. "I live here. Where else would I be?"

"Um...do you know Wilbur Jenkins?" Danielle asked.

The smile disappeared from Beau's face. "Why do you ask?"

"We're trying to find him," Danielle said.

"Why are you looking here?" Beau asked.

"We saw him here earlier and wondered if he was still around."

"It wasn't my fault. I didn't want to do it." Beau shook his head frantically.

"You didn't want to do what?" Danielle asked.

"I told Pa it wasn't right. I tried to stop them. Maybe I could have fought that old man, but not Ambrose and Baxter. They beat the crap outa me. When I woke up, he was already dead. Honest. They made me bury him. Ambrose said if he had to dig the grave himself, he'd make it large enough for both of us. He might be my little brother, but he would've done it."

"It was Wilbur's grave, right?" Danielle asked in a whisper.

Beau nodded. "I didn't have a choice."

"Who dug the grave, you or your brother?" Danielle asked softly.

"I did," Beau said before disappearing.

"Now we know who those remains belong to," Walt said.

"Yes, unless there's another Porter out here with a bullet in his skull."

"Looks like you were right, they killed Wilbur," Walt said.

"Does this mean after Ambrose made his brother dig the grave, he shot him? Were Beau and Wilbur buried together?" Danielle asked.

Walt considered the question for a moment, thinking back on past events, and then shook his head. "I don't think so. Ian emailed me everything he found in the search he told us about last night. I reviewed it this morning while you were still sleeping. Obviously, Wilbur wasn't the one on that ship to Australia. I'd say they killed Wilbur around the same time that land transferred from Jenkins to Porter. Beau was alive for at least another month after that."

"Are you sure?"

"Positive. The last time I saw Beau was at the speakeasy. It was a few days after I got news of the *Eva Aphrodite* going down. It's a date I can't forget. One reason I stopped in that night, I had plans to tie one on and drown my sorrows. But then I ran into Beau, who was already half-seas over."

"I assume that means he was drunk?" Danielle asked.

Walt gave her a nod and said, "I ended up listening to his problems that night instead of dwelling on my own. And that was definitely after Wilbur was murdered."

"I wonder who murdered Beau," Danielle asked.

Walt let out a sigh and said, "It's possible no one murdered him."

"Are you suggesting he committed suicide?"

"He claimed he was desperately in love with someone who took off with another man. He wouldn't be the first person to kill himself over unrequited love. I don't imagine old Beau would want anyone to discover his namesake killed himself over a woman. It would be just like him to bury the body on the property and tell everyone his son took off."

"We have our work cut out for us," Danielle said when they reached the barn door.

"Why do you say that?" Walt asked.

"There are spirits here that need us. We have to help them move on."

Walt rubbed his shoulder and said, "I understand that, but I'm questioning Eva's assertion spirits can't hurt innocents."

"I suppose I could be flippant and make some crack about you not being so innocent. But the truth is, that tree limb could have killed you. It didn't."

Walt let out an uncertain sigh, reached for the barn door, and opened it.

The two stepped inside; the only illumination came from shafts of sunlight streaming through warped planks of siding and the open door. Moments after entering, another apparition appeared before them. This one a woman.

"Charlene Davis?" Walt blurted out in surprise.

THIRTY-THREE

The apparition vanished as quickly as it had appeared, leaving Walt and Danielle standing inside the barn, its door still wide open, letting in the bright sunlight.

"It wasn't?" Danielle gasped.

"It was. Desiree's sister, Charlene," Walt said.

Danielle stepped farther into the barn and glanced around. Hesitantly she called out, "Charlene, please come out. We can help you."

To both Danielle and Walt's surprise, Charlene once again appeared before them, dressed as a flapper with a feathered cap on her short dark hair.

"Who are you?" Charlene asked Danielle. She looked to Walt and said, "Is she a friend of yours, Walt?"

"This is my wife, Charlene. Her name's Danielle," Walt introduced.

Charlene smiled brightly. "You got married? I hadn't heard. I'm getting married too."

"Who are you marrying?" Danielle asked.

Charlene started to say something but hesitated. Shaking her head, she said, "I don't know if I can tell you. It has to remain a secret until we're far away from here."

"You can trust me," Walt told her. "Remember, I'm a friend of your sister's."

"But Desiree doesn't approve of him. She doesn't know I'm eloping. But he's nothing like his father or brother. Nothing at all."

Danielle's eyes widened. "You're in love with Beau Porter!"

Charlene quickly placed a finger over her lips, hushing Danielle. "You can't tell!"

"Why are you here?" Danielle asked.

"I'm waiting for Beau. He's meeting me here."

"In the barn? Is that where you plan to meet him?" Danielle asked.

"Yes, they're all gone. His father, brother, and that fresh nephew of his. They won't be back until morning. By then we'll be far away from here," Charlene told them.

"Charlene, do you know how long you've been waiting for Beau in the barn?" Danielle asked.

Charlene frowned and shook her head. "I...I...I'm not sure." She turned around, revealing the knife handle protruding from the back of her dress, blood staining the blue fabric. The ghost vanished.

"Now we know how she died, but we don't know who killed her," Danielle said. "My guess, they agreed to meet here, but the killer arrived first, murdered Charlene, and somehow made Beau believe she'd taken off with another lover."

"Which was probably old man Porter," Walt suggested. "If that was the case, then he found out Charlene was part black. There was no way in hell Porter would have allowed his son to marry a black woman."

"So much sadness here," Danielle said.

Walt glanced at the open door. "But if both spirits are here, and if they loved each other, then why aren't they together?"

Danielle shrugged. "It's possible Charlene is confined to the barn, like you were to Marlow House. And Beau can't come in here, like Stoddard's ghost wasn't able to enter Marlow House. You know what we need to do?"

"I don't want to ask," Walt groaned.

"We need to get those two to understand what happened, that way they won't be confined and separated, and they can finally be together."

"That sounds romantic, Danielle, but we don't even know for sure if Beau returned Charlene's affections. As far as we know, she met Beau that night in the barn, and he wanted to get her out of the way. Or he found out she was part black; after all, he is a Porter, which meant a Klan member."

"He was?" Danielle sounded disappointed.

"Yes. Old man Porter was high in the local Klan. Damn sure he would have his sons with him."

"I thought you said Beau Junior was the nice one," Danielle asked.

"Compared to his brother, he was. And I felt back then he was only in the Klan because there was no way to avoid it with his father. But I could have been wrong about him, and maybe he had as much hate in his heart as his father."

"Okay, so what's the rest of your depressing alternate scenario?" Danielle asked.

"I would think it's depressing anyway you look at it, since someone put a knife in Charlene's back," Walt reminded her.

"I know. But go on..."

"Your scenario could be accurate. They were in love, and old man Porter interfered. Or Beau could have fallen in love with someone else and got rid of a girlfriend he saw as an embarrassment or in the way. And then the new girlfriend left him."

"You're right, it is depressing either way," Danielle agreed. "But we still have to help Charlene and the others. Even Beau."

"Yes, I know," Walt said with a sigh.

Danielle shouted, "Charlene!"

Walt stood and watched as she circled the barn, calling out Charlene's name over and over again and receiving no answer.

"Perhaps she's not confined to the barn," Walt suggested.

"Or she doesn't want to talk."

"Possible."

Hands on hips, Danielle surveyed her surroundings. "They must not have kept animals in here."

"They used to," Walt said.

"With a concrete floor?" Danielle asked. "Of course, someone after Beau Porter's time could have added it. I could see pouring concrete if you used the barn for storage or a shop." She spied a nearby section of the floor covered with a tarp. By the visible lumps, the tarp covered more than a bare floor. "Wonder what's under there."

To answer her question, Walt willed the tarp up into the air. A moment later it floated some six feet over the section it had been covering, hovering overhead like a cloud.

Both Danielle and Walt stared, trying to understand what exactly they were seeing. Chiseled-out chunks of concrete formed one lump previously concealed by the tarp. The second lump was a large bucket. They didn't look to see what the bucket held; instead, their attention focused on the remaining concrete in the floor and its secrets someone had revealed by removing the floor's top layer.

"Is that what I think it is?" Danielle asked nervously.

"The question should be, who was it?" Walt muttered.

"Or who were they? There's at least two of them; look." Danielle pointed first to what appeared to be a human skull still embedded in the concrete floor, yet partially revealed. She then pointed to the bucket. It held bones, including a second human skull.

"What the hell is going on here?" Danielle asked, stepping back from the tarp.

"I think we should go now. Let the chief take care of this," Walt suggested.

They watched as the tarp drifted back down to the floor, once again concealing the gruesome scene.

"The Stewarts know it's here, and they're digging it up," Walt said.

"I understand the lure of home improvement," Danielle said. "There are enough DIY shows on cable to prove it's popular. But once you uncover multiple graves, I'd think the normal thing to do would be to call the authorities."

"It confirms our suspicions on who tossed those remains in the ocean," Walt said, giving Danielle a gentle nudge and pointing to a dark section of the barn she hadn't yet inspected. Piled in the corner were several burlap bags. "Come on. I don't have a good feeling about this. Let's get out of here."

Danielle nodded. "I agree, let's go find the chief."

Together, Walt and Danielle hurried toward the open barn door. Once they got outside, they quickly shut the door and continued on their way, retracing their steps, but avoiding the apple tree.

When they were almost at the outbuilding where they had seen Dolly, Wilbur suddenly appeared.

"You were in the barn," Wilbur said. "They don't let anyone in the barn."

"Wilbur, we need to leave, but I beg you to come back to Marlow House so we can talk, please," Danielle said.

"You can't leave yet," Wilbur said. "Dolly wants to talk to you. I told her you'd help her."

"I'll come back later," Danielle promised.

"Come on, Danielle," Walt urged, taking her hand and gently giving it a tug, wanting her to keep walking toward their car.

Wilbur glared at Walt. "I don't understand. Are you a ghost?"

"No, I'm not a ghost," Walt said.

"Then none of this makes sense. I'm dead, but you're alive?"

"He's not the same Walt Marlow," Danielle lied.

Wilbur looked at Danielle and frowned. "What do you mean?"

"Marie explained you're a ghost. You've been a ghost for over ninety years. That would make Walt how old? Almost one hundred twenty? Does he look one hundred twenty?"

"So you're a relative of that Walt Marlow?" Wilbur asked.

"Something like that," Walt said.

"Your relative, that other Walt Marlow, he's the reason I got into this mess. If it wasn't for him, they wouldn't have murdered me."

"How was Walt Marlow responsible for your death?" Walt asked.

Before Wilbur could answer, a woman called out, "Walt, come over here!"

They turned toward the outbuilding that had once housed the Porters' hogs. Dolly stood by the building, waving him over.

"She wants you to see. But she thinks you're that other Walt Marlow," Wilbur explained.

"We can help Dolly before we leave," Danielle said.

"There isn't time. It can take hours; look how long it took Cheryl. We'll come back later, after we let the chief know what's out here," Walt insisted.

"She just wants to show you something," Wilbur said. "It won't take long."

Wilbur vanished.

"Walt, here!" Dolly called out.

Walt groaned. "Okay, let's see what she wants to show us, and then we're leaving. Please don't tell Dolly she's dead. Not yet. Okay?"

"Okay, Walt, I promise."

Together Walt and Danielle hurried over to Dolly, who now stood by the entrance to the dilapidated outbuilding.

"What did you want to show me?" Walt asked Dolly when they reached the spirit.

"It's inside. Come look," Dolly said, floating into the building and disappearing.

Walt looked at Danielle and asked, "Are you sure a ghost can't hurt a living person?"

Danielle shrugged. "According to Eva, the universe won't let a spirit hurt an innocent. But why would Dolly's spirit hurt you? Spirits don't suddenly become evil, unless they were evil during their life."

"She did throw a tree branch at me," he reminded her.

"Even living people who aren't evil have angry outbursts. And it didn't land on your head."

Walt let out a deep breath, reached out, and took hold of Danielle's right hand. Hesitantly, they stepped into the dilapidated small building, standing just inside its open doorway. They found Dolly hovering inside, her illusion a golden glow. She pointed down to a section of the dirt floor. A portion of it had been dug up.

"There, look," Dolly urged.

Both Danielle and Walt looked down and found a human skull peeking up at them from the hole.

"That's me," Dolly told them. "That's where they put me."

Danielle looked to Walt. "I think she knows she's dead."

THIRTY-FOUR

Dolly vanished, leaving Walt and Danielle alone in the shabby outbuilding. The only light came from the late morning sunlight streaming through the open doorway.

"This place is a freaking house of horrors," Danielle told Walt.

WHEN TWO MEN had pulled up to the rear of the property ten minutes earlier, they found a Ford Flex parked along the road. After parking behind the Flex, they got out of their vehicle and had a closer look.

"I know whose car that is," the older man said in a low voice. "That belongs to the Marlows."

Both men looked up toward the path leading to the rear of the property and the first outbuilding. The older man placed a finger over his lips, signaling to the other man to be quiet. The younger man gave a nod, and together they stealthily made their way onto the property, each excruciatingly careful not to make a sound.

As they arrived at the rear of the building, they heard a woman's voice say, "This place is a freaking house of horrors."

The younger man looked at his companion and mouthed the words, "Danielle Marlow." The other man nodded in agreement, and they both listened.

"How many do you think there are?" they heard Danielle say.

"We have Dolly, Charlene, Wilbur, the hippy," a male voice said.

Again, the younger man mouthed words, this time, "Walt Marlow."

The older man pointed to some debris on the ground, a section of pipe and a weathered piece of wood that had once been the handle of a boat oar. As they each grabbed a makeshift weapon, they heard Danielle say, "We're fairly certain Beau Porter was here until one of the Stewarts dumped his remains. But I wonder, are there more?"

"I imagine the chief will have this entire place torn up," Walt said.

"Do you think they'll find more than what's in the barn and here?" Danielle asked.

The taller man pointed for the other man to go in one direction while he headed in another, each moving around the shed, heading to its entrance.

"I suppose it's possible. Let's get out of here," Walt said.

"You drive. I'll call the chief on the way home," Danielle said.

"The chief will not be happy with you when he discovers we came out here," Walt said.

"Are you saying he won't be unhappy with you?" Danielle asked.

"Oh, I'll make sure he knows this was your idea. And now that I think about it, we probably should have told someone we were coming out here."

"They're gone for the weekend. Anyway, I have you," they heard Danielle say.

———

PEARL HUCKABEE WORE A WIDE-BRIMMED straw hat to keep the sun out of her eyes while she trimmed the shrubs along her southern property line, and she wore leather gloves to protect her hands. Clad in faded overalls, a blue work shirt, and a pair of Keds with white socks, she efficiently moved down the row of bushes, letting the trimmed leaves and stems fall to the ground to rake up later.

She paused when she heard a voice next door shout, "Dammit, Marie, you scared the crap out of me!" Putting down her shears, Pearl used her gloved hands to separate two bushes so she could see into her neighbor's yard. There stood Heather Donovan, hands on hips, ranting to herself. She was alone—except for the calico cat standing by Heather's feet. But she wasn't ranting at the cat; it was the flowerpot that had the odd girl in a tizzy, cursing up a storm and stomping her feet, giving that darn ol' flowerpot a good what for. And who names their flowerpot Marie?

Pearl shook her head and thought, *That girl is crazy*. She continued to listen.

"YOU NEED NOT GET SO HUFFY!" Marie told Heather as she stood next to a flowerpot.

"I swear, Marie, you will seriously give me a heart attack one of these days, the way you just pop in unannounced!" Heather told her.

"Oh, posh. You're young, healthy, all that jogging you do. You're not going to have a heart attack. But I need your help."

Heather let out a sigh and calmed down. "Okay, what do you need?"

"I can't find Walt and Danielle anywhere. I spent the last evening and most of this morning over at the Kings'. I'm convinced they aren't who we're looking for. But they aren't home, and Max doesn't know where they went."

"Did you try across the street at Lily and Ian's?"

"Yes. They're not there, and I couldn't ask Lily and Ian about Walt and Danielle," Marie explained.

"You could have written something on the dry-erase board," Heather reminded her.

"I suppose, but that can be so tedious in a case like this. Can't you please just go across the street with me and play translator?"

"Why don't you ever ask Chris to do this stuff?" Heather asked.

"Your house is closer," Marie said.

"But maybe they're over at Chris's place," Heather suggested.

"No, after I checked at Lily and Ian's, I looked in the garage, and Danielle's car is gone. I looked down the street; it's not parked by Chris's house."

"Fine," Heather said with a sigh. "But do me a favor first, tell Bella I want her to go in the house before we leave. I don't want her outside alone, and I don't want her crossing the street."

"Certainly…"

While waiting for Marie to relay the entire message to her calico cat, motion from the bushes caught Heather's attention.

"I DON'T KNOW where they went," Lily told Heather fifteen minutes later when she led them into the living room. Sadie tagged along after greeting both Heather and Marie. When they walked into the living room, they found Ian sitting on the floor with Connor, playing with toy trucks.

"Oh, fun!" Heather said, joining the pair on the floor and giving Connor a quick kiss on the forehead.

"Hello, Marie, wherever you are," Ian greeted her after saying hello to Heather.

"I can try calling her," Lily said, picking up her cellphone as she took a seat on one chair.

"I tried both her and Walt's number on the way over," Heather said. "It went to voicemail. They could be ignoring me."

"They're not ignoring you," Lily said. Yet she wasn't entirely certain that was true, and she told herself if they answered, she would make up an excuse why they hadn't answered the phone earlier.

A few minutes later, Lily found no need to fabricate an excuse. "Went to voicemail for me too."

A suspicious sound came from Connor, and Heather gasped, "Oh, kid, that was a stinker!"

"Tell them I'll take care of it," Marie told Heather.

Ian was reaching for Connor when Heather conveyed Marie's message. The next moment Ian and Lily watched their son float from the living room to the nursery, giggling and kicking his feet in delight.

After Marie and Connor left the room, Lily asked, "I wonder why Dani and Walt aren't answering their phones."

"They probably went for a drive and are in a dead spot," Ian suggested. "But I'll call Chris, see if he knows where they went."

While Ian called Chris, Heather told Lily, "I imagine old Pearl will be spreading some rumors about me."

"Why, what happened?" Lily asked.

"When I was talking to Marie in my backyard before coming over here, I didn't know Pearl was listening."

Lily giggled and said, "Poor Pearl doesn't seem to have much in her life, so look at it as giving her something interesting to talk about."

Heather gave a shrug and said, "I guess there's some truth to that. Sort of like when she saw Connor flying around Walt and Danielle's living room."

"I still can't believe she bought that whole 'it's a magic trick' story," Lily said. "But like we all say—"

"People believe what they want to believe," both Heather and Lily chorused.

"Chris doesn't know where they are," Ian told them when he got off the phone. "But he said they should be home in an hour. He talked to Walt early this morning about dropping Hunny off with them while he goes to Astoria."

———————

THE MAN with the hook nose cleaned the blood and fingerprints off the piece of pipe and oar handle before dropping them into the burlap bag. He wiped down Walt's and Danielle's cellphones, then tossed them atop the pipe and oar handle. He handed the bag to the younger man and said, "Whatever you do, dump these out of the bag before dropping them off the pier, and don't let anyone see you. Bring the bag back so I know you didn't do something stupid again."

"What are you going to do?" the younger man asked.

"First, I'll move their car into the garage before someone sees it. Now get going. Once someone knows the Marlows are missing, they can use their phones to try tracing them."

"What about the car? They can trace the car too."

"I'll take care of it. Just get going."

THIRTY-FIVE

At first Danielle wondered if it was a nightmare, one triggered by a past trauma. Kidnapped and forced to sleep while chained on the concrete floor in Lake Havasu City, Arizona, before the police rescued them. She couldn't remember her head throbbing back then as it did now.

Danielle opened her eyes and winced. Wherever she was, there was little light, and while the space above her reminded her of that past imprisonment, it was not the same location. It took a moment for her eyes to adjust to the dim lighting. The shafts of sunlight slipping through ill-fitting wallboards helped break up the darkness.

Reaching for the pain, her hand touched her hair. It felt wet and sticky. Still lying flat on her back, she moved her hand to see her fingers. Blood covered her fingertips.

Wincing, Danielle forced herself to sit up. She heard it, a long-ago familiar sound, the rattling of a chain. Confused, Danielle didn't know where she was. She couldn't remember what had happened. Her head spun, and she felt as if she might vomit.

Attempting to steady her breathing, she closed her eyes and sat there a moment. Then she heard it, a low moan. Was that her or someone else? she wondered. Opening her eyes, she tried moving her head to take in her surroundings. Forcing herself to turn to the right, wincing in pain, she looked to the sound of another moan.

"Walt!" Danielle cried out, reaching for the man lying next to her on the concrete floor. But there was no response. He remained lifeless next to her; the faint sound of his breathing and an intermittent groan told her he was still alive.

Leaning closer to Walt, she touched his head and discovered that, like her, blood covered his hair. Gently, she turned his face to hers. His eyes remained closed, and the wide gash along the top of his head was visible.

She realized the blood also covered his shirt, and she worried about how much he had already lost. Glancing down at their feet, she saw they were both chained to a pipe sticking out of the floor.

Afraid to cry out for help, for fear whoever chained them would appear, she looked around frantically, trying to get her bearings. Slowly, it all came back to her.

They had come to the old Porter place because they had heard it was haunted, and she had hoped the spirits could help them unravel the mystery. Walt had not wanted to go—this was all her fault. Now chained up in the barn, close to where they had discovered skeletal remains, they could die if Walt didn't wake up.

Danielle had believed it would be safe. Not only were the Stewarts gone for the weekend, but she had Walt with her. Walt, who could easily pick up a tree from the road to get Lily to the hospital in time to have Connor. Walt, who could snatch a loaded pistol from a killer's grasp and send it flying across the room. But this Walt was in no shape to do any of those things, and she feared if they didn't get him to the hospital in time, he might die.

She sat quietly and listened. Whoever had hit them both over the heads, knocked them unconscious, and chained their ankles was obviously not in the barn with them. If Stewart and his family were out of town for the weekend, who were their attackers?

Whoever they were, they had taken their cellphones. While she couldn't call her friends for help, there was always one of the ghosts. If she could get Wilbur, he could return to Beach Drive and tell one of the mediums what had happened and where they were. Or better yet, get Marie. Marie could save them.

First, she would start with the one spirit she had seen in the barn.

"Charlene! Please, Charlene, I need your help! Walt needs your help!" Danielle called out.

Charlene did not materialize, but a few minutes later the barn door opened. Danielle turned toward the light now streaming into the building. A man's silhouette blocked a portion of the incoming light. She couldn't see his face.

"What's with all the noise?" a familiar voice asked.

He stepped into the barn and walked toward her and Walt. When he got a few feet closer, she realized the information given to the chief had been wrong. Beau Stewart had not left town for the weekend.

"You?" Danielle said in surprise.

"You've made this easy for me," Beau said when he got closer, an unsettling smile on his face.

Danielle looked to Walt and back to Beau. "Walt could die if we don't get him to the hospital."

Beau shrugged. "Walt will die anyway. So will you." He casually grabbed hold of a folding chair and dragged it closer to Danielle. He sat on it and looked down at his prisoners.

"Why?" Danielle asked.

"Obviously I'm not comfortable with how much you know."

"What do we know that would be worth killing us?" Danielle asked.

"I always assumed you knew about Charlene, after reading *Moon Runners*. I wasn't sure how much information old Marlow left behind, and unfortunately there was a minor accident with those letters, so I couldn't be sure."

"Letters?"

"The ones from the safe," he explained.

"You took those letters?" Danielle asked, finally realizing he was the one Wilbur had overheard. *Yet why hadn't Wilbur recognized Beau?* she wondered. Surely Wilbur had seen Beau Stewart. Or, in his confused state, did he believe he was the Beau who had murdered him?

"Brad and Kathy did that job for me. They had a minor accident on the way back from your house. It had been a while since Kathy's ridden a bike. She took a little tumble. The bundle of letters landed in a puddle of water, and by the time they got them to me, the letters were soaked, illegible. All the ink had run."

"I still don't understand why you want to kill us. They murdered Charlene before you were even born—so were the rest of them."

"You don't have to understand," he said calmly. "Would you like to know how I plan to kill you?" He smiled.

"I would rather know why," she said.

"You need not know why, but I'll tell you how. You're chained up now because I'm not ready to kill you. First, we need to finish removing a few things…" He glanced briefly to the tarp Walt had lifted earlier and looked back to Danielle. "And we should be done by tomorrow night. I'd rather not wait much longer than that, because someone might come looking for you. But just in case they look earlier, I had my son get rid of your cellphones, dropped them off the pier. They won't be tracking you. I even turned off the GPS in your car."

"People know we're here," Danielle said. "It's not too late. You can let us go now. You don't want to face double homicide charges."

He laughed. "We overheard you and your husband out at the shed. You didn't tell anyone where you were going. In fact, according to your husband, the police chief will be annoyed when he finds out you came here."

"You will not get away with this."

Again he laughed. "Sweetheart, my family has an extensive history of getting away with this. And tomorrow night, when we're finished removing everything, there will be a little fire after I move your car from the garage to this barn. Not sure what you and Walt were up to, but I know you have a history of snooping around in places you don't belong. Didn't you almost get trapped in a fire a few years back? I read about that. You barely got out in time. That's what gave me the idea. I think you had been missing a few days that time. You really don't learn your lesson, do you?"

"Exactly how do you intend to explain the fire?" Danielle asked.

"You foolishly parked your car in the barn. I guess you didn't want anyone to see it while you were snooping around. You got a little close to some flammable material we had stored in here. Really a shame."

Speechless, Danielle stared at Beau as he laughed over her and Walt's imminent death. Before she could respond, Beau's son walked into the barn, carrying a burlap bag.

Beau glanced over to his son and asked, "Did you do it?"

"Yes. The phones and the other stuff are at the bottom of the ocean." He tossed his father the burlap bag and looked at Danielle, his expression chillingly calm.

To both of the men's astonishment, Danielle broke into a smile. "You shouldn't have dumped our phones off the pier."

The son frowned at her comment, and the father asked, "Exactly, why is that?"

"Cellphones rarely burn completely in a fire—and not two of them. Everyone knows both Walt and I each carry a cellphone. They'll wonder what happened to them. And who do you think will be the first people they look at? You. This is your property. And they also know about Beau Porter."

"What do they know about Beau Porter?" Brad asked.

"Those skeletal remains found across the street from Marlow House, the DNA results are back. That's why I thought you were out of town for the weekend. The police chief stopped by the rental to tell you they had a DNA match. You weren't there. A neighbor said you'd gone out of town for the weekend."

"What do you mean a DNA match? They don't have any DNA on the Porters," Brad snapped.

"They have cousin Earl's DNA. He willingly gave it to them a few years back," Danielle said.

"That fool," Beau grumbled.

"So I imagine they'll do some serious looking out here—especially after this barn burns down, they discover our bodies, and there's no sign of our cellphones."

"You think you're so smart," Beau snarled. He turned to his son and said, "Brad, you're going to have to take a quick trip back to Portland, pick up your scuba equipment at your apartment. There's some diving you need to do tomorrow before we have our little bonfire."

Beau reached out and gave his son a shove toward the door for him to start walking. He followed Brad and paused before stepping outside.

Looking back to Danielle, Beau said, "Thanks for the heads-up on the minor glitch in our plan. But it's an easy fix."

Danielle watched the pair leave the barn, closing and locking the door behind them.

"It was just to buy some time, you idiots," Danielle said aloud. "If you kill us, you can bet I'll stick around and let my friends know exactly what happened. You won't get away with this."

THIRTY-SIX

C upping his face in her hands, careful not to move his head for fear of inflicting more damage, Danielle whispered, "I'm so sorry, Walt."

"I warned you it wasn't safe. You shouldn't be here," a male voice said.

Gently releasing hold of Walt, Danielle turned toward the voice. Standing before her was the one she and Walt had called a hippy.

"Who are you?" she asked.

"I wondered at first if you were dead, like me," he said.

"You know you're dead?" Danielle asked.

"Yes. Didn't I say there was no hope for me?" He sat down in the chair Beau had been using earlier. "You're the first one I've met. First medium, I mean. That's what you are, right?"

"Yes. My name is Danielle Marlow."

"I know, your husband introduced you both when we met." He nodded to Walt's lifeless body. "I assume he's still alive since I haven't seen his spirit."

"Yes, but will you please help me?" she begged.

"If I can, but I'm not sure how," he said.

"There are others like me and Walt, who can see spirits. If you can get them a message, then they can send help," Danielle urged.

"I'm so sorry. I would if I could, but years ago I made a vow that until the truth came out about the Porter family, I wouldn't leave this place. I'm ashamed to admit that many years ago, in frustration, I tried to break that vow, but it seems I can't. Whenever I step off the property, I find myself back here."

"Oh my," Danielle muttered. "What about Wilbur?"

"Do you know Wilbur?" he asked.

"We've met. And I know he can help me if he's willing."

"None of them know they're dead. But I suspect Wilbur understands now," he told her.

"Wilbur knows. He understands, and that's why I'm sure he can help us. Can you get him for me? Please."

"He's not here at the moment, but I'll know when he returns. I'll see what I can do then," he promised.

"Do you know the person responsible for putting us here—Beau Stewart?" Danielle asked.

"I know who he is. But I've only seen him here once before. He drove off a little while ago with his son. The son has been here about every day for the last week. At least, I think it's been about a week. I'm not so good with time anymore."

"What has the son been doing here?" Danielle asked.

"He's the one doing the excavating. Trying to dig us all up."

"Um…do you have any…gifts?"

He frowned. "Gifts?"

"Powers. Can you move objects, for example?"

"Oh, not really. I've slammed a door or two. It's Dolly who gets worked up sometimes, gets things moving. She has a temper, but I can't say I blame her."

"Who are you? I know who the others are, but who are you?" Danielle asked.

He smiled. "I'm sorry, that's rude of me. My name is Earl, Earl Barr."

"Are you the other Earl's father? The one who used to live here?"

"Yes, that's my son. He's not doing very well. I'm glad my granddaughters moved him someplace safe. And I'm grateful they've made a life away from this place. That's one blessing I can count in all this." Earl let out a deep sigh and leaned back in his chair.

"Why are you here? Why did you vow to stay? How did you die?"

"I'll start with the last question because it leads to the others. I'm here because my wife murdered me and buried me behind the house. Rumor has it I deserted my family."

"Why did she murder you?" Danielle asked.

"I refused to keep the family secret. When I married Georgia, I was unaware of the secret, but then I decided to clean up the old hog shed and found Dolly's remains. I wanted to call the authorities, but she had other ideas."

"That makes no sense, just like Beau Stewart. Dolly was killed long before your wife was born."

"Ahh...it wasn't just about Dolly; it was the family secret. Had I been willing to keep it, then there would've been no reason to kill me. She explained everything after I discovered Dolly's remains. When she realized I wasn't on board, she did what the descendants of Beau Porter do. In her case, she hit me over the head with a cast-iron skillet while I was tying my shoe."

"What secret is that?" Danielle asked.

"It's a family of serial killers. And each generation finds it necessary to educate the next generation on their ancestors' evil deeds and to, well, keep it all in the family."

"Serial killers?" Danielle squeaked.

Earl let out a sigh and said, "Yes. When I first set eyes on my Georgia, she was such a pretty little thing. Sweet, innocent—I later learned as sweet as a viper."

"Who else did she kill?" Danielle asked.

"Aside from me and our son's hopes and dreams, no one that I'm aware of."

"You said serial killers?"

"Ahh...well, I meant more in a collective sense. It first started with the patriarch of the family, Beau Porter. He, with the help of his son Ambrose, murdered Wilbur. Ambrose was the overachiever of the group. Before he helped kill Wilbur, he'd strangled poor Dolly after he caught her trying to run away with their son, Baxter. Old man Porter helped him bury the body and backed up his story about the girl running off."

"Horrible," Danielle muttered.

"Then there was Charlene. According to family legend, Beau Junior shamed the Porter name by planning to elope with a colored woman. Beau Senior took care of Charlene, and Ambrose got rid of the body. They both convinced Beau she had run off with another man."

"So who killed Beau junior?" Danielle asked.

"That was Ambrose. According to the story—and they loved passing those gruesome tales down in the family—Walt Marlow, I assume not your husband but someone with the same name…" He paused a moment and chuckled at the absurdity of the Marlow of the family story being the same man lying unconscious a few feet away. "Anyway, Walt Marlow brought Beau home one night, drunk out of his mind, crying over Charlene and how she had left him. Ambrose got sick of him crying, shot him in the head, and convinced their father Beau had committed suicide. Old man Beau didn't want the world to know how weak his son had been that he had taken his own life, so they told everyone he took off."

"Wow."

"Dolly keeps looking for her baby, but if she found Baxter, it would break her heart. He was a kid when they killed Wilbur, and he helped them bury the body. He also helped his father get rid of Charlene, and he knew his father had murdered his uncle, and he never told his grandfather. He even knew about his old man killing his mother."

"I was right when I called this a house of horrors." Danielle looked to Walt and reached out, gently touching him, wanting to assure herself he was still alive.

"Baxter was my father-in-law. I never met him. But he and his wife had twins, my wife, Georgia, and Beau Stewart's mother, Ida. Ida married later in life, and from what I've picked up over the years, he fit into this family. In fact, from what I've overheard, Beau's father parlayed Ida's inheritance into a fortune."

"Your son, Earl, knew all of this?" Danielle asked.

"Yes. Baxter told his daughters everything, passing down the family secrets—secrets to keep and only share with their children and maybe a spouse. When he died, he divided up his estate, left half to each daughter. Georgia got this property along with others, and Ida stayed on until she married. Did I mention she helped her sister bury my body?"

"Lovely," Danielle said with a grimace. "And did Earl pass this all on to your granddaughters?"

"Thankfully, no. The boy had some problems. Gambled away his inheritance. Got rough with his wife once in a while. But you have to understand, when he was fourteen, he learned what his mother had done to me. While he never told the authorities, he refused to pass down the ugliness of his family to his daughters. He wanted to break that cycle. So he did what he could to push them away. He didn't know how to be a loving father. He believed he was toxic."

"How sad," Danielle murmured.

"One blessing I had by staying here, I watched my granddaughters grow up. They were good girls. They had a good mother. She knew nothing about her husband's family. She only knew he had a cousin he didn't like."

Danielle started to ask a question, but Earl hushed her and said, "It's Wilbur. He's back." The next moment Earl disappeared.

Turning to Walt, Danielle ran her fingertips down his face and silently prayed Wilbur would help her. Several minutes later Earl appeared back in the barn, with Wilbur by his side.

"What happened?" Wilbur asked when he took in the sight of Danielle and Walt, both with head injuries and chained to the floor, and one unconscious. Before she could answer, he said, "I came back here looking for you. I saw him again, the one with the hook nose who I overheard at the pier. He was with the man who took the gunnysack and threw it in the ocean."

"Hook nose? You never mentioned the man at the pier had a hook nose," Danielle said. Had Wilbur thought to mention that before, she might not be here now, Danielle thought.

"I didn't? Well, that doesn't matter now. I saw them driving down the street and recognized him. So I followed them. They ended up at a house in Frederickport. The younger one—the one I've seen here before—he was on his way to Portland. And they said something about hook nose's wife and daughter already being in Portland, and him wanting them to stay a few extra days."

"Hook nose, as you call him, that's Beau Stewart. He's the great-great-grandson of Beauregard Porter Senior," Danielle explained.

"Beau Porter murdered me!" Wilbur growled.

"Yes, and the other Beau wants to murder me and Walt. Please help us. Go find Marie or one of the mediums on Beach Drive. Tell them Walt and I are being held prisoner at the old Barr place in the barn, and that he plans to murder us. Hurry. Tell them Walt needs medical attention. I'm so worried about him."

The next moment Wilbur agreed to help and vanished.

CHRIS CANCELLED his drive to Astoria when Danielle and Walt never showed up to watch Hunny. Heather returned to Lily and Ian's house to discuss their missing friends. Chris joined them. Marie had taken off to look for Walt and Danielle, yet when she returned to Ian and Lily's, about thirty minutes after Chris and Heather's arrival, she only had Eva with her.

"Any news?" Marie asked when she and Eva appeared in the middle of the living room.

"Marie and Eva are here," Chris told Lily and Ian.

"None. We were hoping you'd know something," Heather said.

"I'm sorry I'm barging in like this," a male voice said. Yet only the spirits and mediums could hear him. "But I saw Marie through the window."

The spirits and mediums turned to the voice and found a man standing just inside the living room.

"Wilbur?" Marie said.

"Danielle sent me. She and Walt are in trouble."

THIRTY-SEVEN

It didn't take Lily and Ian long to figure out another ghost had joined them. Chris played interpreter while Wilbur explained the situation.

Once realizing Danielle and Walt were in danger, Lily said, "We need to call the police!" She stood up to grab her cellphone off the coffee table, but Chris stopped her from making the call.

"We don't have time, and if the police charge up there, sirens on, it could get them both killed. Plus, if we can't reach the chief, how do we explain to the dispatcher how we know where they are?" Chris said.

"We have to do something!" Lily cried.

"We will. We'll do what Danielle wanted." Chris looked at Marie. "Marie can get up there faster than anyone. Heather and I will follow."

"Where exactly are they? I need to hurry!" Marie said.

"They're in the barn, but I'll go with you, show you where they are," Wilbur offered.

"Wait a second," Chris said, looking from Wilbur to Eva. "Eva, please go with Marie and meet us at the road to let us know when it's safe for us to come up."

"I should probably go instead," Ian suggested.

Heather shook her head. "No, Chris is right. You won't be able to communicate with the spirits."

"And stay here, try to get the chief on the phone; let him know what's going on," Chris told Ian. "We'll figure out what we need to tell the police if you can't get ahold of him. But first, we need to make sure Danielle and Walt are safe."

As the three spirits prepared to leave, Wilbur paused a moment and smiled at Eva. "You're really Eva Thorndike. I'm an enormous fan."

"You are?" Eva said with a smile as the three spirits disappeared.

WHEN DANIELLE HAD BEEN TRAPPED in Presley House, almost four years earlier, she had been unbelievably thirsty—as thirsty as she was now. But back then she didn't have Walt to worry about, and she could not dwell on her own discomfort, not when the man she loved remained so still next to her. She kept praying he would wake up. While there was some comfort in knowing their death was not the end, and they would still be together, she was not ready to move on. Life was precious, she told herself, even when death provided new adventures. She was not ready to say goodbye to this world and to her friends.

Danielle glanced down at her stomach and touched it lightly with one hand. "Walt," she whispered, "we need to get out of this mess, and then, I think you're right, time to stop using birth control."

A creaking sound interrupted her thoughts, and she looked over to the barn door. Someone was opening it. Danielle's heart lurched, and for a moment she imagined their rescuers had arrived. But the silhouette that appeared soon proved to be foe, not friend. Beau Stewart stood in the doorway, and he carried a pillow.

"I bet you didn't expect to see me back so soon." He sauntered toward her, carrying the pillow in his left hand while absently giving it punches with his right fist.

"Beau is back," Earl announced when he appeared a moment later. He looked at Beau and cringed. "I see he's already here. I saw his car parked out back."

"Why are you here?" Danielle asked him.

"There's a change of plans," Beau said, giving the pillow another punch. "When we first chained you up, my son wanted to get his pistol and take care of you. I had to explain to him, we really don't want the coroner to find your charcoaled skull with a bullet hole. Rather defeats the purpose." He laughed.

"I don't feel good about this," Earl groaned. "I hope Wilbur gets back here soon with your friends."

"And now?" Danielle asked, feeling sick inside.

"Before he took off to Portland to get his scuba gear—oh, and I do want to thank you for pointing out that minor flaw in our plan. You probably saved us from getting caught. Anyway, he really didn't like leaving you alive. He tends to be a worrier, like his mother. He had a point, and I realized, who needs a gun when you have one of these?" He held up the pillow.

"You plan to smother us?" Danielle asked.

"You catch on quick. I'll do you first. I figure you'll put up a fight, and with Walt there, he'll be easy."

Motion behind Beau caught Danielle's attention. Standing in the open doorway, a scant distance from Beau, stood the image of Dolly Porter, a confused and troubled spirit. She was also a spirit who could harness energy.

"Dolly! Please help me! He plans to kill me! Like Ambrose killed you!" Danielle called out frantically.

"Oh, shut up. Stop with your hysterics," Beau said, moving to Danielle with the pillow.

"Dolly, please!" Danielle pleaded.

"Help her, Dolly!" Earl cried out. "He *is* just like Ambrose!"

Now standing over Danielle, Beau said, "Why don't you make this easier on yourself and lie still. Less painful than burning alive. You should actually thank me. It'll be over in a minute."

"Dolly, please!" Still sitting on the floor, her ankle chained to the pipe, Danielle raised her arms to shield herself from the attack.

Beau laughed as he forced himself on her, covering her face with the pillow and pushing her head down to the concrete floor while using his weight to hold down her body. He was there only a moment when the pillow was ripped from his grasp and sailed across the barn while his body flew in the opposite direction, landing violently against one barn wall, knocking all the breath from his lungs as his body fell to the hard floor in a battered heap.

Her heart racing, Danielle lowered her arms and looked up. Dolly hovered over her, bathed in a golden glow, wearing a somber expression.

"Will you see I have a proper burial?" Dolly asked.

"I promise," Danielle said as a groan came from Beau. She looked to him and watched in horror as he stumbled to his feet, a determined look on his face as he glared in her direction. He did not understand what had just happened, but he was damn sure going to finish it.

Dolly didn't need to intervene again, for in the next moment Marie, Eva, and Wilbur appeared in the barn, standing between an angry and dazed Beau and his intended victim.

"Thank God you're here, Marie!" Danielle called out, relief washing over her.

"I don't know what your problem is, lady, but if you believe making me think you talk to imaginary people will save your neck, you're crazy." Beau took one step toward Danielle but soon found himself flung upward to the high ceiling, where he remained, looking down at everyone. However, the only ones he could see were Danielle and Walt. He did not understand the spirits of Marie, Eva, Dolly, Wilbur and Earl curiously watched him. Had there been more lighting in the barn, they would have seen the color in Beau's face drain away. Terror filled his now wide eyes as the hands on his outstretched arms tried desperately to grasp for anything to keep him from falling, yet nothing was there.

Gripped with fear, Beau cried out, "Someone help me!" A more rational Beau, one not floating at the ceiling of a barn, would understand making such a plea was futile when the only people within hearing were the two he had attacked, restrained, and whom he had moments earlier prepared to smother. Sobs followed the plea.

Those gathered in the barn were more concerned with the two people bloodied and restrained than the man hovering overhead. Marie urged Eva to check on Walt and Danielle while she kept her attention on Beau to keep him from plummeting to the concrete floor. Not that she cared about the horrid man's safety, but she had no desire for him to avoid the punishment of the living world by escaping to the spirit realm, and a splattered Beau would be difficult for Danielle and Walt to explain. Of course, once Beau moved over to her side, he would probably find the consequences for his actions dire.

Eva knelt by Walt and Danielle's side.

"We need to get Walt to the hospital. He's been unconscious for hours. I'm so worried about him!" Danielle sobbed, no longer able to maintain her composure.

"Chris and Heather are on their way. They'll call for someone. I need to see if they're here yet. It will be okay, Danielle, I promise," Eva vowed in a gentle voice.

AFTER GHOSTLY INTRODUCTIONS, Dolly stayed by Walt and Danielle's side while Eva went to find Heather and Chris. Earl and Wilbur stood with Marie, looking up at Beau Stewart, who hovered overhead.

"I'm impressed," Wilbur said. "How do you do that?"

"Watch this," Marie said. Beau started spinning like a top for several moments and then stopped. They all laughed.

"Be careful with that. He might puke," Earl said. "While it would go right through us, it would still be gross."

Minutes later Eva returned with Chris and Heather. The pair rushed to Walt and Danielle.

"Oh no, Walt, is he dead?" Heather cried.

"No, he's not dead," Eva assured her, giving them a brief introduction to Dolly.

"Thank God you're here," Danielle sobbed.

Heather reached out and took Danielle's hand while Chris checked Walt's vitals. Danielle hastily told them what had happened. Chris pulled out his cellphone and said, "I'm calling for the police and paramedics."

Heather glanced up at the man hovering overhead and said, "Yeah, well, while you do that, we need to get that sleaze down and tied up. I hope there's some rope around here."

There wasn't.

SOMEONE MUST HAVE SLIPPED him some hallucinogenic drugs, Beau thought. One minute he was preparing to get rid of the Marlows and the next he was up on the ceiling looking down. And then he started spinning. It was worse than carnival rides he had ridden as a child.

Once he realized this was all some bad trip, he pulled himself together and stopped sobbing like a little wimp. He would get through this, he told himself. The next moment he plummeted to the floor, stopping just inches from full impact.

Beau's heart raced as he lay flat on the cold concrete, unable to move. It felt as if someone was restraining his arms and legs, but no one was there. He was no longer alone in the barn with Walt and Danielle. Chris Johnson and the woman Kathy thought looked like a witch had showed up, and the witch blabbered on about not being able to find any rope.

He heard sirens. They grew louder. Turning his head to one side, he watched as the witch jumped up and yelled, "I'll show them where we are." She raced out of the barn.

Chris Johnson stood over him, talking to himself, like he was trying to figure out what to do. The next moment Beau found himself flipped on his belly and his arms pulled behind his back. Squirming wildly, Beau still could not move his arms or legs.

Beau heard Chris say, "Marie, whatever you do, don't let him go," before climbing on his back and taking hold of his wrists. Several minutes later police and paramedics filled the barn, and he found himself being pulled to a standing position after Chris moved off him and allowed several police officers to take charge.

Still trying to grasp the series of events following his failed attempt to smother Danielle, Beau recognized one of the police officers in the group. It was Brian Henderson, who in the next moment asked, "What the hell is going on here?"

THIRTY-EIGHT

The police did not understand the situation in the barn, yet the paramedics deemed it urgent to get Walt to the hospital, considering his condition. Danielle also required medical attention.

Before they could take either person to the waiting ambulance, there was the matter of removing the chains, which required keys to unlock the padlocks. When one officer asked Beau where the keys were, he yelled, "How would I know? I had nothing to do with this!" While it took more time, they freed Walt and Danielle without keys.

Beau demanded they remove his handcuffs. "I had nothing to do with what happened here!" he said belligerently. "Do you know who I am?"

"We know who you are, Mr. Stewart," Sergeant Joe Morelli said politely as the paramedics removed Walt and Danielle from the barn. "But according to Mrs. Marlow, you were the one who attacked them."

"Even if I did, which I didn't, this is my property. They were trespassing!" Beau said. "I've been with my family in Portland, and I came back to check on things. We recently purchased this property, and we're renting a house in Frederickport while we remodel this place. I worry about vandalism while we're away."

"Vandalism?" Chris interrupted. "You told us the other day you intended to tear all the buildings down. Why would you be so concerned about vandalism?"

"Because when vandals come on your property, people can get hurt, and obviously that's what happened with the Marlows. But I had nothing to do with it! Now let me go!" Beau ranted.

"We'll discuss this down at the police station," Joe said, passing Beau to two of his officers. Beau continued to rant as they took him away.

Joe looked at Chris and said, "I've already told Heather I don't want either of you to leave yet. I intend to interview both of you in a minute, you first and then Heather. So stay right there." Joe turned away and walked to Brian.

"Marie, Eva," Chris whispered. Dolly had disappeared when the responders had arrived, but Marie and Eva remained standing by Chris with Wilbur and Earl.

"Yes?" Marie asked.

Keeping his voice down and turning so none of the remaining responders would think he was talking to himself, Chris said, "I need you both to listen to what I tell the police when they interview me. And then let Heather know before they interview her, so our stories match. And then one of you needs to get to the hospital and tell Danielle what I said."

"You also need to tell them about the human remains," Wilbur added.

Chris looked questioningly at Wilbur and Earl. The two ghosts began filling Chris in on what he hadn't yet been told.

BRIAN AND JOE silently listened to Chris's version of the day's events.

"Walt and Danielle agreed to watch Hunny today while I went to Astoria. But when I got over there, they weren't home. And they weren't answering their cellphones. I went over to see if Lily and Ian had heard from them; they hadn't. So I asked Heather. She told me she was in the alley behind her house when they were driving away this morning. They stopped a moment to talk to her. Said they were taking a drive over here."

"Why did they come over here?" Brian asked.

"At the party Beau had talked about all the work they were doing on the property. I assume they were just curious about what he had done so far."

"Where's their car?" Joe asked.

"I haven't seen it." Chris shrugged. He really didn't know where their car was.

"Then what happened?" Brian asked.

"Heather and I drove over here to see if we could find them. We came up the back way, parked. We didn't think anything about not seeing their car. Figured it could be out front. We got out for a moment, just intending to look around, when we heard screaming."

"Screaming?" Brian asked.

"Yeah. Someone was shouting for help. Turned out it was Danielle. We found her and Walt chained up in here. She told us Beau had attacked them, chained them up, and intended to smother them and burn down the barn. But when she started yelling, and then we showed up, it scared him off."

"But you had him when we got here?" Joe said.

"About five or ten minutes after I called 911, Heather started yelling. She saw Beau trying to sneak out of a stall. I guess he hid after we got here. So I tackled him and held him until you arrived."

"Is there anything else?" Joe asked.

"Well, there's the human remains buried in that shed out back, and then the ones under there." Chris pointed to the tarp.

HEATHER SAT on the lone folding chair in the barn and watched as Brian and Joe interviewed Chris. She couldn't hear their conversation, yet with the double doors pushed wide open and the position of the late afternoon sun, light streamed into the old barn, providing ample illumination for Heather to see Chris and the two officers. Focusing on Chris's lips, she tried figuring out what he was saying, yet soon admitted she sucked at lip-reading. Heather dreaded being interviewed, not knowing what Chris had told them. Why hadn't they gotten their stories straight before the police had arrived?

"Why the worried face?" Wilbur asked when he appeared by Heather's side. After she told him her concern, he smiled and said, "Don't worry, Chris already thought of that."

"EVA THORNDIKE, IS THAT YOU?" a woman's voice called out amongst the commotion in the barn. Only the remaining spirits heard. Marie had already left to the hospital to check on Walt and Danielle, and to tell Danielle what Chris had told the police. Dolly had not returned, and Chris and Heather were outside, walking back to Chris's car. The remaining police officers were currently taking a closer look at the skeletal remains found under the tarp and concrete.

"Charlene?" Eva said.

"It is you!" Charlene gasped.

Eva reached out her hand to Charlene. "Come, we need to talk."

"I'M afraid you can't see Mrs. Marlow now," the nurse told Joe and Brian. They stood in front of the nurses' station on the third floor. "She was just given a sedative."

"We understand Walt Marlow is in intensive care?" Brian asked.

"Yes," the nurse said, offering no additional information.

Brian spied Lily and Heather sitting together in the small waiting area next to the nurses' station. He nudged Joe and nodded toward the women.

"LOOK WHO'S HERE," Marie chirped when Brian and Joe walked up to Lily and Heather in the waiting room. The two women looked up at the officers, who did not understand the spirit of Marie Nichols sat with them.

"How's Danielle doing?" Joe asked.

Lily looked up to Joe. "They just gave her a sedative. But they said she would be all right. It's Walt we're worried about. Chris just went to talk to the doctors in ICU about him."

"They won't say anything to Chris," Joe told her. "He's not a family member."

Lily smiled wearily up to Joe, her bloodshot eyes free of any makeup, washed clean by her tears. "They will. Both Chris and I have a medical power of attorney for Walt and Danielle, and they have it on Chris."

"Did you find their car?" Heather asked. Wilbur had already told her the answer. But she was curious if they would tell them.

"Yes. We found it in the garage, with the keys in it. Beau Stewart claims Walt or Danielle must have parked it there. But his fingerprints were all over the car and keys," Brian said.

"Beau Stewart is a homicidal maniac," Heather said. "I assume you found the skeletal remains?"

"Yes. The ones Chris told us about, in the shed, and in the barn. Our team is still out there."

"They need to check behind the house, too," Marie said.

"I bet you'll find more," Heather said. "You need to dig around the house."

AFTER BRIAN and Joe left the waiting room, they headed for intensive care. En route, they ran into Chris.

"Lily said you were checking on Walt," Joe said when they stopped in the hall to talk with him. "How's he doing?"

"Good, actually. He finally came to. But they're still running some tests. I've arranged for them to move Walt and Danielle into the same hospital room," Chris said. "Hopefully within the next couple of hours."

"They'll do that?" Joe asked.

"He really doesn't need to be in ICU," Chris said. "And both of them will heal faster if they're together, not worrying about the other one."

FIFTEEN MINUTES LATER, Brian and Joe stood together in front of the hospital elevator, waiting for its door to open so they could go down to the first floor and head to the police station.

"Chris and Heather told the exact same story when we questioned them," Brian noted.

"Almost like they rehearsed it," Joe said.

"Do we want to place bets that Beau Stewart is the one the chief wanted us to be on the lookout for on Wednesday?" Brian asked.

"It looks that way, considering what they've been digging up. And the burlap sacks we found in the barn, we already knew the remains were related to Barr; now we know where they came from before they got tossed in the ocean."

"This entire thing is crazy," Brian said.

"You know what else is crazy," Joe asked.

"What?"

"That Chris would have a medical power of attorney over Walt and Danielle, and they would have it over him."

"I know it used to be that way, before Walt came along," Brian said.

"Right, when Chris and Danielle were dating. And neither one had any family. But seriously? Would you feel comfortable having the guy who used to date your wife have the power to pull the plug? Or let your old girlfriend's new husband have that power?"

Brian chuckled. "Yeah, when you put it like that, it's weird."

"That entire Beach Drive group, I don't know, it's like they have some secret club. Kelly often feels like an outsider. Ian's her brother, and she shouldn't have to feel that way."

"They invite you guys to all their parties," Brian reminded him.

"Yeah, because Ian is Kelly's brother," Joe grumbled. "When I first met Ian, back when Danielle and Lily moved to town, I felt closer to Ian. We had a lot of fun."

"Then we arrested Danielle for murder and the fun ended," Brian said with a laugh as the elevator door opened.

"We've gone beyond that," Joe said as he stepped into the empty elevator. "They even invite you to their parties now."

Brian followed Joe into the elevator but didn't respond to his comment because he spied two nurses running in their direction. He held the elevator open for them. Once inside, the nurses thanked Brian, punched in their desired floor number, and then began chatting amongst themselves. The door closed.

"It must be nice to have that much money," one nurse said to the other.

"I don't think it's his money, it's the foundation's. But that generous donation will be appreciated by the hospital."

"All I can say, the Marlows must be close friends if he's willing to risk his job just to change around some hospital rooms."

"I thought it was against hospital protocol. But hey, who says no to a generous benefactor? I'd like to have a friend like that," the other nurse said.

The elevator stopped on the second floor. The door opened, and the nurses stepped out. When the door closed again, Brian said, "I don't think Chris has to worry about losing his job with the foundation."

THIRTY-NINE

W hen the sedative finally wore off and Danielle woke up, she was not alone in the hospital room. Marie sat by her side. Danielle was both disoriented and confused, but Marie held her hand and gently explained what had happened and why she was in the hospital. While Danielle understood Marie's body was only an illusion, and there was no actual hand holding hers, only the pressure of energy exerted by Marie to give the illusion of the intimacy, Danielle appreciated the gesture. While she had lost her own beloved grandmother years before, and then her parents, there was comfort knowing a grandmotherly figure was by her side, one who sincerely cared for her.

"And Walt?" Danielle asked.

"Walt's awake. While you were sleeping, they moved you to another room, and they're bringing Walt down from ICU to share this room with you. He should be here soon. I checked on him just a while ago."

"And he's okay?" Danielle asked.

"Yes, dear. They want to keep him over for observation. In fact, they want to keep both of you. But the tests have all come back, and there doesn't seem to be anything of significant concern. You need to rest."

"Oh, Max," Danielle said, remembering he had been alone all day.

"I already popped over there and let Max know what was going on, and I fed him," Marie said. "He just wants you to get better so you can get back home."

"Thank you, Marie. Do you know what happened to Beau Stewart?" Danielle asked.

"I know they've arrested him. He left the barn kicking and screaming, saying *'Don't you know who I am!'* But I've been at the hospital since they brought you here, so I'm afraid I don't know. But I imagine Chris or Lily will stop by later and update you. They were here earlier, but you had just had a sedative, so they couldn't come in. Heather was here too."

"I wish I had my phone." Danielle groaned and said, "I just remembered, they dropped it off the pier."

"You can get another phone, dear. Just as long as you're both okay. That's what's important."

Commotion from the open doorway caught their attention, and they looked to see Walt being wheeled into the hospital room.

"Walt!" Danielle cried out.

He reached his hand out to her, and she to him, yet they were not close enough to touch.

After the nurses settled Walt into his hospital bed and left the room, Marie said, "I'll let you two have some privacy." She vanished.

"Oh, Walt, I'm so sorry," Danielle said, bursting out in tears.

"Why are you sorry? And please don't cry!" He looked to the table next to him and willed a tissue from its box, sending it floating across the room to Danielle.

She snatched the tissue from midair, gave a sniffle, and smiled before using it to wipe her eyes and blow her nose. "This is all my fault."

"It's not. It's Beau Stewart's fault. I'm just sorry I wasn't listening to myself, and they got the jump on us."

"What do you mean, listening to yourself?" Danielle asked.

"I had a premonition when we were standing in that shed. I knew something was about to happen, but I brushed it off, told myself I was letting my imagination run away with me. I should have listened."

"What kind of premonition?"

"It's not that I saw what was about to happen, but I felt something bad was about to happen. That's why I was eager to leave."

Danielle let out a sigh and said, "You don't understand how relieved I am that you're okay."

"And you don't understand how annoyed I am with Chris," he countered.

"Chris? Why?" Danielle asked.

"First, he races to our rescue with Heather and helps save us. Then, according to the nurses, he pulled some strings, along with some bribery—by a donation to the hospital—to get you and me moved to the same room."

"You didn't want to be saved? You don't want to share a room with me?"

"Yes, of course. But now I have to be nice to Chris." He laughed.

Danielle rolled her eyes. "You're always nice to Chris."

Walt grinned. "He's a good friend."

A knock came at the door. They looked over and saw the chief standing just inside the room.

"I hope you're up for a visit?" the chief said.

"Come in, Edward," Walt said.

"Hey, Chief, so you're back," Danielle greeted him. "Heather told me at the barn Ian couldn't get ahold of you."

"That's what I get for turning off my phone so I can spend some quality time with the boys." He walked over to Danielle and gave her hand a gentle squeeze and then shook Walt's hand before pulling up a chair and sitting between them.

"We are a pain," Danielle said.

"Yes, you are," the chief agreed. "Ian called me before Brian did. He filled me in on what happened, and I went right down to the station."

"Marie said they arrested Beau?"

The chief nodded. "He's not talking until his lawyer gets here, and that won't be until Monday morning. But they've uncovered the skeletal remains for four people over there. Two in the barn, one in the shed and another behind the house. They're looking for more."

"I don't think they'll find more," Danielle told him.

"Are you sure?" the chief asked.

"I suppose it's possible there are others, and their spirits moved on. But we only saw five spirits over there, and that includes Beau Porter Junior, who I assume belongs to the remains that washed up on shore."

"So who are they; do you know?" the chief asked.

"Dolly Porter, Earl Barr and Beau Stewart's great-grandmother, who I assume you'll at least be able to determine they're related by a DNA test. She was the one in the shed. Then Earl Barr Senior, who is the father to Earl Barr, whose DNA you already have. I'm sure he's the one you found behind the house. Wilbur's remains should show a match with the one Betty White has on file, and then you probably want to ask the Kings for a DNA match. I assume one is Charlene Davis."

"What I'm trying to understand, why exactly did Beau Stewart want you dead?" the chief asked.

"He was definitely the one Wilbur overheard at the pier, and I assume his daughter was the woman he was talking to. She was the one who broke into Marlow House with her brother and took the letters," Danielle said. "But I still don't understand why."

"Those deaths all happened years ago," the chief said. "I can understand he wouldn't want the world knowing about the murders his ancestors committed, with him running for Congress. But killing you is extreme."

BACK ON BEACH DRIVE, the friends asked the same question. Why was Beau Stewart so desperate to get Walt's diary? Why was he prepared to kill them? It was a question they feared would not get answered, and one Heather woke up Sunday morning thinking about.

She had just poured herself some hot tea when Marie appeared in her kitchen to give her an update on Walt and Danielle.

"Glad you're here!" Heather said.

"You are?" Marie asked in surprise.

Heather sipped her tea and said, "Actually, I wanted to talk to you. But why are you here?"

"To tell you Walt and Danielle are doing very well this morning."

"That's a relief. Walt had me worried." Heather took another sip of tea.

"Why did you want to see me?" Marie asked.

"I need you to help me do something," Heather said.

"What?"

"I want to convince Beau Stewart to explain why he wanted to kill Walt and Danielle."

"And exactly how do you expect to do that?" Marie asked.

"Show him his daughter was right. I'm a witch."

HEATHER SAT with Marie in her car in the police station parking lot thirty minutes later.

"I don't believe you thought this out very well. How do you expect to get in there to talk to him?" Marie asked. "Edward's car isn't even here, so he can't help you."

"I don't want to involve the chief. But I know Stewart's here in lockup, and according to what Joe once told me, a prisoner can normally have visitors, but only if they agree to see them."

"Do you honestly think he'll agree to see you?" Marie asked.

Gnawing on her right thumbnail, Heather scrunched up her nose as she stared out the windshield, looking at the police station entrance. "Let me think a minute; I'll figure something out."

A car pulled into the parking lot and drove by Heather's car, parking behind her. Abruptly she sat up straight. "That was Beau's son," she said excitedly.

"How is that going to help?" Marie asked.

"Watch," Heather said, rolling down her driver's side window.

Just as Brad walked by, she called out, "Hey, I have a message for your father."

He stopped and looked her way but said nothing and didn't approach the window.

Heather smiled at him and said, "If your father wants to get out of this, he needs to talk to me."

"What are you up to?" Marie asked.

Hesitantly, Brad walked to her car. "Why would my dad need to talk to you?"

"I was there yesterday when your father got arrested. But I'm willing to change my story, which will help your dad get off. I know something about Chris and Danielle that'll help him."

"What do you know?"

"I'm not telling you. I'll only talk to your father."

"Why would you want to help him?" he asked.

"I'll do about anything for the right price," Heather told him.

HE HAD TO ADMIT; he was curious to hear what she had to say. Sitting alone in the jail cell, he watched as the door opened and a police officer led Heather to his cell.

Her complexion was paler than he remembered, a stark contrast to her inky black hair, its length straight and falling past her shoulders. She wore thick dark eyeliner and blood red lipstick. He thought her dress more appropriate for a Halloween costume, fashioned from black crepe and just short enough to show off black boots. Beau remembered what his daughter had said in jest about Heather being a witch, and he wondered what she would say if she saw her now. He wanted to laugh at the thought, but he didn't think it prudent to insult her before she helped him. And if Heather Donovan imagined herself a witch, he really didn't care, as long as he got out of this mess.

"You have ten minutes," the officer told her before leaving them alone.

Beau stood up and walked closer to Heather; bars separated them. "How can you help me?"

"Oh, I lied about that. I just needed to talk to you."

He frowned and started to yell for the guard. She pointed a finger at him and wiggled it upwards. He flew up to the ceiling and hovered there a moment before coming back down. His feet landed on the floor. No longer calling for the guard, he stared at her, wide-eyed.

"Don't do that again or you'll be sorry," Heather said in a low menacing voice.

"What are you?" he stammered.

"I'm a witch," Heather said brightly.

He opened his mouth to say something, but she pointed her finger at him again, and he could feel himself lifting off the ground. He immediately stopped talking.

"That's better," she said. "I have something to tell you, and then I'll leave. Don't interrupt me, or I'll put you up there and send you spinning like I did at the barn."

Beau swallowed nervously and said nothing.

"I put a curse on you. You will starve yourself. From this moment on, you'll be unable to eat or drink. You'll either starve to death or die of dehydration…although now that I think about it, it will probably be from dehydration. I'm pretty sure a person can go without food longer than water. Either way, you'll be dead. Unless you break the curse."

"How do I do that?" he asked dully. He didn't know if he should laugh or cry. It all sounded absurd, but he didn't know how he could explain what had happened back at the barn and just a minute ago.

"There is only one way to break the curse. You must tell Police Chief MacDonald why you wanted to kill the Marlows, and why you wanted Walt Marlow's diary, and you need to tell him every-thing. Until you do that—until you tell him everything—you won't be able to eat or drink. Do you understand?"

Beau stared at Heather yet said nothing. She flashed him a smile and turned, heading for the door. Just as she was about to ring the buzzer for the guard, she looked back to Beau and said, "By the way, you really shouldn't hit yourself."

The next moment his right hand flew up and smacked him in the face.

FORTY

Heather Donovan must have hypnotized him. That was the only thing that could explain what he had experienced. Plus, she had been there at the barn. While he remembered her coming after he first experienced the floating and spinning, she could have made a suggestion for him to forget when she had arrived. Yes, he told himself, that was exactly what happened. But whatever power of suggestion she had over him was certainly gone now. He took a deep breath and told himself to stop being foolish. There was nothing Heather Donovan could do to him unless he allowed it. Closing his eyes, he breathed deeply, cleansing himself of whatever influence she had exerted over him. After fifteen minutes he took a deep breath, opened his eyes, and smiled.

Standing up, he walked over to the sink in his cell and picked up the cup. He filled it with water. But before he could get it to his mouth, it flew out of his hand and out of his cell, spilling all the water before rolling to a corner across the room. He stared at the cup and then looked at his hand.

When a guard brought lunch a few hours later, Beau made some excuse for dropping the cup and how it had rolled out of his cell, and asked if they could hand it to him. The guard looked at him suspiciously and warned him not to throw things.

After the guard left him alone, Beau sat in his cell, looking at his

BOBBI HOLMES

lunch. He remembered what she had said, "You will starve yourself." He thought about the water glass and how it had flown out of his hand. After a moment he laughed at himself and said, "You just dropped it, you fool."

He picked his sandwich up from the plate and brought it to his mouth. Before taking a bite, he felt pressure on his hands, and to his horror, he watched as his own fingers squished the sandwich and then threw its pieces from his cell, landing on the floor just out of his reach.

***

EDWARD JUNIOR WAS SPENDING the night with a friend, so Police Chief MacDonald took his youngest, Evan, to dinner at Lucy's Diner. Just as they finished eating, he received a call from Brian; Beau Stewart wanted to confess, but he would only talk to the police chief.

MacDonald took Evan with him to the station. They had already brought Beau to the interrogation room, and he was waiting there with Brian when the chief and Evan arrived. Father and son paused at the door leading to the interrogation room while the chief gave Evan instructions on where to wait. MacDonald noticed his son was not paying attention to him, but looking at the closed door behind him, leading to the interrogation room.

MacDonald was about to reprimand his son for not paying attention when Evan grinned and said, "Hi, Marie, what are you doing here?"

"Helping your father," Marie told him, giving the boy a little wink.

"Marie's here?" the chief asked.

With a grin, Evan looked up at his father. "Yes, she said she's helping you."

Furrowing his brows, the chief looked at the space where his son had been staring and asked, "What are you up to, Marie?"

***

BRIAN LEFT the chief alone in the interrogation room with Beau Stewart and went to the adjacent office so he could watch the exchange through the two-way mirror. Stewart had been in their

236

custody for a little more than twenty-four hours, but he looked horrible; confinement did not agree with him, which confused Brian because lockup in their station was fairly tame. Currently, there were no other prisoners, they kept it clean, and the staff never mistreated inmates. If convicted, Stewart would never handle the big house.

Looking into the interrogation room, Brian watched as the chief took a seat across from Beau, who sat with his hands on the table as his fingers fidgeted nervously.

"I see you've waived your right to an attorney," the chief said.

Beau nodded. "I want to tell you everything. Why I wanted Walt Marlow's diary. Why I wanted to kill them. But I don't know where to start."

"The beginning is a good place," the chief suggested.

Beau told the chief about the murders committed in his family. Knowledge of those murders stayed in the family and passed to the next generation with the understanding to keep the family secret. One reason had to do with Wilbur Jenkins's death.

"Our family never bought the land from Jenkins. Jenkins wanted cash and agreed to take less than market value because he wanted to travel and needed the money quickly. He took his papers to Beau Porter, but instead of paying him, they murdered him, buried his body on the property. They forged purchases of sale. Our family built our entire fortune on that land."

"And you could have lost everything if the truth came out?" the chief asked.

"When I read *Moon Runners*, I recognized so many stories my mother told me. Events you wouldn't find in a newspaper. I figured Marlow had to have taken his story from a diary or letters left behind from Walt Marlow. My mother told me about Ambrose murdering his brother after he came home drunk—after crying on Walt Marlow's shoulder over Charlene leaving him. Beau Junior didn't know they had killed Charlene. But that night, when he told Walt about Charlene leaving him, he must have also told Walt about how Ambrose and his father had murdered Jenkins for the land. He must have, because Walt obviously figured if they had murdered Jenkins, they probably murdered Charlene too. Walt Marlow was friends with Charlene; he undoubtably knew she was black and that she didn't have another lover. He must have written it in those letters, because there wasn't a diary."

"Why did you buy the land from your cousin?" the chief asked.

"Earl was a weak man. He told me years ago he would never share the family secret with his daughters. I didn't trust him to keep it. He'd already squandered away his share of the inheritance, so he wouldn't lose anything if it came out. I'd been trying to buy that property for years. I feared once he died, his daughters would sell it, and then whoever bought it would learn our family secret. Once the authorities started doing DNA matches on the remains, I figured if Marlow came forward, told them what he had read in those letters about Jenkins's murder, they could get a match for Jenkins's remains and prove that story true. We would lose everything."

"You planned to remove the remains and dispose of them?" the chief asked.

"Yes. I remember the selling agent making a comment about the barn having a concrete floor; he found that unusual. At the time, I wanted to laugh. He did not understand why that concrete was really there."

When Beau finished telling the chief all he had to say, he asked timidly, "May I have a drink of water, please?"

Brian continued to watch from the adjacent office and thought it odd how hesitantly Beau took the glass of water the chief handed him. The manner in which he brought it to his lips, it was as if he was reluctant to take a sip. When he finally did, Beau's expression transformed, as if all his troubles had melted away, and he wasn't facing prison time. He finished the entire glass and then asked if he could have more. He was practically giddy. When he finished, he leaned across the table and whispered something to the chief, but Brian couldn't hear what he said.

"WHAT DID Stewart whisper to you at the end?" Brian asked the chief after they returned Beau to lockup. The chief had already gotten Evan from the lunchroom, and they were getting ready to head home, but first Evan visited the bathroom while his father waited in the hallway, talking to Brian.

The chief didn't answer immediately, but finally said, "He told me Heather Donovan is a witch, and we need to watch her."

"Did he say witch or bitch? I know she visited him in lockup this morning. I don't understand what that was about, but he said he wanted to see her."

"It was witch," the chief said with a smile.

———————

LATE TUESDAY AFTERNOON, Pearl Huckabee stood on her back porch and sniffed the air. Someone was barbecuing steaks. Closing her eyes, she breathed in deeply, and her stomach growled. She hadn't eaten since breakfast at Pier Café that morning. That was when Carla, the waitress with the purple-this-week hair, told her how someone had attacked the Marlows over the weekend, and they ended up in the hospital. Apparently, they'd released Danielle yesterday, but Walt Marlow wouldn't be home until today, according to Carla. Pearl suspected he was already home, and the aroma of steaks cooking was probably coming from their yard. Leaving her patio, Pearl went inside to see what she had in her freezer for dinner.

———————

THEY HAD GATHERED for an impromptu barbecue, the friends of Beach Drive, along with Marie and Eva. It was early for dinner, but too late for lunch. Yet they figured after three days of hospital food, Walt would probably appreciate a steak, no matter what the time.

Lily and Ian provided the steaks, Heather picked up salads, bread and dessert at the deli, and Chris brought wine—the good stuff, Danielle's favorite. Chris and Ian barbecued in the outdoor kitchen while the others sat nearby, discussing recent events.

"I can't believe the police found Charlene's trunk in the barn after all these years. Why didn't they just get rid of it?" Heather asked. "And why did they have it in the first place?"

"Charlene had her trunk with her because she was meeting Beau in the barn, and they planned to run away together. She showed up early, and his father came home unexpectedly," Eva said. "According to Charlene, they stored it up in the attic rafter for years, but the Stewarts took it down and looked through it, which did not make her happy. But I don't know why they kept it initially."

After Chris repeated Eva's words, Ian said, "They probably kept it as a trophy,"

"The chief tells me the Kings have agreed to a DNA test,"

Danielle said. "Which doesn't surprise me. All along, they just wanted to find out what really happened to Charlene."

"I wish I could tell them Charlene's happy now, and she has moved on with her beloved, Beau Junior," Eva said. Chris continued to play interpreter, letting the non-mediums know what Eva had said.

"I don't get how they both haunted the old Barr place yet didn't know the other one was there," Heather said.

"It works that way sometimes," Eva explained.

"Raven told the chief when she learned of Beau Stewart's involvement, it didn't surprise her," Danielle said. "Not that she had any idea Charlene's lover had been his distant cousin, but she knew about the family's history with the Klan. It was something her grandmother had told her about when she had interviewed her for their family history. None of them were happy when he announced his bid for the Senate, and it looked like he had an excellent chance of winning."

"I guess they don't have to worry about that now," Chris said.

"There was another thing the chief told me," Danielle said. "There was a photograph of Charlene and Desiree Davis in the trunk, and Kiara King looks a lot like Desiree."

"There was something familiar about Kiara when I first saw her," Walt said. "When I learned about her connection to Desiree, I realized why she had looked familiar. I'm surprised I didn't figure it out sooner."

The conversation turned back to the ghosts haunting the property, and Heather said, "Most of them didn't even realize they were dead."

"Which lends to the confusion," Danielle said.

"But Earl understood he was dead. He knew everything about all of them," Heather said. "Why didn't he tell them?"

"I don't think he understood how to go about it," Danielle suggested. "And I believe Dolly understood she was dead. She knew those were her remains. But she had so much anger. She couldn't move on. I think saving us helped her put some of that anger to good use, and she was able to accept what happened and finally continue on her journey."

"Did you ever find out why Wilbur attached himself to Beau's remains? Did he think they were his?" Ian asked.

"He knew they belonged to Beau. He wanted to return them.

Wilbur felt obligated to Beau since he had tried to save him. And poor Beau was perhaps the most confused of all the spirits there," Danielle explained.

"But I thought Wilbur didn't even realize he was dead when Marie first met him, and he was looking for that bag," Heather said.

"Heather, don't you understand by now? A spirit who is not completely aware of his death might in some way understand he's dead, yet in another way still believe he's alive. While Wilbur felt obligated to Beau for trying to save his life, it didn't mean he understood he was dead," Eva explained. Once again, Chris repeated the words for the non-mediums.

"Wilbur visited me in the hospital before he moved on," Walt told them. "He explained why he blamed me for getting himself killed."

"Yes, Walt, the poor example," Danielle teased.

Walt gave her a playful nudge and said, "It was because he heard how I sold my grandfather's business after I inherited everything, and then traveled abroad for a year. He said he wanted to do that too. He didn't want to be tied down with the responsibility of a family inheritance, but he wanted more than a year."

"Sadly, it didn't work out for him," Danielle said.

"Did they all move on?" Lily asked.

"Yes," Eva said. "Earl was especially excited to go; he's been waiting for years. I imagine it's rather quiet over at the old Porter place about now." Again, Chris repeated her words.

"So what happens to Beau Stewart now?" Lily asked.

"I don't know what will happen with him. But they have arrested his kids, too. Not sure how they feel about their father rolling on them," Danielle said.

"You can all thank witchy woman for that," Chris said, waving his spatula in Heather's direction. They all laughed.

"That was rather brilliant of you," Lily told Heather.

Heather gave Lily a slight bow and said, "Thank you."

"What about me?" Marie asked.

"We make a good team, Marie," Heather said.

"I wonder what will happen to the Stewart estate?" Ian said. "That will be a legal nightmare."

Lily looked at Danielle, who sat on the end of Walt's lounge, and asked, "What I want to know, what has any of this taught you, Dani?"

"Like don't go poking around in a serial killer's backyard," Chris suggested.

"What it taught me?" Danielle repeated the question and looked to Walt with a soft smile. Resting her right hand on her stomach, she said, "It's reminded me how uncertain this life is, and there are some things…some things I don't want to put off any longer."

THE GHOST AND THE WITCHES' COVEN

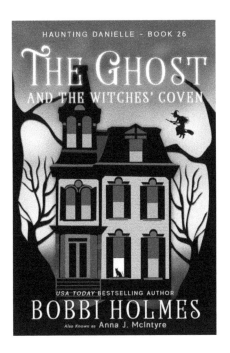

RETURN TO MARLOW HOUSE IN

THE GHOST AND THE WITCHES' COVEN

HAUNTING DANIELLE, BOOK 26

The mediums of Beach Drive don't take rumors of a witches' coven seriously—not until it threatens one of their own.

Meanwhile, Officer Brian Henderson can no longer ignore the secrets of Marlow House. Can he handle the truth?

NON-FICTION BY

BOBBI ANN JOHNSON HOLMES

Havasu Palms, A Hostile Takeover
Where the Road Ends, Recipes & Remembrances
Motherhood, a book of poetry
The Story of the Christmas Village

BOOKS BY ANNA J. MCINTYRE

COULSON FAMILY SAGA

Coulson's Wife

Coulson's Crucible

Coulson's Lessons

Coulson's Secret

Coulson's Reckoning

Now available in Audiobook Format

UNLOCKED ♡ HEARTS

Sundered Hearts

After Sundown

While Snowbound

Sugar Rush

Lightning Source UK Ltd.
Milton Keynes UK
UKHW010637240820
368739UK00001B/70